Sue
A Little Heroine

By

L. T. Meade

SUE - A LITTLE HEROINE

CHAPTER I

BIG BEN'S VOICE

Sue made a great effort to push her way to the front of the crowd. The street preacher was talking, and she did not wish to lose a word. She was a small, badly made girl, with a freckled face and hair inclined to red, but her eyes were wonderfully blue and intelligent. She pushed and pressed forward into the thick of the crowd. She felt a hand on her shoulder, and looking up, saw a very rough man gazing at her.

"Be that you, Peter Harris?" said Sue. "An' why didn't yer bring Connie along?"

"Hush!" said some people in the crowd.

The preacher raised his voice a little higher:

"'Tell His disciples and Peter that He goeth before you into Galilee.'"

Peter Harris, the rough man, trembled slightly. Sue found herself leaning against him. She knew quite well that his breath was coming fast.

"His disciples and Peter," she said to herself.

The street preacher had a magnificent voice. It seemed to roll above the heads of the listening crowd, or to sink to a penetrating whisper which found its echo in their hearts. The deep, wonderful eyes of the man had a power of making people look at him. Sue gazed with all her might and main.

"Father John be a good un," she said to herself. "He be the best man in all the world."

After the discoursewhich was very brief and full of stories, and just the sort which those rough people could not help listening toa hymn was sung, and then the crowd dispersed.

Sue was amongst them. She was in a great hurry. She forgot all about John Atkins, the little street preacher to whom she had been listening. She soon found herself in a street which was gaily lighted; there was a gin-palace at one end, another in the middle, and another at the farther end. This was Saturday night: Father John was fond of holding vigorous discourses on Saturday nights. Sue stopped to make her purchases. She was well-known in the neighborhood, and as she stepped in and out of one shop and then of another, she was the subject of a rough jest or a pleasant laugh, just as the mood of the person she addressed prompted2 one or other. She spent a few pence out of her meager purse, her purchases were put into a little basket, and she found her way home. The season was winter. She turned into a street back of Westminster; it went by the name of Adam Street. It was very long and rambling, with broken pavements, uneven roadways, and very tall, narrow, and dirty houses.

In a certain room on the fourth floor of one of the poorest of these houses lay a boy of between ten and eleven years of age. He was quite alone in the room, but that fact did not at all insure his being quiet. All kinds of sounds came to himsounds from the street, sounds from below stairs, sounds from overhead. There were shrieking voices and ugly laughter, and now and then there were shrill screams. The child was accustomed to these things, however, and it is doubtful whether he heard them.

He was a sad-looking little fellow, with that deadly white complexion which children who never go into the fresh air possess. His face, however, was neither discontented nor unhappy. He lay very still, with patient eyes, quite touching in their absolute submission. Had any one looked hard at little Giles they would have noticed something else on his faceit was a listening look. The sounds all around did not discompose him, for his eyes showed that he was waiting for something. It came. Over and above the discord a Voice filled the air. Nine times it repeated itself, slowly, solemnly, with deep vibrations. It was "Big Ben" proclaiming the hour. The boy had heard the chimes which preceded the hour; they were beautiful, of course, but it was the voice of Big Ben himself that fascinated him.

"Ain't he a real beauty to-night?" thought the child. "How I wishes as Sue 'ud hear him talk like that! Sometimes he's more weakly in his throat, poor fellow! but to-night he's in grand voice."

The discord, which for one brief moment was interrupted for the child by the beautiful, harmonious notes, continued in more deafening fashion than ever. Children cried; women scolded; men cursed and swore. In the midst of the din the room door was opened and a girl entered.

"Sue!" cried Giles.

"Yes," answered Sue, putting down her basket as she spoke. "I'm a bit late; there wor a crowd in the street, and I went to hear him. He wor grand."

"Oh, worn't he?" said Giles. "I never did know him to be in such beautiful voice."

Sue came up and stared at the small boy. Her good-natured but somewhat common type of face was a great contrast to his.

"Whatever are you talking about?" she said. "You didn't hear him; you can't move, poor Giles!"

"But I did hear him," replied the boy. "I feared as I'd get off to sleep, but I didn't. I never did hear Big Ben in such voicehe gave out his text as clear as could be."

"Lor', Giles!" exclaimed Sue, "I didn't mean that stupid clock; I means Father John. I squeezed up as close as possible to him, and I never missed a word as fell from his lips. Peter Harris were there too. I wonder how he felt. Bad, I 'spect, when he remembers the way he treated poor Connie. And oh, Giles! what do yer think? The preacher spoke to him jest as clear as clear could be, and he called him by his namePeter. 'Tell His disciples and Peter,' Father John cried, and I could feel Peter Harris jump ahind me."

"Wor that his text, Sue?"

"Yes, all about Peter. It wor wonnerful."

"Well, my text were, 'No more pain,'" said the boy. "I ache bad nearly always, but Big Ben said, 'No more pain,' as plain as he could speak, poor old fellow! It was nine times he said it. It were werry comforting."

Sue made no reply. She was accustomed to that sort of remark from Giles. She busied herself putting the kettle on the fire to boil, and then cleaned a little frying-pan which by-and-by was to toast a herring for Giles's supper and her own.

"Look what I brought yer," she said to the boy. "It were turning a bit, Tom Watkins said, and he gave it me for a ha'penny, but I guess frying and a good dash of salt 'ull make it taste fine. When the kettle boils I'll pour out your tea; you must want it werry bad."

"Maybe I do and maybe I don't," answered Giles. "It's 'No more pain' I'm thinking of. Sue, did you never consider that maybe ef we're good and patient Lord Christ 'ull take us to 'eaven any day?"

"No," answered Sue; "I'm too busy." She stood for a minute reflecting. "And I don't want to go to 'eaven yet," she continued; "I want to stay to look after you."

Giles smiled. "It's beautiful in 'eaven," he said. "I'd like to go, but I wouldn't like to leave you, Sue."

"Take your tea now, there's a good fellow," answered Sue, who was nothing if not matter-of-fact. "Aye, dear!" she continued as she poured it out and then waited for Giles to raise the cup to his lips, "Peter Harris do look bad. I guess he's sorry he was so rough on Connie. But now let's finish our supper, and I'll prepare yer for bed, Giles, for I'm desp'rate tired."

CHAPTER II

A SERVANT OF GOD

John Atkins, the street preacher, was a little man who led a wonderful life. He was far better educated than most people of his station, and in addition his mind was tender in feeling and very sensitive and loving. He regarded everybody as his brothers and sisters, and in especial he took to his heart all sorrowful people. He never grumbled or repined, but he looked upon his life as a pilgrimage to a better country, and did not, therefore, greatly trouble if things were not quite smooth for him. This little man had a very wide circle of friends. The fact is, he had more power of keeping peace and order in the very poor part of London, back of Westminster, where he lived, than had any dignitary of the Church, any rector, any curate, or any minister, be he of what persuasion he might. Father John was very humble about himself. Indeed, one secret of his success lay in the fact that he never thought of himself at all.

Having preached on this Saturday evening, as was his wont, to a larger crowd than usual, he went home. As he walked a passer-by could have seen that he was lame; he used a crutch. With the winter rain beating on him he looked insignificant. Presently he found the house where he had a room, went up the stairs, and entered, opening the door with a latch-key. A fire was burning here, and a small paraffin lamp with a red shade over it cast a warm glow over the little place. The moment the light fell upon Father John his insignificance vanished. That was a grand head and face which rose above the crippled body. The head was high and splendidly proportioned. It was crowned with a wealth of soft brown hair, which fell low on the shoulders. The forehead was lofty, straight, and full; the mouth rather compressed, with firm lines round it; the eyes were very deep setthey were rather light gray in color, but the pupils were unusually large. The pupils and the peculiar expression of the eyes gave them a wonderful power. They could speak when every other feature in the face was quiet.

"I don't like themI dread them," said Peter Harris on one occasion. "Aye, but don't I love 'em just!" remarked little Giles.

Giles and Sue were special friends of John Atkins. They had, in fact, been left in his care by their mother three years before this story begins. This was the way they had first learned to know Father John.

The man had a sort of instinct for finding out when people were in trouble and when they specially needed him. There was a poor woman lying on her dying bed, and a boy and a girl were kneeling close to her.

"Keep a good heart up, Giles," she said to the boy. "I know I'm goin' to leave yer, and you're as lame as lame can be, but then there's Sue. Sue has a deal o' gumption for such a young un. Sue won't let yer want, Giles, lad; you need never go to the workhouse while Sue's alive."

"No, that he needn't, mother," answered Sue.

"Can't yer get back on to yer sofa, Giles?" she added, turning to the boy. "You'll break your back kneeling by mother all this time."

"No, I won't; I'd rather stay," answered the boy. His eyes were full of light; he kept on stroking his mother's hand.

"Go on, mother," he said. "Tell us more. You're goin'5 to 'eaven, and you'll see father." A sob strangled his voice for a minute.

"Yes, I'll see my good 'usbandthat is, I hope so; I can but trustI allus have trusted, though often, ef I may say the truth, I couldn't tell what I were a-trusting to. Somehow, whatever folks say, there is a Providence."

"Oh, mother!" said Giles, "God is so beautifulwhen you see father again you'll know that."

"Mother," interrupted Sue, "does yer think as Providence 'ull get me constant work at the sewing, enough to keep Giles and me?"

"I dunno, Sue," answered the woman. "I've trusted a good bit all my life, and more specially since your father was took, and somehow we haven't quite starved. Happen it'll be the same with Giles and you."

The boy sighed. His back was aching terribly. His heart was breaking at the thought of losing his mother; he struggled to continue kneeling by the bedside, but each moment the effort became greater.

The children were kneeling so when a quick, light step was heard on the stairs, and a little man entered. It was too dark in the room for the children to see his face; they heard, however, a very pleasant voice. It said in cheerful tones:

"Why haven't you fire here, and a candle? Can I help you?"

"There ain't much candle left," answered Giles.

"And mother's dying," continued Sue. "She don't mind the darkdo yer, mother?"

The little man made no reply in words, but taking some matches from his pocket, and also a candle, he struck a light. He placed the candle in a sconce on the wall, and then turned to the three.

"Be yer a parson?" asked the woman.

"I am a servant of God," answered Atkins.

"I'm real glad as you're a parson," she answered; "you can make it all right between Almighty God and me."

"You are mistaken; I can't do that. That is Jesus Christ's work. But I will pray with youlet me hold your hand, and we will pray together."

Then and there in the dismal attic Father John spoke out his heart in the following simple words. Even Sue never forgot those words to the latest day she lived:

"Lord God Almighty, look down upon this dying woman. Thy Son died for her and she knows it not. Lord, she is in great darkness, and she is so near death that she has no time to learn the truth in its fullness; but Thou who art in the light can show some of Thy light to her. Now, in her dying hour, reveal to her Thyself."

The dying woman fixed her glittering eyes on the strange man. When he ceased speaking she smiled; then she said, slowly:

"I allus felt that I could trust in Providence."

She never spoke after that, and half an hour afterwards she died.

This was the beginning of Father John's friendship with Giles and Sue.

The next day Sue, by dint of many and anxious inquiries, found him out, and put her queer little unkempt head into his room.

"Ef yer please, parson, may I speak to yer 'bout Giles and me?"

"Certainly, my little girl. Sit down and tell me what I can do for you."

"Parson," said Sue, with much entreaty in her voice and many a pucker on her brow, "what I wants to say is a good deal. I wants ter take care o' Giles, to keep up the bit o' home and the bit o' victual. It 'ud kill Giles ef he wor to be took to the work'us; and I promised mother as I'd keep 'im. Mother wor allers a-trustin', and she trusted Giles ter me."

Here Sue's voice broke off into a sob, and she put up her dirty apron to her eyes.

"Don't cry, my dear," answered Atkins kindly; "you must not break your word to your mother. Will it cost you so much money to keep yourself and Giles in that little attic?"

"It ain't that," said she, proudly. "It ain't a bit as I can't work, fur I can, real smart at 'chinery needlework. I gets plenty to do, too, but that 'ere landlady, she ain't a bit like mother; she'd trusten nobody, and she up this morning, and mother scarce cold, and says as she'd not let her room to Giles and me 'cept we could get some un to go security fur the rent; and we has no un as 'ud go security, so we must go away the day as mother is buried, and Giles must go to the work'us; and it 'ull kill Giles, and mother won't trust me no more."

"Don't think that, my child; nothing can shake your mother's trust where God has taken her now. But do you want me to help you?"

Sue found the color mounting to her little, weather-beaten face. A fear suddenly occurred to her that she had been audaciousthat this man was a stranger, that her request was too great for her to ask. But something in the kindness of the eyes looking straight into hers brought sudden sunshine to her heart and courage to her resolve. With a burst, one word toppling over the other, out came the whole truth:

"Please, sirplease, sir, I thought as you might go security fur Giles and me. We'd pay real honest. Oh, sir, will you, jest because mother did trusten so werry much?"

"I will, my child, and with all the heart in the world. Come home with me now, and I will arrange the whole matter with your landlady."

CHAPTER III

GOOD SECURITY

John Atkins was always wont to speak of Sue and Giles as among the successes of his life. This was not the first time he had gone security for his poor, and many of his poor had decamped, leaving the burden of their unpaid rent on him. He never murmured when such failures came to him. He was just a trifle more particular in looking not so much into the merits as the necessities of the next case that came to his knowledge. But no more, than if all his flock had been honest as the day, did he refuse his aid. This may have been a weakness on the man's part; very likely, for he was the sort of man whom all sensible and long-headed people would have spoken about as a visionary, an enthusiast, a believer in doing to others as he would be done by a person, in short, without a grain of everyday sense to guide him. Atkins would smile when such people lectured him on what they deemed his folly.

Nevertheless, though he took failure with all resignation, success, when it came to him, was stimulating, and Giles and Sue he classed among his successes.

The mother died and was buried, but the children did not leave their attic, and Sue, brave little bread-winner, managed not only to pay the rent but to keep the gaunt wolf of hunger from the door. Sue worked as a machinist for a large City house.

Every day she rose with the dawn, made the room as tidy as she could for Giles, and then started for her long walk to the neighborhood of Cheapside. In a room with sixty other girls Sue worked at the sewing-machine from morning till night. It was hard labor, as she had to work with her feet as well as her hands, producing slop clothing at the rate of a yard a minute. Never for an instant might her eyes wander from the seam; and all this severe work was done in the midst of an ear-splitting clatter, which alone would have worn out a person not thoroughly accustomed to it.

But Sue was not unhappy. For three years now she had borne without breaking down this tremendous strain on her health. The thought that she was keeping Giles in the old attic made her bright and happy, and her shrill young voice rose high and merry above those of her companions. No; Sue, busy and honest, was not unhappy. But her fate was a far less hard one than Giles's.

Giles had not always been lame. When first his mother held him in her arms he was both straight and beautiful. Though born of poor parents and in London, he possessed a health and vigor seldom bestowed upon such children. In those days his father was alive, and earning good wages as a fireman in the London Fire Brigade. There was a comfortable home for both Sue and Giles, and Giles was the very8 light and sunshine of his father's and mother's life. To his father he had been a special source of pride and rejoicing. His beauty alone would have made him so. Sue was essentially an everyday child, but Giles had a clear complexion, dark-blue eyes, and curling hair. Giles as a baby and a little child was very beautiful. As his poor, feeble-looking mother carried him aboutfor she was poor and feeble-looking even in her palmy dayspeople used to turn and gaze after the lovely boy. The mother loved him passionately, but to the father he was as the apple of his eye.

Giles's father had married a wife some degrees below him both intellectually and socially. She was a hard-working, honest, and well-meaning soul, but she was not her husband's equal. He was a man with great force of character, great bravery, great powers of endurance. Before he had joined the Fire Brigade he had been a sailor, and many tales did he tell to his little Giles of his adventures on the sea. Sue and her mother used to find these stories dull, but to Giles they seemed as necessary as the air he breathed. He used to watch patiently for hours for the rare moments when his father was off duty, and then beg for the food which his keen mental appetite craved for. Mason could both read and write, and he began to teach his little son. This state of things continued until Giles was seven years old. Then there came a dreadful black-letter day for the child; for the father, the end of life.

Every event of that torturing day was ever after engraved on the little boy's memory. He and his father, both in high spirits, started off for their last walk together. Giles used to make it a practice to accompany his father part of the way to his station, trotting back afterwards safely and alone to his mother and sister. To-day their way lay through Smithfield Market, and the boy, seeing the Martyrs' Monument in the center of the market-place, asked his father eagerly about it.

"Look, father, look!" he said, pointing with his finger. "What is that?"

"That is the figure of an angel, lad. Do you see, it is pointing up to heaven. Do you know why?"

"No, father; tell us."

"Long ago, my lad, there were a lot of brave people brought just there where the angel stands; they were tied to stakes in the ground and set fire to and burnedburned until they died."

"Burned, father?" asked little Giles in a voice of horror.

"Yes, boy. They were burned because they were so brave they would rather be burned than deny the good God. They were called martyrs, and that angel stands there now to remind people about them and to show how God took them straight to heaven."

"I think they were grand," answered the boy, his eyes kindling. "Can't people be like that now?"

"Any one who would rather die than neglect a duty has, to my mind, the same spirit," answered the man. "But now, lad, run home, for I must be off."

"Oh, father, you are going to that place where the wonderful new machinery is, and you said I might look at it. May I come?"

The father hesitated, finally yielded, and the two went on together. But together they were never to come back.

That very day, with the summer sun shining, and all the birds in the country far away singing for joy, there came a message for the brave father. He was suddenly, in the full prime of his manly vigor, to leave off doing God's work down here, doubtless to take it up with nobler powers above. A fireman literally works with his life in his hands. He may have to resign it at any moment at the call of duty. This trumpet-call, which he had never neglected, came now for Giles Mason.

A fire broke out in the house where little Giles watched with keen intelligence the new machinery. The machinery was destroyed, the child lamed for life, and the brave father, in trying to rescue him and others, was so injured by falling stones and pieces of woodwork that he only lived a few hours.

The two were laid side by side in the hospital to which they were carried.

"Father," said the little one, nestling close to the injured and dying man, "I think people can be martyrs now!"

But the father was past words, though he heard the child, for he smiled and pointed upwards. The smile and the action were so significant, and reminded the child so exactly of the angel who guards the Martyrs' Monument, that ever afterwards he associated his brave father with those heroes and heroines of whom the sacred writer says that "the world is not worthy."

CHAPTER IV

SOLITARY HOURS

Giles was kept in the hospital for many weeks, even months. All that could be done was done for him; but the little, active feet were never to walk again, and the spine was so injured that he could not even sit upright. When all that could be done had been done and failed, the boy was sent back to his broken-down and widowed mother.

Mrs. Mason had removed from the comfortable home where she lived during her husband's lifetime to the attic in a back street of Westminster, where she finally died. She took in washing for a livelihood, and Sue, now twelve years old, was already an accomplished little machinist.

They were both too busy to have time to grieve, and at night were too utterly worn-out not to sleep soundly. They were kind to Giles lying on his sick-bed; they both loved him dearly, but they neither saw, nor even tried to understand, the hunger of grief and longing which filled his poor little mind.

His terrible loss, his own most terrible injuries, had developed in the boy all that sensitive nerve organism which can render life so miserable to its possessor. To hear his beloved father's name mentioned was a torture to him; and yet his mother and Sue spoke of it with what seemed to the boy reckless indifference day after day. Two things, however, comforted himone the memory of the angel figure over the Martyrs' Monument at Smithfield, the other the deep notes of Big Ben. His father, too, had been a martyr, and that angel stood there to signify his victory as well as the victory of those others who withstood the torture by fire; and Big Ben, with its solemn, vibrating notes, seemed to his vivid imagination like that same angel speaking.

Though an active, restless boy before his illness, he became now very patient. He would lie on his back, not reading, for he had forgotten what little his father taught him, but apparently lost in thought, from morning to night. His mother was often obliged to leave him alone, but he never murmured at his long, solitary hours; indeed, had there been any one by to listen to all the words he said to himself at these times, they would have believed that the boy enjoyed them.

Thus three years passed away. In those three years all the beauty had left little Giles's face; all the brightness had fled from his eyes; he was now a confirmed invalid, white and drawn and pinched. Then his poor, tired-out mother died. She had worked uncomplainingly, but far beyond her strength, until suddenly she sickened and in a few days was dead. Giles, however, while losing a mother, had gained a friend. John Atkins read the sensitive heart of the boy like a book. He came to see him daily, and soon completed the reading-lessons which his father had begun. As soon as the boy could read he was no longer unhappy. His sad and troubled mind need no longer feed on itself; he read what wise and great men thought, for Atkins supplied him with books. Atkins's books, it is true, were mostly of a theological nature, but once he brought him a battered Shakespeare; and Sue also, when cash was a little flush, found an old volume of the Arabian Nights on a book-stall. These two latter treasures gave great food to the active imagination of little Giles.

In July arrangements were made to provide for the families of firemen who were killed in the performance of their duty, but nothing was done for them before that date.

CHAPTER V

EAGER WORDS

When John Atkins was quite young he was well-to-do. His father and mother had kept a good shop, and not only11 earned money for their needs but were able to put by sufficient for a rainy day. John was always a small and delicate child, and as he grew older he developed disease of the spine, which not only gave him a deformed appearance but made him slightly lame. Nevertheless, he was an eager little scholar, and his father was able to send him to a good school. The boy worked hard, and eagerly read and learned all that came in his way.

Thus life was rather pleasant than otherwise with John Atkins up to his fifteenth year, but about then there came misfortunes. The investment into which his father had put all his hard-won earnings was worthless; the money was lost. This was bad enough, but there was worse to follow. Not only had the money disappeared, but the poor man's heart was broken. He ceased to attend to his business; his customers left him to go elsewhere; his wife died suddenly, and he himself quickly followed her to the grave.

After these misfortunes John Atkins had a bad illness himself. He grew better after a time, took to cobbling as a trade, and earned enough to support himself. How he came to take up street preaching, and in consequence to be much beloved by his neighbors, happened simply enough.

On a certain Sunday evening he was walking home from the church where he attended, his heart all aglow with the passionate words of the preacher he had been listening to. The preacher had made Bunyan the subject of his discourse, and the author of the Pilgrim's Progress was at that time the hero of all heroes in the mind of Atkins. He was thinking of his wonderful pilgrimage as he hurried home. He walked on. Suddenly, turning a corner, he knocked up against a man, who, half-reeling, came full-tilt against him.

"Aye, Peter," he said, knowing the man, and perceiving that he was far too tipsy to get to his home with safety, "I'll just walk home with you, mate. I've got an apple in my pocket for the little wench."

The man made no objection, and they walked on. At the next corner they saw a crowd, all listening eagerly to the words of a large, red-faced man who, mounted on a chair, addressed them. On the burning, glowing heart of John Atkins fell the following terrible words:

"For there be no God, and there be nothing before us but to die as the beasts die. Let us get our fill of pleasure and the like of that, neighbors, for there ain't nothing beyond the grave."

"It's a lie!" roared Atkins.

The words had stung him like so many fiery serpents. He rushed into the midst of the crowd; he forgot Peter Harris; he sprang on to the chair which the other man in his astonishment had vacated, and poured out a whole string of eager, passionate words. At that moment he discovered that he had a wonderful gift. There was the message in his heart which God had put there, and he was able to deliver it. His words were powerful. The crowd, who had listened without any great excitement to the unbeliever, came close now to the man of God, applauding him loudly. Atkins spoke of the Fatherhood of God and of His love.

"Ain't that other a coward?" said two or three rough voices when Atkins ceased to speak. "And he comes here talking them lies every Sunday night," said one poor woman. "Come you again, master, and tell us the blessed truth."

This decided Atkins. He went to his parish clergyman, an overworked and badly paid man, and told him the incident. He also spoke of his own resolve. He would go to these sheep who acknowledged no Shepherd, and tell them as best he could of a Father, a Home, a Hope. The clergyman could not but accept the services of this fervent city missionary.

"Get them to church if you can," he said.

"Aye, if I can," answered Atkins; "but I will compel them to enter the Church abovethat is the main thing."

Soon he began to know almost all the poor folks who crowded to hear him. In their troubles he was with them; when joy came he heard first about it, and rejoiced most of all; and many a poor face of a tired woman or worn-out man, or even a little child, looking into his, grew brighter in the presence of death.

CHAPTER VI

DIFFERENT SORT OF WORK

Connie was a very pretty girl. She was between thirteen and fourteen years of age, and very small and delicate-looking. Her hair was of a pale, soft gold; her eyes were blue; she had a delicate complexion, pink and whitealmost like a china figure, Sue said; Giles compared her to an angel. Connie was in the same trade that Sue earned her bread by; she also was a machinist in a large warehouse in the City. All day long she worked at the sewing-machine, going home with Sue night after night, glad of Sue's sturdy support, for Connie was much more timid than her companion.

Connie was the apple of Harris's eye, his only child. He did everything he could for her; he lived for her. If any one could make him good, Connie could; but she was sadly timid; she dreaded the terrible moments when he returned home, having taken more than was good for him. At these times she would slink away to visit Giles and Sue, and on more than one occasion she had spent the night with the pair rather than return to her angry father. Some months, however, before this story begins, a terrible misfortune had come to Peter Harris. He had come home on a certain evening worse than usual from the effects of drink. Connie happened to be in. She had dressed herself with her usual exquisite neatness. She always kept the place ship-shape. The13 hearth was always tidily swept. She managed her father's earnings, which were quite considerable, and the wretched man could have had good food and a comfortable home, and been happy as the day was long, if only the craze for drink had not seized him.

Connie was very fond of finery, and she was now trimming a pretty hat to wear on the following Sunday. Not long ago she had made a new friend, a girl at the warehouse of the name of Agnes Coppenger. Agnes was older than Connie. She was the kind of girl who had a great admiration for beauty, and when she saw that people turned to look at pretty Connie with her sweet, refined face and delicate ways, she hoped that by having such a pleasant companion she also might come in for her share of admiration. She therefore began to make much of Connie. She praised her beauty, and invited her to her own home. There Connie made companions who were not nearly such desirable ones as Sue and Giles.

She began to neglect Sue and Giles, and to spend more and more of her time with Agnes.

On a certain day when the two girls were working over their sewing-machines, the whir of the numerous machines filling the great warehouse, Agnes turned to Connie.

"When we go out at morning break I 'ave a word to say to yer."

Connie's eyes brightened.

"You walk with me," whispered Agnes again.

An overseer came round. Talking was forbidden in the great room, and the girls went on with their mechanical employment, turning out long seam after long seam of delicate stitches. The fluff from the work seemed to smother Connie that morning. She had inherited her mother's delicacy. She coughed once or twice. There was a longing within her to get away from this dismal, this unhealthy life. She felt somehow, down deep in her heart, that she was meant for better things. The child was by nature almost a poet. She could have worshiped a lovely flower. As to the country, what her feelings would have been could she have seen it almost baffles description.

Now, Sue, working steadily away at her machine a little farther down the room, had none of these sensations. Provided that Sue could earn enough money to keep Giles going, that was all she asked of life. She was as matter-of-fact as a young girl could be; and as to pining for what she had not got, it never once entered her head.

At twelve o'clock there was a break of half-an-hour. The machinists were then turned out of the building. It did not matter what sort of day it was, whether the sun shone with its summer intensity, or whether the snow fell in thick flakeswhatever the condition of the outside world, out all the working women had to go. None could skulk behind; all had to seek the open air.

Connie coughed now as the bitter blast blew against her cheeks.

"Isn't it cold?" she said.

She expected to see Agnes by her side, but it was Sue she addressed.

"I've got a penny for pease-pudding to-day," said Sue. "Will you come and have a slice, Connie? Or do yer want somethin' better? Your father, Peter Harris, can let yer have more than a penny for yer dinner."

"Oh, yes," answered Connie; "'tain't the moneyI 'aven't got not a bit of happetite, not for nothing; but I want to say a word to Agnes Coppenger, and I don't see her."

"Here I be," said Agnes, coming up at that moment. "Come right along, Connie; I've got a treat for yer."

The last words were uttered in a low whisper, and Sue, finding she was not wanted, went off in another direction. She gave little sighs as she did so. What was wrong with pretty Connie, and why did she not go with her? It had been her custom to slip her hand inside Sue's sturdy arm. During the half-hour interval, the girls used to repair together to the nearest cheap restaurant, there to secure what nourishing food their means permitted. They used to chatter to one another, exchanging full confidences, and loving each other very much.

But for some time now Connie had only thought of Agnes Coppenger, and Sue felt out in the cold.

"Can't be helped," she said to herself; "but if I am not mistook, Agnes is a bad un, and the less poor Connie sees of her the better."

Sue entered the restaurant, which was now packed full of factory girls, and she asked eagerly for her penn'orth of pease-pudding.

Meanwhile Connie and Agnes were very differently employed. When the two girls found themselves alone, Agnes looked full at Connie and said:

"I'm going to treat yer."

"Oh, no, you ain't," said Connie, who was proud enough in her way.

"Yes, but I be," said Agnes; "I ha' lots o' money, bless yer! Here, we'll come in here."

An A.B.C. shop stood invitingly open just across the road. Connie had always looked at these places of refreshment with open-eyed admiration, and with the sort of sensation which one would have if one stood at the gates of Paradise. To enter any place so gorgeous as an A.B.C., to be able to sit down and have one's tea or coffee or any other refreshment at one of those little white marble tables, seemed to her a degree of refinement scarcely to be thought about. The A.B.C. was a sort of forbidden fruit to Connie, but Agnes had been there before, and Agnes had described the delight of the place.

"The quality come in 'ere," said Agnes, "an' they horders all sorts o' things, from mutton-chops to poached heggs. I am goin' in to-day, and so be you."

"Oh, no," said Connie, "you can't afford it."

"That's my lookout," answered Agnes. "I've half-a-crown in my pocket, and ef I choose to have a good filling meal, and ef I choose that you shall have one too, why, that is my lookout."

As Agnes spoke she pulled her companion through the swinging door, and a minute later the two young girls had a little table between them, not far from the door. Agnes called in a lofty voice to one of the waitresses.

"Coffee for two," she said, "and rolls and butter and poached heggs; and see as the heggs is well done, and the toast buttered fine and thick. Now then, look spruce, won't yer?"

The waitress went off to attend to Agnes's requirements. Agnes sat back in her chair with a sort of lofty, fine-lady air which greatly impressed poor Connie. By-and-by the coffee, the rolls and butter, and the poached eggs appeared. A little slip of paper with the price of the meal was laid close to Agnes's plate, and she proceeded to help her companion to the good viands.

"It's this sort of meal you want hevery day," she said. "Now then, eat as hard as ever you can, and while you're eating let me talk, for there's a deal to say, and we must be back in that factory afore we can half do justice to our wittles."

Connie sipped her coffee, and looked hard at her companion.

"What is it?" she asked suddenly. "What's all the fuss, Agnes? Why be you so chuff to poor Sue, and whatever 'ave you got to say?"

"This," said Agnes. "You're sick o' machine-work, ain't you?"

"Oh, that I be!" said Connie, stretching her arms a little, and suppressing a yawn. "It seems to get on my narves, like. I am that miserable when I'm turning that horrid handle and pressing that treadle up and down, up and down, as no words can say. I 'spect it's the hair so full of fluff an' things, too; some'ow I lose my happetite for my or'nary feed when I'm working at that 'orrid machine."

"I don't feel it that way," said Agnes in a lofty tone. "But then, I am wery strong. I can heat like anything, whatever I'm a-doing of. There, Connie; don't waste the good food. Drink up yer corffee, and don't lose a scrap o' that poached egg, for ef yer do it 'ud be sinful waste. Well, now, let me speak. I know quite a different sort o' work that you an' me can both do, and ef you'll come with me this evening I can tell yer all about it."

"What sort of work?" asked Connie.

"Beautiful, refinedthe sort as you love. But I am not going to tell yer ef yer give me away."

"What do you mean by that, Agnes?"

"I means wot I sayI'll tell yer to-night ef yer'll come 'ome with me."

"Yer mean that I'm to spend all the evening with yer?" asked Connie.

"Yesthat's about it. You are to come 'ome with me, and we'll talk. Why, bless yer! with that drinkin' father o' yourn, wot do you want all alone by yer lonesome? You give me a promise. And now I must pay hup, and we'll be off."

"I'll come, o' course," said Connie after brief reflection. "Why shouldn't I?" she added. "There's naught to keep me to home."

The girls left the A.B.C. shop and returned to their work.

Whir! whir! went the big machines. The young heads were bent over their accustomed toil; the hands on the face of the great clock which Connie so often looked at went on their way. Slowlyvery slowlythe time sped. Would that long day ever come to an end?

The machinists' hours were from eight o'clock in the morning to six in the evening. Sometimes, when there were extra lots of ready-made clothes to be produced, they were kept till seven or even eight o'clock. But for this extra work there was a small extra pay, so that few of them really minded. But Connie dreaded extra hours extremely. She was not really dependent on the work, although Peter would have been very angry with his girl had she idled her time. She herself, too, preferred doing this to doing nothing. But to-night, of all nights, she was most impatient to get away with Agnes in order to discover what that fascinating young person's secret was.

She looked impatiently at the clock; so much so that Agnes herself, as she watched her eyes, chuckled now and then.

"She'll be an easy prey," thought Agnes Coppenger. "I'll soon get 'er into my power."

At six o'clock there was no further delay; no extra work was required, and the machinists poured into the sloppy, dark, and dreary streets.

"Come along now, quickly," said Agnes. "Don't wait for Sue; Sue has nothing to do with you from this time out."

"Oh dear! oh dear!" said Connie. "But I don't want to give up Sue and Giles. You ha' never seen little Giles Mason?"

"No," replied Agnes, "and don't want to. Wot be Giles to me?"

"Oh," said Connie, "ef yer saw 'im yer couldn't but love 'im. He's the wery prettiest little fellow that yer ever clapped yer two eyes onwith 'is delicate face an' 'is big brown eyesand the wonnerful thoughts he have, too. Poetry ain't in it. Be yer fond o' poetry yerself, Agnes?"

"I fond o' poetry?" almost screamed Agnes. "Not I! That is, I never heerd itdon't know wot it's like. I ha' no time to think o' poetry. I'm near mad sometimes fidgeting and17 fretting how to get myself a smart 'at, an' a stylish jacket, an' a skirt that hangs with a sort o' swing about it. But you, nowyou never think on yer clothes."

"Oh yes, but I do," said Connie; "and I ha' got a wery pwitty new dress now as father guv me not a fortnight back; and w'en father don't drink he's wery fond o' me, an' he bought this dress at the pawnshop."

"Lor', now, did he?" said Agnes. "Wot sort be it, Connie?"

"Dark blue, with blue velvet on it. It looks wery stylish."

"You'd look like a lydy in that sort o' dress," said Agnes. "You've the face of a lydythat any one can see."

"Have I?" said Connie. She put up her somewhat roughened hand to her smooth little cheeks.

"Yes, you 'ave; and wot I say is thisyer face is yer fortoon. Now, look yer 'ere. We'll stand at this corner till the Westminster 'bus comes up, and then we'll take a penn'orth each, and that'll get us wery near 'ome. Yer don't think as yer father'll be 'ome to-night, Connie?"

"'Tain't likely," replied Connie; "'e seldom comes in until it's time for 'im to go to bed."

"Well then, that's all right. When we get to Westminster, you skid down Adam Street until yer get to yer diggin's; an' then hup you goes and changes yer dress. Into the very genteel dark-blue costoom you gets, and down you comes to yer 'umble servant wot is waitin' for yer below stairs."

This programme was followed out in all its entirety by Connie. The omnibus set the girls down not far from her home. Connie soon reached her room. No father there, no fire in the grate. She turned on the gas and looked around her.

The room was quite a good one, of fair size, and the furniture was not bad of its sort. Peter Harris himself slept on a trundle-bed in the sitting-room, but Connie had a little room all to herself just beyond. Here she kept her small bits of finery, and in especial the lovely new costume which her father had given her.

She was not long in slipping off her working-clothes. Then she washed her face and hands, and brushed back her soft, glistening, pale-golden hair, and put on the dark-blue dress, and her little blue velvet cap to match, andlittle guessing how lovely she appeared in this dress, which simply transformed the pretty child into one of quite another rank of lifeshe ran quickly downstairs.

A young man of the name of Anderson, whom she knew very slightly, was passing by. He belonged to the Fire Brigade, and was one of the best and bravest firemen in London. He had a pair of great, broad shoulders, and a very kind face. It looked almost as refined as Connie's own.

Anderson gave her a glance, puzzled and wondering. He felt half-inclined to speak, but she hurried by him, and the next minute Agnes gripped her arm.

"My word, ain't you fine!" said that young lady. "You18 be a gel to be proud of! Won't yer do fine, jest! Now then, come along, and let's be quick."

Connie followed her companion. They went down several side-streets, and took several short cuts. They passed through the roughest and worst part of the purlieus at the back of Westminster. At last they entered a broader thoroughfare, and there Agnes stopped.

"Why, yer never be livin' here?" asked Connie.

"No, I bean't. You'll come to my 'ome afterwards. I want to take yer to see a lydy as maybe'll take a fancy to yer."

"Oh!" said Connie, feeling both excited and full of wonder.

The girls entered a side passage, and presently Connie, to her astonishment, found herself going upwardsup and up and upin a lift. The lift went up as far as it would go. The girls got out. Agnes went first, and Connie followed. They walked down the passage, and Agnes gave a very neat double knock on the door, which looked like an ordinary front door to a house.

The door was opened by a woman rather loudly dressed, but with a handsome face.

"How do you do, Mrs. Warren?" said Agnes. "I ha' brought the young lydy I spoke to yer about. Shall us both come in?"

"Oh, yes, certainly," said Mrs. Warren.

She stood aside, and Connie, still following her companion, found herself at the other side of the neat door. The place inside was bright with electric light, and the stout, showily dressed lady, going first, conducted the girls into a room which Agnes afterwards spoke of as the dining-room. The lady sat down in a very comfortable arm-chair, crossed her legs, and desired Connie to come forward and show herself.

"Take off yer 'at," she said.

Connie did so.

"You're rather pretty."

Connie was silent.

"I want," said the stout woman, "a pretty gel, something like you, to come and sit with me from ten to two o'clock hevery day. Yer dooties'll be quite light, and I'll give yer lots o' pretty clothes and good wages."

"But what'll I have to do?" asked Connie.

"Jest to sit with me an' keep me company; I'm lonesome here all by myself."

Connie looked puzzled.

"You ask wot wages yer'll get," said Agnes, poking Connie on the arm. Connie's blue eyes looked up. The showy lady was gazing at her very intently.

"I'll give yer five shillin's a week," she said, "and yer keep, and some carst-off clothesmy ownnow and again; and ef that bean't a bargain, I don't know wot be."

Connie was silent.

"You 'ad best close with it," said Agnes. "It's a charnce19 once in a 'undred. Yer'll be very 'appy with Mrs. Warrenher's a real lydy."

"Yes, that I be," said Mrs. Warren. "I come of a very hold family. My ancestors come hover with William the Conqueror."

Connie did not seem impressed by this fact.

"Will yer come or will yer not?" said Mrs. Warren. "I'll take yer jaunts, tooI forgot to mention that. Often on a fine Saturday, you an' mewe'll go to the country together. You don't know 'ow fine that 'ull be. We'll go to the country and we'll 'ave a spree. Did yer never see the country?"

"No," said Connie, in a slow voice, "but I ha' dreamt of it."

"She's the sort, ma'am," interrupted Agnes, "wot dreams the queerest things. She's hall for poetry and flowers and sech like. She's not matter-o'-fack like me."

"Jest the sort I want," said Mrs. Warren. "II loves poetry. You shall read it aloud to me, my gelor, better still, I'll read it to you. An' as to flowerswhy, yer shall pluck 'em yer own self, an' yer'll see 'em a-blowin' an' a-growin', yer own self. We'll go to the country next Saturday. There, nowain't that fine?"

Connie looked puzzled. There certainly was a great attraction at the thought of going into the country. She hated the machine-work. But, all the same, somehow or other she did not like Mrs. Warren.

"I'll think o' it and let yer know," she said.

But when she uttered these words the stately dressed and over-fine lady changed her manner.

"There's no thinking now," she said. "You're 'ere, and yer'll stay. You go out arter you ha' been at my house? You refuse my goodness? Not a bit o' it! Yer'll stay."

"Oh, yes, Connie," said Agnes in a soothing tone.

"But I don't want to stay," said Connie, now thoroughly frightened. "I want to goand to go at once. Let me go, ma'am; II don't like yer!"

Poor Connie made a rush for the door, but Agnes flew after her and clasped her round the waist.

"Yer be a silly!" she said. "Yer jest stay with her for one week."

"But II must go and tell father," said poor Connie.

"You needn'tI'll go an' tell him. Don't yer get into such a fright. Don't, for goodness' sake! Why, think of five shillin's a week, and jaunts into the country, and beautiful food, and poetry read aloud to yer, and hall the rest!"

"I has most select poetry here," said Mrs. Warren. "Did yer never yere of a man called Tennyson? An' did yer never read that most touching story of the consumptive gel called the 'May Queen'? 'Ef ye're wakin' call me hearly, call me hearly, mother dear.' I'll read yer that. It's the most beauteous thing."

"It sounds lovely," said Connie.

She was always arrested by the slightest thing which touched her keen fancy and rich imagination.

"And you 'ates the machines," said Agnes.

"Oh yes, I 'ates the machines," cried Connie. Then she added after a pause: "I'm 'ere, and I'll stay for one week. But I must go back first to get some o' my bits o' duds, and to tell father. You'd best let me go, ma'am; I won't be long away."

"But I can't do that," said Mrs. Warren; "it's a sight too late for a young, purty gel like you to be out. Agnes, now, can go and tell yer father, and bring wot clothes yer want to-morrow.Agnes, yer'll do that, won't yer?"

"Yesthat I will."

"They'll never let me stay," said Connie, reflecting on this fact with some satisfaction.

"We won't ax him, my dear," said Mrs. Warren.

"I must go, really, now," said Agnes. "You're all right, Connie; you're made. You'll be a fine lydy from this day out. And I'll come and see yer. W'en may I come, Mrs. Warren?"

"To-morrer evenin'," said Mrs. Warren. "You and Connie may have tea together to-morrer evenin', for I'm goin' out with some friends to the thayertre."

Poor Connie never quite knew how it happened, but somehow she found herself as wax in the strong hands of Mrs. Warren. Connie, it is true, gave a frightened cry when she heard Agnes shut the hall door behind her, and she felt positive that she had done exceedingly wrong. But Mrs. Warren really seemed kind, although Connie could not but wish that she was not quite so stout, and that her face was not of such an ugly brick red.

She gave the girl a nice supper, and talked to her all the time about the lovely life she would have there.

"Ef I takes to yer I'll maybe hadopt yer as my own daughter, my dear," she said. "You're a wery purty gel. And may I ax how old you are, my love?"

Connie answered that she was fourteen, and Mrs. Warren remarked that she was small for her age and looked younger. She showed the girl her own smart clothing, and tried the effect of her bit of fur round Connie's delicate throat.

"There," she said; "you can keep it. It's only rabbit; I can't afford no dearer. But yer'll look real foine in it when we goes out for our constooshionul to-morrow morning."

Connie was really touched and delighted with the present of the fur. She got very sleepy, too, after supper—more sleepy than she had ever felt in her life—and when Mrs. Warren suggested that her new little handmaid should retire early to bed, the girl was only too glad to obey.

CHAPTER VII

SHOPPING

Connie slept without dreams that night, and in the morning awoke with a start. What was the matter? Was she late? It was dreadful to be late at the doors of that cruel factory. Those who were late were docked of their pay.

Peter Harris was always very angry when his daughter did not bring in her full earnings on Saturday night. Connie cried out, "Father, father!" and then sat up in bed and pushed her golden hair back from her little face. What was the matter? Where was she? Why, what a pretty room! There was scarcely any light yet, and she could not see the different articles of furniture very distinctly, but it certainly seemed to her that she was in a most elegant apartment. Her room at home was—oh, so bare! just a very poor trundle-bed, and a little deal chest of drawers with a tiny looking-glass on top, and one broken chair to stand by her bedside. This was all.

But her present room had a carpet on the floor, and there were pictures hanging on the walls, and there were curtains to the windows, and the little bed on which she lay was covered with a gay counterpane—soft—almost as soft as silk.

Where could she be? It took her almost a minute to get back the memory of last night. Then she shuddered with the most curious feeling of mingled ecstasy and pain. She was not going to the factory to-day. She was not going to work at that horrid sewing-machine. She was not to meet Sue. She was not to be choked by the horrid air. She, Connie, had got a new situation, and Mrs. Warren was a very nice woman, although she was so fat and her dress was so loud that even Connie's untrained taste could not approve of it.

Just then a voice called to her:

"Get up, my dear; I'll have a cosy breakfast ready for yer by the time yer've put yourself tidily into yer clothes."

"Yes," thought Connie to herself, "I've done well to come. Agnes is right. I wonder what she'll say when she comes to tea this evening. I wonder if she met father. I do 'ope as father won't find me. I'd real like to stay on here for a bit; it's much, much nicer than the cruel sort of life I 'ave to home."

Connie dressed by the light which was now coming in more strongly through the window. Mrs. Warren pushed a can of hot water inside the door, and the girl washed with a strange, unwonted sense of luxury. She had no dress but the dark-blue, and she was therefore forced to put it on.

When she had completed her toilet she entered the sitting-room. Mrs. Warren, in her morning déshabille, looked a more unpleasing object than ever. Her hair was in tight22 curl-papers, and she wore a very loose and very dirty dressing-gown, which was made of a sort of pattern chintz, and gave her the effect of being a huge pyramid of coarse, faded flowers.

There was coffee, however, which smelled very good, on the hearth, and there was some toast and bacon, and some bread, butter, and jam. Connie and Mrs. Warren made a good meal, and then Mrs. Warren began to talk of the day's programme.

"I have a lot of shopping to do this morning," she said, "and we'll go out not later than ten o'clock sharp. It's wonderful wot a lot o' things I has to buy. There's sales on now, too, and we'll go to some of 'em. Maybe I'll get yer a bit o' ribbonyou're fond o' blue ribbon, I take it. Well, maybe I'll get it for yerthere's no saying. Anyhow, we'll walk down the streets, and wot shops we don't go into we'll press our noses against the panes o' glass and stare in. Now then, my dear, yer don't s'pose that I'll allow you to come out walking with the likes o' me with yer 'air down like that."

"Why, 'ow is it to be done?" said Connie. "I take it that it's beautiful; I ha' done it more tidy than ever."

"But I don't want it tidy. Now then, you set down yere close to the fire, so that you can toast yer toes, and I'll see to yer 'air."

Connie was forced to obey; more and more was she wax in the hands of her new employer. Mrs. Warren quickly took the hair-pins out of Connie's thick plait. She let it fall down to her waist, and then she unplaited it and brushed out the shining waves of lovely hair, and then said, with a smile of satisfaction:

"Now, I guess there won't be anybody prettier than you to walk abroad to-day."

"But I can't," said Connie"I don't ever wear my 'air like that; it's only young lydies as does that."

"Well, ain't you a lydy, and ain't I a lydy? You're going out with one, and yer'll wear yer 'air as I please."

Connie shivered; but presently the little dark-blue cap was placed over the masses of golden hair, the gray fur was fastened round the slender throat, and Connie marched out with Mrs. Warren.

Mrs. Warren's own dress was in all respects the reverse of her pretty young companion's. It consisted of a very voluminous silk cloak, which was lined with fur, and which gave the already stout woman a most portly appearance. On her head she wore a bonnet covered with artificial flowers, and she enveloped her hands in an enormous muff.

"Now, off we go," said Mrs. Warren. "You'll enjoy yerself, my purty."

It is quite true that Connie didat least, at first. This was the time of day when, with the exception of Sundays, she was always buried from view in the ugly warehouse. She was unaccustomed to the morning sunshine, and she was23 certainly unaccustomed to the handsome streets where Mrs. Warren conducted her.

They walked on, and soon found themselves in crowded thoroughfares. At last they stopped before the doors of a great shop, into which crowds of people were going.

"Oh, what a pretty girl!" said Connie to her companion.

A young girl, very like Connie herselfso like as to make the resemblance almost extraordinarywas entering the shop, accompanied by an old gentleman who was supporting himself by the aid of a gold-headed stick. The girl also had golden hair. She was dressed in dark blue, and had gray fur round her neck. But above the fur there peeped out a little pale-blue handkerchief made of very soft silk.

"That's purty," whispered Mrs. Warren to Connie. "Yer'd like a 'andkercher like thatyer shall 'ave one. Get on in front o' me; you're slimmer nor me; I want to push into the shop."

Connie obeyed. As she passed the fair young girl, the girl seemed to notice the extraordinary likeness between them, for she turned and looked at Connie and smiled. She also said something to her companion, who also stared at the girl. But stout Mrs. Warren poked Connie from behind, and she had to push forward, and presently found herself in the shop.

There it seemed to her that Mrs. Warren did very little buying. It is true she stopped at several counters, always choosing those which were most surrounded by customers; it is true she pulled things about, poking at the goods offered for sale, and making complaints about them, but always keeping Connie well to the fore.

A delicate color had sprung into the girl's cheeks, and almost every one turned to look at her. The shopmen turned; the shopgirls gazed; the customers forgot what they wanted in their amazement at Connie's beauty. Her hair, in especial, was the subject of universal admirationits thickness, its length, its marvelous color. The girl herself was quite unconscious of the admiration which her appearance produced, but Mrs. Warren knew well what a valuable acquisition she had made in little Connie.

When they left the shop she seemed to be in high good-humor. But, lo and behold! a change had taken place in the outside world. The sun, so bright and glorious, had hidden himself behind a murky yellow fog, which was coming up each moment thicker and thicker from the river.

"Oh dear!" said Mrs. Warren.

"Oh dear!" cried Connie too. "We won't get lost, will us, ma'am?"

"Lost?" cried Mrs. Warren, with a sniff. "Now, I call this fog the most beautiful fortunation thing that could have 'appened. We'll have a real jolly morning now, Connie. You come along o' me. There, childwalk a bit in front. Why, ye're a real, real beauty. I feel sort of ashamed to be walkin' with yer. Let folks think that you're out with yer nurse, my pretty. Yes, let 'em think that, and that she's screening yer from misfortun' wid her own ample person."

Thus Connie walked for several hours that day. In and out of crowded thoroughfares the two perambulated. Into shops they went, and out again they came. Everywhere Connie went first, and Mrs. Warren followed very close behind.

At last the good lady said that she had done her morning's shopping. Connie could not well recall what she had bought, and the pair trudged soberly home.

When they got there Mrs. Warren went straight to her own bedroom, and Connie sat down by the fire, feeling quite tired with so much exercise. Presently Mrs. Warren came out again. She had changed her dress, and had put on an ample satin gown of black with broad yellow stripes. She was in high good-humor, and going up to Connie, gave her a resounding smack on the cheek.

"Now," she said, "yer won't think 'ard of poor Mammy Warren. See wot I've gone an' got an' bought for yer."

Connie turned quickly. A soft little blue handkerchief, delicately folded in tissue-paper, was laid on the table by the girl.

"Whywhythat ain't for me!" said Connie.

"Yes, but it be! Why shouldn't it be for you? I saw yer lookin' at that purty young lydy who was as like yer as two peas. I watched 'ow yer stared at the blue 'andkercher, and 'ow yer sort o' longed for it."

"But indeedindeed I didn't."

"Anyhow, here's another, and yer can have it, and wear it peeping out among yer fur. I take it that yer blue 'andkercher'll take the cake."

"Then you've bought it for me?" said Connie.

"Yusdidn't I zay so?"

"But I never seen yer do it," said Connie.

"Seen me do it?" said Mrs. Warren, her eyes flashing with anger. "You was too much taken up with yer own conceits, my gelhevery one staring at yer, 'cos poor old Mammy Warren 'ad made yer so beautiful. But though you was full to the brim o' yourself, I warn't so selfish; I were thinkin' o' youand yere's yer 'andkercher."

Connie took up the handkerchief slowly. Strange as it may seem, it gave her no pleasure. She said, "Thank you, Mrs. Warren," in a subdued voice, and took it into her little bedroom.

Connie felt that she did not particularly want to wear the handkerchief. She did not know why, but a trouble, the first of the many troubles she was to undergo in the terrible society of Mrs. Warren, came over her. She went back again and sat down by the fire. During the greater part of the afternoon the stout woman slept. Connie watched her furtively. A strong desire to get up and run away seized her. Could she not get out of that house and go back to Sue and25 Giles? How happy she would feel in Giles's bare little room! How she would enjoy talking with the child! With what wonder they would both listen to Big Ben as he spoke in that voice of his the number of the hours! Giles would make up fairy-tales for Connie to listen to. How Connie did love the "wonnerful" things he said about the big "Woice"! One day it was cheerful, another day sad, another day very encouraging, another day full of that noble influence which the child himself so largely exercised. At all times it was an angel voice, speaking to mankind from high above this sordid world.

It helped Giles, and it helped Connie too. She sat by the fire in this well-furnished room and looked anxiously towards the door. Once she got up on tiptoe. She had almost reached the door, but had not quite done so, when Mrs. Warren turned, gave a loud snore, and opened her eyes. She did not speak when she saw Connie, but her eyes seemed to say briefly, "Well, don't you go any farther"; and Connie turned back into her small bedroom.

Sharp at four o'clock Mrs. Warren started up.

"Now then," she said, "I'm goin' to get the tea ready."

"Can I help you, ma'am?" asked Connie. "Shall I make you some toast, ma'am?"

"Toast?" cried Mrs. Warren. "Toast? Do you think I'd allow yer to spile yer purty face with the fire beatin' on it? Not a bit o' it! You set down thereit's a foine lydy you be, and I ha' to take care of yer."

"But why should yer do that, ma'am? I ain't put into the world to do naught. I ha' always worked 'ardfather wanted me to."

"Eh?" said Mrs. Warren. "But I'm yer father and mother both now, and I don't want yer to."

"Don't yer?" said Connie.

She sank down and folded her hands in her lap.

"I must do summut to whiten them 'ands o' yours," said Mrs. Warren; "and I'm goin' to get yer real purty stockings an' boots to wear. You must look the real lydya real lydy wears neat boots and good gloves."

"But I ain't a lydy," said Connie; "an' wots more," she added, "I don't want to be."

"You be a lydy," said Mrs. Warren; "the Halmighty made yer into one."

"I don't talk like one," said Connie.

"No; but then, yer needn't speak. Oh lor'! I suppose that's Agnes a-poundin' at the door. Oh, stand back, child, and I'll go to her."

Mrs. Warren opened the door, and Agnes stepped in.

"I ha' took French leave," she said. "I dunno wot they'll say at the factory, but yere I be. You promised, you know, Mrs. Warren, ma'am, as I shouldn't 'ave naught to do with factory life, niver no more."

"You needn't," said Mrs. Warren. "I ha' a deal o' work for yer to get through; but come along into my bedroom and we'll talk over things."

Mrs. Warren and Agnes disappeared into the bedroom of the former, Mrs. Warren having first taken the precaution to lock the sitting-room door and put the key into her pocket. Poor Connie felt more than ever that she was a prisoner. More than ever did she long for the old life which she had lived. Notwithstanding her father's drinking bouts, notwithstanding his cruelty and neglect, the free life, the above-board lifeeven the dull, dull factory lifewere all as heaven compared to this terrible, mysterious existence in Mrs. Warren's comfortable rooms.

CHAPTER VIII

COMPARISONS

Mrs. Warren and Agnes talked together for quite three quarters of an hour. When they came out of the bedroom, Mrs. Warren was wearing a tight-fitting cloth jacket, which made her look more enormous even than the cloak had done. She had a small black bonnet on her head, over which she had drawn a spotted net veil. Her hands were encased in decent black gloves, her skirt was short, and her boots tidy. She carried in her hand a fair-sized brown leather bag; and telling Connie that she was "goin' out," and would be back when she saw her and not before, left the two girls alone in the little sitting-room.

After she had shut the door behind her, Agnes went over to it, and possessing herself of the key, slipped it into her pocket. Then she stared hard at Connie.

"Well," she said, "an' 'ow do yer like it?"

"I don't like it at all," answered Connie, "I want to goI will go. I'd rayther a sight be back in the factory. Mrs. Warrenshe frightens me."

"You be a silly," said Agnes. "You talk like that 'cos you knows no better. Why, 'ere you are as cosy and well tended as gel could be. Look at this room. Think on the soft chair you're sittin' upon; think on the meals; think on yer bedroom; think on the beautiful walk you 'ad this morning. My word! you be a silly! No work to do, and nothing whatever to trouble yer, except to act the lydy. My word! ef you're discontent, the world'll come to an end. Wish I were in your shoesthat I do."

"Well, Agnes, get into them," said Connie. "I'm sure you're more than welcome. I'm jestjest pinin' for wot you thinks naught on. I want to see Giles and Sue andandfather. You git into my shoesyou like itI don't like it."

Agnes burst into a loud laugh.

"My word!" she said, "you're be a gel and a 'arf. Wouldn't I jest jump at gettin' into your shoes if I could? But there! yer shoes don't fit me, and that's the truth."

"Don't fit yer, don't they?" exclaimed Connie. "Wot do yer mean by that?"

"Too small," said Agnes, sticking out her ugly foot in its broken boot"too genteeltoo neat. No one could make a lydy o' me. Look at my 'ands." She spread out her coarse, stumpy fingers. "Look at my face. Why, yere's a glass; let's stand side by side, an' then let's compare. Big face; no nose to speak of; upper lip two inches long; mouthslit from ear to ear; freckles; eyes what the boys call pig's eyes; 'air rough and coarse; figure stumpy. Now look at you. Face fair as a lily; nose straight and small; mouth like a rosebud; eyes blue as the sky. No, Connie, it can't be done; what with that face o' yourn, and that gold 'air o' yourn, you're a beauty hout and hout. Yer face is yer fortoon', my purty maid."

"My face ain't my fortune."

"Things don't fit, Connie. You ha' got to stay yereand be a fine lydy. That's the way you works for yer livin'I ha' to work in a different sort."

"What sort? Oh, do tel me!"

"No; that's my secret. But I've spoke out plain with the old woman, and I'm comin' yere Saturday nightnot to stay, bless yer! no, but to do hodd jobs for her; for one thing, to look arter you when she's out. I 'spect she'll get Ronald back now you ha' come."

"Ronald!" cried Connie. "Who's he?"

"Never you mind; you'll know when yer see of 'im."

"Then I'm a prisoner," said Connie"that's what it means."

"Well, well! take it like that ef yer like. Ain't it natural that Mrs. Warren should want yer to stay now she ha' got yer? When yer stays willin'-like, as yer will all too soon, then yer'll 'ave yer liberty. Hin an' out then yer may go as yer pleases; there'll be naught to interfere. Yer'll jest do yer dooty then, and yer dooty'll be to please old Mammy Warren."

"Has my father missed me?" asked Connie, who saw by this time that she could not possibly cope with Agnes; if ever she was to effect her escape from this horrible place, it must be by guile.

"'Ow is father?" she asked. "'Ave he missed me yet?"

"Know nothing 'bout him. Don't think he have, for the boys, Dick and Hal, was 'ome when I come back. They 'ad no news for me at all."

"You saw Sue to-day?"

"Yus, I saw her, an' I kep' well away from her."

"Agnes," said Connie in a very pleading voice, "ef I must stay 'erean' I don't know wot I ha' done to be treated like thiswill yer take a message from me to little Giles?"

"Wot sort?" asked Agnes.

"Tell 'im straight from me that I can't come to see 'im for28 a few days, an' ax him to pray for me; an' tell him that I 'ears the Woice same as he 'ears the Woice, and tell 'im as it real comforts me. Wull yer do that, Agneswull yer, now?"

"Maybe," said Agnes; then after a pause she added, "Or maybe I won't. I 'ates yer Methody sort o' weak-minded folks. That's the worst o' you, Connie; you're real weak-minded, for all ye're so purty, what wid yer 'prays' an' yer Woice, indeed!"

"Hark! it's sounding now," said Connie.

She raised her little delicate hand, and turned her head to listen. The splendid notes filled the air. Connie murmured something under her breath.

"I know wot Giles 'ud say 'bout the Woice to-night," she murmured.

But Agnes burst into a loud laugh.

"My word!" she said. "You 're talkin' o' Big Ben. Well, you be a caution."

"He that shall endure," whispered Connie; and then a curious hidden sunshine seemed to come out and radiate her small face. She folded her hands. The impatience faded from her eyes. She sat still and quiet.

"Wot hever's the matter with yer?" asked Agnes.

"Naught as yer can understand, Aggie."

"Let's get tea," said Agnes. She started up and made vigorous preparations. Soon the tea was served and placed upon the little centre-table. It was an excellent tea, with shrimps and bread-and-butter, and cake and jam. Agnes ate enormously, but Connie was not as hungry as usual.

"Prime, I call it!" said Agnes. "My word! to think of gettin' all this and not workin' a bit for it! You be in luck, Connie Harrisyou be in luck."

When the meal was over, and Agnes had washed up and made the place tidy, she announced her intention of going to sleep.

"I'm dead-tired," she said, "and swallerin' sech a fillin' meal have made me drowsy. But I ha' the key in my pocket, so don't you be trying that little gime o'running away."

Agnes slept, and snored in her sleep, and Connie restlessly walked to the window and looked out. When Big Ben sounded again her eyes filled with tears. She had never spent such a long and dismal evening in her life.

Mammy Warren did not return home until between ten and eleven o'clock. Immediately on her arrival, Agnes took her departure. Mammy Warren then locked the door, and having provided herself with a stiff glass of whisky-and-water, desired Connie to hurry off to bed.

"Yer'll be losing yer purty sleep," she said, "and then where'll yer be?"

The next day Connie again walked abroad with Mrs. Warren. Once more she was dressed in the dark-blue costume, with her golden hair hanging in a great fleece down her back. But when she made her appearance without the little blue handkerchief, Mrs. Warren sent her back for it.

"I know wot I'm about," she said. "The blue in the 'andkercher'll add to the blue in yer eyes. Pop it on, gel, and be quick."

Connie obeyed.

"I don'twant to," she said.

"And w'y don't yer?"

The woman's voice was very fierce.

"I'm somehow sort o' feared."

"Take that for bein' sort o' feared," said Mrs. Warren; and she hit the child so fierce a blow on the arm that Connie cried out from the pain.

Poor Connie was a very timorous creature, however, and the effect of the blow was to make her meek and subservient. The blue handkerchief was tied on and arranged to Mrs. Warren's satisfaction, and they both went out into the open air.

They went by 'bus to quite a different part of the town on this occasion, and Mrs. Warren again assured her little companion that she had a great deal of shopping to get through.

"That is why I wear this cloak," she said; "I ha' bags fastened inside to hold the things as I buy."

Once again they got into a crowd, and once again Connie was desired to walk on a little way in front, and once again people turned to look at the slim, fair child with her beautiful face and lovely hair. Once more they entered several shops, and invariably chose the most crowded partsso crowded that Mrs. Warren whispered to Connie:

"We must wait till our turn, honey. We must ha' patience, dearie."

They had patience. Mrs. Warren did absolutely purchase half-a-dozen very coarse pocket-handkerchiefs, keeping Connie close to her all the time. One of these she straightway presented to the girl, saying in a loud voice as she did so to the attendant:

"I'm out with the purty dear to give her exercise. I am her nurse. She mustn't walk too far. No, thank you, mum, I'll carry the 'andkerchers 'ome myself; I won't trouble yer to send them to Portland Mansions.Now, come along, my dear; we mustn't waste our time in this 'ot shop. We must be hout, taking of our exercise."

They walked a very, very long way that morning, and Mrs. Warren, contrary to her yesterday's plan, did now and then expend a few pence. Whenever she did so she drew the shop people's attention to Connie, speaking of her as her charge, and a "dear, delicate young lydy," and begging of the people to be quick, as "'ot air" was so bad for the dear child; and invariably she refused to allow a parcel to be sent to Portland Mansions, saying that she preferred to carry it. At last, however, she seemed to think that Connie had had sufficient exercise, and they went home from the corner of Tottenham Court Road on the top of a 'bus.

On their way Connie turned innocently to her companion and said:

"Why ever did yer say as we lived in Portland Mansions?" But a sharp pinch on the girl's arm silenced her, and she felt more nervous and frightened than ever.

The moment they got home, Mrs. Warren again returned to her bedroom, and came back neatly dressed in a black and yellow silk, with a keen appreciation of roast pork and apple sauce, which had been preparing in the oven all the morning. Connie too was hungry.

When the meal came to an end Mrs. Warren said:

"More like a lydy you grows each minute. But, my dear, I must thank yer nivver to open yer mouth when you're out, for yer ain't got the accent. Yer must niver do it until yer has acquired the rightful accent."

"Was that why yer pinched me so 'ard when I axed why yer spoke o' Portland Mansions?" asked Connie.

Mrs. Warren burst into a loud laugh.

"Course it were," she said. "Don't yer nivver do nothing o' that sort agin."

"But we don't live in Portland Mansions. Why did yer say so?" asked Connie.

"Ax no questions and yer'll be told no lies," was Mrs. Warren's response.

She accompanied this apparently innocent speech with a look out of her fierce black eyes which caused poor Connie's heart to sink into her shoes. After a minute Mrs. Warren said:

"To-morrer's Saturday; we'll go out a bit in the morning, and then we'll take train into the country. I promised yer a jaunt, and yer shall 'ave it. I'm thinking a lot o' yer, my dear, and 'ow I can best help such a beautiful young gel. Yer accent must be 'tended to, and the best way to manage that is for you to have a refoined sort o' companion. Ronald is that sort. We'll go and fetch 'im 'ome to-morrer."

"Whoever is Ronald?" asked Connie. "Do tell me, please," she added in an interested voice, "for Agnes spoke of him yesterday."

"You wait till yer see," said Mrs. Warren. She nodded good-humoredly.

The rest of the day passed very much like the day before. It was again intensely dull to poor Connie. She had nothing whatever to do but to feed and sit still. Again Mrs. Warren slept until tea-time. Then Agnes made her appearance, and Mrs. Warren went out in a tight-fitting coat, and with a leather bag in her hand. Agnes made tea and scolded

Connie; and Connie grumbled and cried, and begged and begged to be given back her liberty.

Mrs. Warren returned a little later than the night before. Agnes went away; Mrs. Warren drank whisky-and-water, and Connie was sent to bed. Oh, it was a miserable night! And would her own people ever find her? Would Sue be satisfied that Connie was not quite lost? And would Father John look for her? Dear, kind, splendid Father John! What would she not give to hear his magnificent voice as he preached to the people once again? Would not her own father search heaven and earth to find his only child? He was so good to Connie when he was not drunkso proud of her, too, so glad when she kissed him so anxious to do the best he could for her! Would he give her up for ever? "Oh dear, dear!" thought the poor child, "if it was not for the Woice I believe I'd go mad; but the Woiceit holds me up. I'm 'appy enough w'en I 'ears it. Oh, little Giles, thank yer for telling me o' the wonnerful Woice!"

CHAPTER IX

A TRIP INTO THE COUNTRY

Saturday dawned a very bright and beautiful day. Mrs. Warren got up early, and Connie also rose, feeling somehow or other that she was going to have a pleasanter time than she had yet enjoyed since her imprisonment. Oh yes, she was quite certain now that she was imprisoned; but for what object it was impossible for her even to guess.

Mrs. Warren bustled out quite an hour earlier than usual. She did not go far on this occasion. She seemed a little anxious, and once or twice, to Connie's amazement, dodged down a back street as though she were afraid. Her red face turned quite pale when she did this, and she clutched Connie's arm and said in a faltering voice:

"I'm tuk with a stitch in my side! Oh, my poor, dear young lydy, I'm afeered as I won't be able to take yer for a long walk this blessed morning."

But when Connie, later on, inquired after the stitch, she was told to mind her own business, and she began to think that Mrs. Warren had pretended.

They reached Waterloo at quite an early hour, and there they took third-class tickets to a part of the country about thirty miles from London. It took them over an hour to get down, and during that time Connie sat by the window wrapped in contemplation. For the first time she saw green grass and hills and running water, and although it was midwinter she saw trees which seemed to her too magnificent and glorious for words. Her eyes shone with happiness, and she almost forgot Mrs. Warren's existence. At last they reached the little wayside station to which Mrs. Warren had taken tickets. They got out, and walked down a winding country lane.

"Is this real, real country?" asked Connie.

"Yustoo real for me."

"Oh ma'am, it's bootiful! But I dunna see the flowers."

"Flowers don't grow in the winter, silly."

"Don't they? I thought for sure I'd see 'em a-blowin' and a-growin'. Yer said soyer mind."

"Well, so yer wull, come springtime, ef ye're a good gel. Now, I want to talk wid yer wery serious-like."

"Oh ma'am, don't!" said poor Connie.

"None o' yer 'dont's' wid me! You ha' got to be very thankful to me for all I'm a-doin' for yerfeedin yer, and cockerin' yer up, and makin' a fuss o' yer, and brushing out yer 'air, and giving yer blue ties, and boots, and gloves."

"Oh ma'am, yes," said Connie; "and I'm wery much obleegedI am, trulybut I'd rayther a sight rayther, go 'ome to father; I would, ma'am."

"Wot little gels 'ud like isn't wot little gels 'ull get," said Mrs. Warren. "You come to me of yer own free will, and 'avin' come, yer'll stay. Ef yer makes a fuss, or lets out to anybody that yer don't like it, I've a little room in my housea room widdout no light and no winder, and so far away from any other room that yer might scream yerself sick and no one 'ud 'ear. Into that room yer goes ef yer makes trouble. And now, listen."

Mrs. Warren gripped Connie's arm so tight that the poor child had to suppress a scream.

"I know wot ye're been saying to Agnesa-grumblin' and a-grumblin' to Agnes, instead o' down on yer knees and thankin' the Almighty that yer've found Mammy Warren. I know all about it: Yer'll stop thatd'yer 'eard'yer 'ear?"

"Yus, ma'am," said Connie.

"Do yer, promise?"

"Yus, ma'am," said the poor child again.

"I'll see as yer keeps ityer little good-for-nothing beggar maid as I'm a-pamperin' of! Don't I work for yer, and toil for yer? And am I to have naught but grumbles for my pains? Yer won't like that rooman' it's there!"

"I won't grumble," said Connie, terrified, and not daring to do anything but propitiate her tyrant.

Mrs. Warren's manner altered.

"Wull," she said, "I ha' brought yer down all this long way to 'ave a plain talk, and I guess we 'ave 'ad it. You please me, and I'll do my dooty by you; but don't please me, and there ain't a gel in the whole of Lunnon'll be more misrubble than you. Don't think as yer'll git aw'y, for yer won'tno, not a bit o' it. And now I've something else to say. There's a young boy as we're goin' to see to-day. 'Is name is Ronald; he's a special friend o' mine. I ha' had that boy a-wisiting o' me afore now, but he were took bad with a sort of fever. My word! din't I nurse himthe best o' good things didn't I give 'im! But his narves went wrong, and I sent him into the country for change of hair. He's all right now. He's a very purty boy, same as you're a purty gel, and I'm goin' to bring him back to be a companion for yer."

"Oh ma'am!"

"Yus," said Mrs. Warren. "Yer'll like that, won't yer?"

"Oh yus, ma'am."

"Wull, nowwe'll be calling at the cottage in a few minutes, and wot I want yer to do is to have a talk with that yer boy. Ye're to tell him as I'm wonnerful good; ye're to tell him the sort o' things I does for yer. The poor boyhe got a notion in his head w'en he had the feverthat IIMammy Warrenwor cruel to him. You tell him as there ain't a word o' truth in it, for a kinder or more motherly body never lived. Ef yer don't tell him that, I'll soon find out; an' there's the room without winders an' without light real 'andy. Nowdo yer promise?"

These words were accompanied by a violent shake.

"Do yer promise?"

"Yus, I promise," said Connie, turning white.

Mrs. Warren had an extraordinary capacity for changing her voice and manner, even the expression of her face. While she had been extracting two promises from poor Connie, she looked like the most awful, wicked old woman that the worst parts of London could produce; but when on two points Connie had faithfully promised to yield to her wishes, she immediately altered her tactics, and became as genial and affectionate and pleasant as she had been the reverse a few minutes back.

"I believes yer," she said, "and you're a real nice child, and there won't be any one in the 'ole of Lunnun 'appier than you as long as yer take the part of poor old Mammy Warren. Now then, yere's the cottage, and soon we'll see the little man. He'll be a nice companion for yer, Connie, and yer'll like that, won't you?"

"Oh yes, ma'am," said Connie.

She was not a London child for nothing. She had known a good deal of its ups and downs, although nothing quite so terrible as her present position had ever entered into her mind. But she saw clearly enough that the only chance of deliverance for her, and perhaps for the poor little boy, was to carry out Mammy Warren's injunctions and to keep her promise to the letter. Accordingly, when Mrs. Warren's knock at the cottage door was answered by a kind-looking, pale-faced woman, Connie raised her bright blue eyes to the woman's face and listened with deep interest when Mrs. Warren inquired how the poor little boy was.

"Is it Ronald?" said the woman, whose name was Mrs. Cricket. "He's ever so much better; he's taken kindly to his food, and is out in the woods now at the back of the house playing all by himself."

"In the woods is he, now?" said Mrs. Warren. "Well, I ha' come to fetch him 'ome."

"Oh ma'am, I don't think he's as strong as all that."

"I ha' come to fetch him 'ome by the wishes of his parients," said Mrs. Warren. "I suppose," she added, "there's no doubt in yer moind that I 'ave come from the parients of the boy?"

"Oh no, ma'amnone, o' course. Will you come in, and I'll fetch him?"

"Is he quite right in the 'ead now?" said Mrs. Warren as she and Connie followed Mrs. Cricket into the cottage.

"He's better," said that good woman.

"No talk o' dark rooms and nasty nightmares and cruel old women? All those things quite forgot?" asked Mrs. Warren.

"He ain't spoke o' them lately."

"Well then, he's cured; he's quite fit to come 'ome. This young lydy is a r'lation o' hisn. I ha' brought her down to see 'im, and we'll all travel back to town together.You might go and find him, my dear," said Mrs. Warren, turning to Connie, and meanwhile putting her finger to her lips when Mrs. Cricket's back was turned in order to enjoin silence on the girl.

"You run out into the woods, my purty, and find the dear little boy and bring him back here as fast as yer like."

"Yes, missy," said Mrs. Cricket, opening the back door of the cottage, "you run out, straight up that path, and you'll find little Ronald."

Connie obeyed. She was glad to be alone in order to collect her thoughts. A wild idea of running away even now presented itself to her. But looking back, she perceived that Mrs. Warren had seated herself by the kitchen window and had her bold eyes fixed on her retreating little figure. No chance of running away. She must trust to luck, and for the present she must carry out Mrs. Warren's instructions.

Presently she came up to the object of her searchan exceedingly pretty, dark-haired boy of about ten years of age. His face was pale, his features regular, his eyes very large, brown, and soft, like rich brown velvet. He did not pay much attention to Connie, but went on laying out a pile of horse-chestnuts which he had gathered in rows on the ground.

"Be your name Ronald?" said Connie, coming up to him.

He looked at her, then sprang to his feet, and politely took off his little cap.

"Yes, my name is Ronald Harvey."

"I ha' come to fetch yer," said Connie.

"What for?" asked the boy.

"It's Mammy Warren," said Connie in a low tone.

"What?" asked the child.

His face, always pale, now turned ghastly white.

"She's such a nice woman," said Connie.

She sat down by Ronald.

"Show me these purty balls," she said. "Wot be they?"

"Chestnuts," said the boy. "Did you ever see them before? That was not true what you said aboutabout"

"Yus," said Connie, "it is true. I'm a little gel stayin' with her now, and youI want you to come back with me. She's real, real kind is Mammy Warren."

The boy put his hand up to his forehead.

"You seem a nice girl," he said, "and you look likelike a lady, only you don't talk the way ladies talk. I'm a gentleman. My father was an officer in the army, and my darling mother died, andand something happenedI don't know whatbut I was very, very, very ill. There was an awful time first, and there seemed to be a woman called Mammy Warren mixed up in the time and"

"Oh, you had fever," said Connie, "and youyou pictured things to yourself in the fever. But 'tain't true," she added earnestly. "I'm wid her, an' she's real, real, wonnerful kind."

"You wouldn't tell a lie, would you, girl?" said the boy.

Connie bit her lip hard.

"No," she said then in a choked voice.

"I wonder if it's true," said the boy. "It seems to me it was much more than the fever, but I can'tI can't quite remember."

"She is very kind," echoed Connie.

"Children, come along in," said a cheerful voice at that moment; and Connie, raising her eyes, saw the sturdy form of Mrs. Warren advancing up the path to meet her.

"She was terrible cruel in my time," said Ronald, glancing at the same figure. "I don't want to go back."

"Oh, dodo come back, for my sake!" whispered Connie.

He turned and looked into the beautiful little face.

"Boys have to be good," he said then, "andand brave. My father was a very brave man." Then he struggled to his feet.

"Well, Ronald," said Mrs. Warren, "and 'ow may yer be, my dear little boy? This is Connie, a cousin o' yourn. Wot playmates you two wull be! Ye're both comin' back with me to my nice 'ome this wery arfternoon. And now Mrs. Cricket 'as got a meal for us all and then yer little things'll be packed, Ronald, and I'll carry 'emfor in course yer nurse ought to carry yer clothes, my boy. We'll get off to the train as fast as ever we can arter we've had our meal. Now, children, foller me back to the cottage."

Mrs. Warren sailed on in front. Connie and Ronald followed after, hand in hand. There was quite a splendid color in Connie's pale cheeks now, for all of a sudden she saw a reason for her present life. She had got to protect Ronald, who was so much younger than herself. She would protect him with her very life if necessary.

CHAPTER X

THE RETURN TO LONDON

Mrs. Warren made a very hearty meal. She swallowed down cup after cup of strong coffee, and ate great hunches of thick bread-and-butter, and called out to the children not to shirk their food.

But, try as they would, neither Connie nor Ronald had much appetite. Connie, in spite of herself, could not help casting anxious glances at the little boy, and whenever she did so she found that Mrs. Warren had fixed her with her bold black eyes. It seemed to Connie that Mrs. Warren's eyes said quite as plainly as though her lips had spoken:

"I'll keep my word; there's the room with no winder and no light in ityer'll find yerself in there ef yer don't look purty sharp."

But notwithstanding the threatening expression of Mrs. Warren's eyes, Connie could not restrain all sign of feeling. Ronald, on the other hand, appeared quite bright. He devoted himself to Connie, helping her in the most gentlemanly way to the good things which Mrs. Cricket had provided.

"The apple jam is very nice," he said. "I watched Mrs. Cricket make it.Didn't I, Mrs. Cricket?"

"That you did, my little love," said the good woman. "And I give you a little saucer of it all hot and tasty for your tea, didn't I, my little love?"

"Oh yes," replied Ronald; "and didn't I like it, just!"

"Jam's wery bad for little boys," said Mrs. Warren at this juncture. "Jam guvs little boys fever an' shockin' cruel dreams. It's bread-and-butter as little boys should heat, and sometimes bread without butter in case they should turn bilious."

"Oh no, ma'am, begging your pardon," here interrupted Mrs. Cricket; "I haven't found it so with dear little Master Ronald. You tell his parients, please, ma'am, that it's milk as he wantslots and lots of country milkandand a chop now and then, and chicken if it's young and tender. That was 'ow I pulled 'im round.Wasn't it, Ronald, my dear?"

"Yes," said Ronald in his gentlemanly way. "You were very good indeed, Mrs. Cricket."

"Perhaps," interrupted Mrs. Warren, drawing herself up to her full height, which was by no means great, and pursing her lips, "yer'll 'ave the goodness, Mrs. Cricket, to put on a piece o' paper the exact diet yer like to horder for this yere boy. I'm a busy woman," said Mrs. Warren, "and I can't keep it in my 'ead. It's chuckens an' chops an' new-laid heggsyer did say new-laid heggs at thruppence each didn't yer, Mrs. Cricket?an' the richest an' best milk, mostly cream, I take it."

"I said nothing about new-laid eggs," said Mrs. Cricket, who was exceedingly exact and orderly in her mind; "but now, as you 'ave mentioned them, they'd come in very 'andy. But I certain did speak of the other things, and I'll write 'em down ef yer like."

"Do," said Mrs. Warren, "and I'll mention 'em to the child's parients w'en I see 'em."

But at this juncture something startling happened, for Ronald, white as a sheet, rose.

"Has my father come back?" he asked. "Have you heard from him? Are you taking me to him?"

Mrs. Warren gazed full at Ronald, and, quick as thought, she adopted his idea. Here would be a waya delightful wayof getting the boy back to her dreadful house.

"Now, ain't I good?" she said. "Don't I know wot a dear little boy wants? Yus, my love, ye're soon to be in the harms of yer dear parient."

"But you said both parients," interrupted Mrs. Cricket.

Mrs. Warren put up her finger to her lips. She had got the boy in her arms, and he found himself most unwillingly folded to her ample breast.

"Ain't one enough at a time?" was her most dubious remark. "And now then, Ronald, hurry up with yer things, for Connie and me, we must be hoff. We could leave yer behind, ef yer so wished it, but Lunnun 'ud be a much more convenient place for yer to meet yer father."

"Oh I'll go, I'll go!" said Ronald. "My darling, darling father! Oh, I did think I'd never see him again! And he's quite well, Mrs. Warren?"

"In splendid, splendid health," said Mrs. Warren. "Niver did I lay eyes on so 'andsome a man."

"And I'll see him to-night?" said Ronald.

"Yusef ye're quick."

Then Ronald darted into the next room, and Mrs. Cricket followed him, and Connie and Mrs. Warren faced each other. Mrs. Warren began to laugh immoderately.

"Young and tender chuckens," she said, "an' chops an' new-laid heggs an' milk. Wotever's the matter with yer, Connie?"

Connie answered timidly that she though Ronald a dear little boy, and very pretty, and that she hoped that he would soon get strong with the nourishing food that Mrs. Warren was going to give him. But here that worthy woman winked in so mysterious and awful a manner that poor Connie felt as though she had received an electric shock. After a time she spoke again.

"I'm so glad about his father!" she said. "His father was a hofficer in the harmy. Will he really see him to-night, Mrs. Warren?"

"Will the sky fall?" was Mrs. Warren's ambiguous answer. "Once for all, Connie, you ax no questions an' you'll be told no lies."

A very few moments afterwards Ronald came out of the little bedroom, prepared for his journey. Mrs. Cricket cried when she parted with him, but there were no tears in the boy's lovely eyeshe was all smiles and excitement.

"I'll bring my own, own father down to see you, Mrs. Cricket," he said; "maybe not to-morrow, but some day next week. For you've been very good to me, darling Mrs. Cricket."

Then Mrs. Cricket kissed him and cried over him again, and the scene might have been prolonged if Mrs. Warren had38 not caught the boy roughly by the shoulder and pulled him away.

As they were marching down the tiny path which led from the cottage to the high-road, Mrs. Cricket did venture to say in an anxious voice:

"I s'pose as Major Harvey'll pay me the little money as I spent on the dear child?"

"That he will," said Mrs. Warren. "I'll see him to-night, most like, and I'll be sure to mention the chuckens and the chops."

"Well then, good-bye again, darling," said Mrs. Cricket. Ronald blew a kiss to her, and then, taking Connie's hand, they marched down the high-road in the direction of the railway station, Mrs. Warren trotting by their side, carrying the small bundle which contained Ronald's clothes all tied up neatly in a blue check handkerchief.

"Yer'll be sure to tell yer father wot a good nurse I were to you, Ronald," she remarked as they found themselves alone in a third-class carriage.

"You're quite sure it was only a dream?" said Ronald then very earnestly.

"Wot do yer mean by that, chile?" inquired Mrs. Warren.

"I mean the dark room without any light, and the dreadful person whowhoflogged me, andthe hunger."

"Poor little kid!" said Mrs. Warren. "Didn't he 'ave the fever, and didn't Mammy Warren hold him in her arms, an', big boy that he be, walked up and down the room wid him, and tried to soothe him w'en he said them nasty lies? It wor a dream, my dear. W'y, Connie here can tell yer 'ow good I am to 'er."

"Wery good," said Connie"so good that there niver were no one better."

She tumbled out the words in desperation, and Mammy Warren gave her a radiant smile, and poked her playfully in the ribs, and said that she was quite the funniest gel she had ever come acrost. After this Connie was quite silent until the little party found themselves at Waterloo.

Here they mounted to the top of a 'bus, and Ronald, trembling with delight, clutched hold of Connie's hand.

"Stoop down," he said; "I want to whisper." Connie bent towards him. "Do you think my father will be waiting for me when we get back to Mrs. Warren's?"

"I don't know," was the only reply poor Connie could manage to give him.

At last the omnibus drive came to an end, and the trio walked the short remaining distance to Mrs. Warren's rooms. Ronald almost tumbled upstairs in his eagerness to get there first.

"Oh, how will he get in? I do hope he's not been waiting and gone away again."

Mrs. Warren opened the door with her latch key. The room was dark, for there was neither fire-light nor gas-light; but39 soon these deficiencies were supplied, for Mrs. Warren was exceedingly fond of creature comforts.

"I wonder when he'll come," said Ronald. He was standing by the table and looking anxiously with his big brown eyes all round him. "I do wonder when he'll come."

Mrs. Warren made no reply. She began to prepare supper. As she did so there came a knock at the door. Mrs. Warren went to open it. She had an eager conversation with some one who stood without, and then she and Agnes entered the room together. Ronald evidently knew Agnes, for he shrank away from her and regarded her arrival with the reverse of pleasure.

"Wulland 'ow yer?" said Agnes in a cheerful tone.

She chucked Ronald under the chin and remarked on his healthy appearance.

"Wull," said Mrs. Warren, "yer can't blame the pore child for that, seein' as he 'ave been cockered up on the best food in the landchuckens and chops, no less."

"Oh, dear me! how shockin' greedy you must be!" said Agnes. "I'm sure, ma'am," she continued, turning to Mrs. Warren, "no one could desire better than wot you 'as to eat."

"I like my own food," said Mrs. Warren, "although it be simplicity itself. There are two red 'errin's for supper to-night, and bread-and-butter and tea, and a little raspberry jam, and ef that ain't enough for anybody's palate, I don't know"

"My father, when he comes"began Ronald, but here Mrs. Warren turned to him.

"You're a manly boy, Ronald," she said, "and I know you'll tike wot I 'ave to say in a manly sperrit. Yer father have been called out o' Lunnon, and won't be back for a day or two. He sent a message by Agnes 'ere. He don't know the exact day as he'll be back, but he'll come wery soon."

"Yes," said Agnes, "I seen him."

"Where?" asked Ronald.

"In the street," said Agnes. "He come along 'ere an hour back. Ef you'd been 'ome he might ha' took yer back with him; but w'en he found that you was still in the country he wor that pleased 'is whole face seemed to smile, and he saidsaid 'e, 'Dear Mammy WarrenI'd like to chuck her under her chin.' Them was his wery words."

"I don't believe my father would say that sort of thing," answered Ronald.

"Oh my!" said Agnes. "Highty-tighty! Don't yer go an' say as I tells lies, young man"

"An' it's the wery thing he would say," interrupted Mrs. Warren, "for a plainer-spoken, more hagreeable man than the Major niver drew breath."

"He left yer a message," continued Agnes, "an' yer can tike it or leave itI don't care. Wot he said wor this. You're to obey Mammy Warren, an' be wery grateful to her, an' do40 jest wot she tells yer until he comes 'ome. He'll be 'ome any day, an' he'll come an' fetch yer then, and the more good yer be to Mammy Warren the better pleased he'll be."

Ronald sat down on a little stool. He had sat on that stool before. He looked with dim eyes across the over-furnished, hot, and terribly ugly room. That vision of delight which had buoyed him up all the way back to London was not to be realized for a few days. He must bear with Mrs. Warren for a few days. It did not enter into his head that the whole story about his father was false from beginning to end. The present disappointment was quite enough for so young a child to bear.

After this Mrs. Warren and Agnes conversed in semi-whispers, and presently they retired into Mrs Warren's bedroom, and Connie and Ronald were alone.

"I am glad yer've come 'ere, Ronald," said Connie.

"Yes," said Ronald. He pressed his little white hand against his forehead.

"You're missing your father, I know," continued Connie, "Somehow I'm a-missing o' mine."

"Have you a father, Connie?" asked the little boy.

"Yusthat I 'ave," said Connie. "Not a great, grand gentleman like yourn, but a father for all that."

"Is your father in London?" asked the boy.

"Oh yes," answered Connie, "and not far from 'ere, nayther."

"Then why aren't you with him?" asked Ronald.

"'Cos I can't be," replied Connie in a low whisper.

"Hush!" said Ronald.

Just then the door opened and Agnes came out. Mrs. Warren followed her. Mrs. Warren wore her usual tight-fitting jacket, but on this occasion Agnes carried a leather bag, which seemed to be stuffed so full that it was with difficulty it could be kept shut.

Mrs. Warren addressed the two children.

"I'm goin' to lock you two in," she said, "an' you'd best go to bed. There's a little bed made up in your room, Connie, for Ronald to sleep in; and as you're a deal older than that sweet little boy, you'll nurse him off to sleep, jest as though he wor your real brother. Arter he's asleep you can go to bed yerself, for there's nothing like early hours for beauty sleep. You yere me, Connie? You know wot to do?"

"Yus," answered Connie. Her voice was almost cheerful. She was so truly glad that Mrs. Warren was going out. When she heard the key turning in the lock, and knew that she and Ronald were locked in all alone, she scarcely seemed to mind, so glad was she of Ronald's company. Neither child spoke to the other until the retreating footsteps of Mrs. Warren and Agnes ceased to sound on the stairs.

Then Connie went up to Ronald, and kneeling down by him put her arms round him and kissed him.

"You're very pretty," said the little boy, "although you41 don't talk like a lady. But that doesn't matter," he added, "for you've got a lady's heart."

"I love you, Ronald," was Connie's answer.

Ronald now put his own arms round Connie's neck and kissed her once or twice on her peach-like cheek, and then they both sat down on the floor and were happy for a few minutes in each other's company. After that Ronald began to speak. He told Connie about his father and about his mother. He did not cry at all, as most children would have done, when he spoke of those he loved so dearly.

"Mother's dead nearly a year now," he said. "It was waiting for father that killed her. Father went out to a dreadful war in South Africa, and we heard that he was killed.

Mother wouldn't believe it; she never did believe it—never—and she taught me not to, and I never did. But, all the same, it killed her."

"And then wot became of you?" asked Connie.

"I was taken here," replied Ronald. "That's three or four months ago now. I remember quite well being out walking with my nurse. She wasn't very nice, my nurse wasn't; but she was—oh, so good and kind compared to—what—what happened afterwards! Darling mother was dead. They had put her body in the grave, and the angels had got her soul. I didn't like to think of the grave, but I did love to remember the angels. The last thing mother said when she was dying was, 'Ronald, when your father comes back, be sure you tell him that I never believed that he was really dead.'"

"I promised her, and then she said again, 'And you'll never believe it either, Ronald.' And I said that I never, never would, if it was a thousand years. And then she kissed me and smiled; and I s'pose the angels took her, for she never spoke any more."

"Well," said Connie, who did not want Ronald to dwell too long on this very sad scene, "tell us 'bout the day you come 'ere."

"Mother was in her grave," said Ronald, "and there was no one who thought very much about me; and my nurse—she was not half as kind as when mother lived. One day she took me for a walk. We went a long, long way, and presently she asked me to wait for her outside one of those awful gin-palaces. She used to go in there sometimes, even when mother was alive. Well, I waited and waited outside, but she never came out. I was not a bit frightened at first, of course, for my father's boy mustn't be a coward, must he, Connie?"

"No," answered Connie.

"But she didn't come out, and it got late, and people began to look at me, and by-and-by Mammy Warren came out of the gin-palace. She was—oh, so red in the face! and I thought I'd never seen so dreadfully stout a woman. She put her hand on my shoulder and said, 'Wotever are you doing here?' And I said, 'I'm waiting for my nurse, Hannah Waters.' And she said, 'Oh, then, you're the little boy!' And I stared at her, and42 she said, 'Pooh Hannah's took bad, and she's asked me to take you home. Come along at once, my dear.'

"I went with her. I wasn't a bit frightened—I had never been frightened in all my life up to then. But she didn't take me home at all. She brought me to this house. She was very kind to me at first, in a sort of a way, and she told me that my relations had given me to her to look after, and that I was to be her little boy for the present, and must do just what she wanted."

"Welland wot did she want?" asked Connie, trembling not a little.

"It wasn't so dreadful bad at first," continued Ronald. "She used to take me out every day for long walks, and she made me look very nice; and we went into shops, for she said she wanted to buy things, but I don't think she ever did buy much. I used to be tired sometimes; we walked such a very long way."

"And did she ever make you go a little, tiny bit in front of her?" said Connie.

"Why, yes," replied Ronald. "But I rather liked that, for, you see, I'm a gentleman, and she's not a lady."

"I wonder," said Connie, "ef she spoke of herself as your old nurse."

Ronald began to laugh.

"How clever of you to think of that, Connie! She always did; and whenever she did buy things she said they were for me; and she used to giveoh, tremendous grand addresses of where I lived."

"Portland Mansions, p'r'aps?" said Connie.

"Sometimes that, and sometimes other places; but of course the parcels were never sent there; she always carried them herself."

"And she wore a big, big cloak, with pockets inside?" asked Connie.

"Yes, she didshe did."

"She does just the same with me now," said Connie. "I go out with her every day, and we go into the big shopsinto the most crowded partsand she doesn't buy much. I like that the best part of the day, for all the rest of the time I have to stay here and do nothing."

"And so had I to stay in these rooms and do nothing," said Ronald. "But I won't have to stay long now," he continued, "as my dear, dear father has come home. Oh! I wish darling mother were alive, that she might feel as happy as I do to-night."

"But tell me, Ronald," continued Connie, "how was it yer got the fever?"

"I don't quite remember that part," said the little boy. "All that part was made up of dreams. There was a dreadful dream when I seemed to be quite well, and when I said something before some one, and Mammy Warren turned scarlet; and when I was alone sheshe flogged me and put me into43 a dark, dark room foroh! it seemed likefor ever. And I had nothing to eat, and I was so frightenedfor she said there was a bogy therethat I nearly died. I didn't like to be frightened, for it seemed as though I couldn't be father's own son if I were afraid. But I was afraid, ConnieI was. I'll have to tell darling father about it when I see him; I'm sure he'll forgive me, more particular when he knows the whole thing was only a fever dreamfor there's not any room in this house like that, is there, Connie."

"Yes, but there be," thought Connie. But she did not say so aloud.

That night Ronald slept as peacefully as though he were really back again with his father. But Connie lay awake. Anxious as she had been before Ronald's arrival, that state of things was nothing at all to her present anxiety.

The next day was Sunday, and if it had not been for Big Ben the two poor children would have had a most miserable time, for they were shut up in Mrs. Warren's room from morning till night. In vain they begged to be allowed to go out. Mrs. Warren said "No," and in so emphatic a manner that they did not dare to ask her twice.

Agnes did not come at all to the house on Sunday, and Connie and Ronald finally curled themselves up in the deep window-ledge, and Connie talked and told Ronald all about her past life. In particular she told him about Big Ben, and little Giles, and the wonderful, most wonderful "Woice." After that the children had a sort of play together, in which Ronald proved himself to be a most imaginative little person, for he invented many fresh stories with regard to Big Ben, assuring Connie that he was much more than a voice. He would not be at all surprised, he said if Big Ben was not a great angel who came straight down from heaven every hour to comfort the sorrowful people in Westminster. Ronald thought it extremely likely that this wonderful angel knew his own mother, and was on this special Sunday telling him to be a brave boy and keep up his heart, for most certainly he would be safe back with his father before another Sunday came.

"That's what he says," continued Ronald, "and that's what'll happen, you'll see, Connie. And when darling father comes here you shall come away too, for I won't leave you alone with Mammy Warren. She's not a real kind person, is she, Connie?"

"Don't ax me," said Connie. Ronald looked up into her face.

"You can't tell a lie at all well," he said. "You're trying to make me think that Mammy Warren's nice, but you're not doing it well, for I don't believe you."

Then the big clock once again tolled the hour, and Ronald laughed with glee.

"There's no doubt about it now," he said. "Father is coming, and very, very soon. Oh I am glad, and happy!"

During that Sunday the children had very little food, for Mrs. Warren seemed all of a sudden to have changed her tactics. Whether it was the fact that she was really angry at Mrs. Cricket's having fed the boy on chicken and mutton-chops, no one could tell; but all he did have on that eventful Sunday was weak tea, stale bread and butter, and a very little jam.

Towards evening the two poor little creatures were really hungry. By-and-by they clasped each other round the neck, and fell asleep in each other's arms. It was in this conditioncurled up near the firethat Mrs. Warren found them when she got home.

CHAPTER XI

A NEW DEPARTURE

With Monday morning, however, all things seemed to have altered. Mrs. Warren was up spry and early. She called Connie to come and help her, but she desired Ronald to lie in bed.

"It's a nasty day," she said; "there's sleet falling. We'll go out, of course, for fresh air is good for children, but we must none of us wear our best clothes."

"What do yer mean by that?" said Connie.

"Don't you go and ax me wot I mean; just do wot I tells yer. No dark-blue dress for yer to-day, missy. I ha' got a old gownd as 'ull fit yer fine."

Poor Connie trembled. Mrs. Warren went into her bedroom.

"'Ere, now," she said, "you put it on."

The old gown was certainly not at all nice. Its color was quite indescribable. It was very ragged and torn, too, round the bottom of the skirt. It dragged down in front so as almost to trip poor Connie when she tried to walk, and was several inches too short in the back.

Mrs. Warren desired Connie to take off her dainty shoes and stockings, and gave her some stockings with holes in them, and some very disreputable shoes down at the heel. She made her pin across her chest a little old shawl of an ugly pale pattern, and instead of allowing her to wear her hair in a golden fleece down her back, she plaited it, and tied it into a little bunch at the back of her head. She then put an old bonnet on the child's heada bonnet which must have once belonged to quite an elderly womanand tied it with strings in front. Connie felt terribly ashamed of herself.

"I'm all in rags," she said, "jest as though I wor a beggar maid."

"I've a fancy that yer shall wear these 'ere clothes to-day," said Mrs. Warren. "Yer've been a fine lydy too long; yer'll be a beggar maid to-day. W'en I tell yer wot to do in the street, yer'll do it. You can sing, I take it. Now then, you learn the words."

Mrs. Warren planted down before Connie the well-known words of "Home, Sweet Home."

"I know this without learning it," said the girl.

"An' you 'as a good woice, I take it."

"Middlin'," replied Connie.

"Wull, sing it for me now."

Connie struck up the familiar words, and so frightened was she that in real desperation she acquitted herself fairly well.

"You'll take a treble, an' the little boy 'ull do likewise, and I'll take a fine, deep second. Ah! I know 'ow to sing," said Mrs. Warren.

"You won't take little Ronald out on a dreadful sort o' day like this," said Connie.

"Wen I want yer adwice I'll ax fur it," said Mrs. Warren, with most withering sarcasm.

Poor Connie felt her heart suddenly fit to burst. What new and dreadful departure was this? Mrs. Warren now brought Ronald into the front room, and there she arrayed him in garments of the poorest type, allowing his little thin legs to be quite bare, and his very thin arms to show through his ragged jacket. She posed, however, a little red cap on the midst of his curly dark hair; and this cap most wonderfully became the child, so that few people could pass him in the street without noticing the sweetness of his angelic face. Then Mrs. Warren prepared herself for the part she was to take. She went into her bedroom for the purpose, and returned looking so exactly like a stout old beggar woman that the children would scarcely have known her. She had covered her left eye with a patch, and now only looked out on the world with her right one. Her hair was knotted untidily under a frowsy old bonnet, and a very thin shawl was bound across her ample breast.

"We'll do fine, I take it," she said to the children. "I am your mother, my dears; you'll both 'old me by the 'and. Purtier little lambs couldn't be seen than the two of yez. And ef poor, ugly Mammy Warren 'ave made herself still uglier for yer sweet sakes, 'oo can but love 'er for the ennoblin' deed? Wull, come along now, children; but first I'll build up the fire, for we'll be 'ungry arter this 'ere job."

The fire was built up to Mrs. Warren's satisfaction, and the three went downstairs. Ronald was quite speechless with shameto go out like this, to disgrace his brave father and his darling mother in this sort of fashion, was pure torture to the boy; but Connie, in the thought of him and the fear that he would take cold, almost forgot her own misery.

The three did not go anywhere by 'bus that day, but hurried down side alleys and back streets until they got into the region of Piccadilly. The children had not the least idea where they were. Suddenly, however, they came to a pause outside a large hotel, and there Mrs. Warren struck up the first note of "Home, Sweet Home."

She had timed everything well. The policeman was at the other end of his beat, and she would not be molested for quite ten minutes. The quavering, ugly notes of the old woman were well subdued, and Connie had a really fine voice, and it rose high on the bitter air in sweet, childish appeal and confidence. Ronald, too, was struck with a sudden thought. That hotel was a sort of place where father used to live when he was alive. Who could tell if his father himself might not have returned, and might not be there, and might not hear him if he sang loud enough and sweet enough?

The voice of the boy and the voice of the girl blended together, and Mrs. Warren skilfully dropped hers so as not to spoil the harmony. The people in the hotel were attracted by the sweet notes, and crowded to the windows. Then Connie's face of purest beautyConnie's face rendered all the more pathetic by the old bonnet and the dreadful, tattered dressand Ronald with his head thrown back, his red cap held in his hand, the white snow falling in flakes on his rich dark hair, made between them a picture which would melt the hardest heart. Sixpences and even shillings were showered from the windows, and as the last note of "Home, Sweet Home" died away Mrs. Warren pocketed quite a considerable harvest.

She and the children then moved on and did likewise before several other large buildings, but they were not so successful again as they had been with their first attempt. The police came back sooner than they were expected. Ronald began to cough, too, and Connie's face looked blue with cold. Mrs. Warren, however, was not disappointed. She spoke encouragingly and protectingly to the children.

"Come 'ome, loveys," she said; "come 'ome, my little dears."

They did get homeor, rather, they got back to the dreadful house where they were imprisonedlate in the afternoon, Ronald almost speechless with cold and fatigue, Connie trembling also, and aching in every limb.

But now unwonted comforts awaited them. Mrs. Warren had no idea of killing off these sources of wealth. She put Ronald into a hot bath, and rubbed his limbs until they glowed, and then moved his little bed in front of the fire and got him into it. Connie was also rubbed and dried and desired to dispense with her beggar's toilet.

Afterwards there was quite a good dinner of roast pork with crackling and apple sauce, and dreadful as their position was, both the poor children enjoyed this meal as they had never enjoyed food before.

Thus a few days went by, the children going out every morning with Mrs. Warren sometimes as beggar children, but sometimes again as children of the well-to-do. These two programmes formed the most interesting part of their little lives. For the rest of the day they sat huddled up together, sometimes talking, sometimes silent, while each day47 a bigger and bigger ache came into Ronald's heart. Why, oh why did not his father come to fetch him?

But as all things come to an end, so the children's life in Mrs. Warren's dreadful attics came to an abrupt conclusion.

One day, just as they were dressed to go out, there came a hurried knock at the door. It seemed to Connie, who was very sharp and observant, that Mrs. Warren did not much like the sound. She went to the door and, before opening it, called out, "Who's there?"

"Agnes," was the reply; whereupon Mrs. Warren opened the door a few inches, and Agnes squeezed in, immediately locking the door behind her. She whispered something into Mrs. Warren's ear, which caused that good woman to turn deadly white and stagger against the wall.

"Yer've no time to faint, ma'am," said Agnes. "'Erelet me slap yer on the back."

She gave two resounding whacks on Mrs. Warren's stout back, which caused that woman to heave a couple of profound sighs and then to recover her presence of mind.

She and Agnes then retired into her bedroom, where drawers were hastily opened, and much commotion was heard by the two prettily dressed and waiting children. In another minute or two Agnes came out alone.

"Wull," she said, "and 'ow be you, Connie?"

"I am all right," said Connie. "Where's Mammy Warren?"

"She's tuk bad, and won't want yer to go out a-walkin' with her to-day. Oh my! oh my! how spry we be! It 'minds me o' the old song, 'As Willikins were a-walkin' wid his Dinah one day.'"

"Agnes," said Connie, "I'm certain sure as there's some'ut wrong."

"Be yer now?" said Agnes. "Wull then, ye're mistook. Wot could be wrong? Ye're a very queer and suspicious gel, Connie Harristhe most suspicious as I hever see'd. Ye're just for all the world the most selfish gel as could be found in the whole o' Lunnun. Pore Mammy Warren was told of the sudden death of her sister, and that's all the sympathy you guvs her. Wery different she behaves to you and Ronald. 'Hagnes,' says she, 'tike those pore children for a run,' says she, 'and bring them 'ome safe in time for dinner,' says she, 'an' give 'em some roast mutton for dinner, poor darlin's,' says Mammy Warren; and then she falls to cryin', and 'Oh, my sister!' she says, and 'Oh, poor Georgina!' she sobs. Now then, the pair of yerout we goes, and I'll go wid yer."

Quick as thought Agnes accomplished her purpose, and the two prettily dressed childrenConnie with her hair down her back, Ronald looking like a little princefound themselves in the street. But if the two children thought that they had the slightest chance of running away they were terribly mistaken, for Agnes proved even a sharper taskmistress than Mrs. Warren. She seemed to Connie to have suddenly got quite old and very cruel and determined. She walked the children here, and she walked them there. They peered into shop windows and got into crowds, but they did no shopping that morning. Connie was rather glad of that, and now she was so accustomed to being stared at that she hardly took any notice; while as to Ronald, his sweet brown eyes looked full up into the face of every gentleman who passed, in the faint hope of discovering his father again.

It seemed to Connie that they were out longer than usual; but at last they did come back. Then, to their great surprise, they found the door of Mammy Warren's sitting-room wide opened.

"My word! 'ow can this 'ave 'appened?" said Agnes.

They all went in, and Agnes went straight to the bedroom. She came out presently, wearing a very grave face, and told the children that she greatly feared poor Mammy Warren had gone off her head with griefthat there wasn't a sign of her in the bedroom, nor anywhere in the house.

"And she's took her things, too," said Agnes. "Wull, now—wull, I must go and search for her. Yer dinner's in the oven, children, and I'll come back to see 'ow yer be sometime to-night, p'rhaps."

"Wull Mammy Warren come back to-night?" asked Connie.

"I don't know—maybe the poor soul is in the river by now. She wor took wery bad, thinkin' of her sister, Georgina. I'll lock yer in, of course, children, and yer can eat yer dinner and think o' yer mercies."

CHAPTER XII

LEFT ALONE

When Agnes went out the two children stared at each other.

"Connie," said Ronald, "I wish you'd tell me the real, real truth."

But Connie was trembling very much. "Don't yer ax me," she said. She suddenly burst into tears. "I am so dreadfully frightened," she cried. "I don't think I ever wor so frightened in all my life before. You're not half so frightened as I am, Ronald."

"Of course not," said Ronald, "for I am a boy, you see, and I'll be a man by-and-by. Besides, I have to think of fatherfather would have gone through anything. Once he was in a shipwreck. The ship was really wrecked, and a great many of the passengers were drowned. Father told me all about it, but it was from a friend of father's that I learned afterwards how splendid he was, savingoh, heaps of people! It was that night," continued Ronald, sitting down by the fire as he spoke, his eyes glowing with a great thought, and his little face all lit up by the fire-light"it was that night that he49 first found out how much he loved mother; for mother was in a great big Atlantic liner, and it was father who saved her life. Afterwards they were married to each other, and afterwards I came to themGod sent me, you know."

"Yus," said Connie.

She dried her eyes.

"Go on talking, Ronald," she said. "I never met a boy like you. I thought there were no one like Giles, but it seems to me some'ow that you're a bit betteryou're so wonnerful, wonnerful brave, and 'ave such a cunnin' way of talkin'. I s'pose that's 'cos youyou're a little gen'leman, Ronald."

Ronald made no answer to this. After a minute he said:

"There's no thanks to me to be bravethat is, when I'm brave it's all on account of father, and 'Like father, like son.' Mother used to teach me that proverb when I was very small. Shall I tell you other things that father did?"

"Oh yus, please," said Connie.

"He saved some people once in a great big fire. No one else had courage to go in, but he wasn't afraid of anything. And another time he saved a man on the field of battle. He got his V. C. for that."

"Wotever's a V. C.?" inquired Connie.

"Oh," said Ronald, "don't you even know that? How very ignorant you are, dear Connie. A V. C.why, it's better to be a Victoria Cross man than to be the greatest noble in the land. Even the King couldn't be more than a Victoria Cross man."

"Still, I don't understand," said Connie.

"It's an honor," said Ronald, "that's given for a very, very brave deed. Father had it; when he comes back he'll show you his Victoria Cross; then you'll know."

"Do yer think as he'll come soon?" asked Connie.

"He may come to-day," said Ronald"or he may not," he added, with a profound sigh.

The little boy had been talking with great excitement, but now the color faded from his cheeks and he coughed a little. He had coughed more or less since that dreadful day when Mrs. Warren had taken him out in the snowstorm. He was always rather a delicate child, and after his bad fever he was not fit to encounter such misery and hardship.

"Connie," he said after a time, "it's the worst of all dreadful things, isn't it, to pretend that you are what you aren't?"

"What do yer mean by that?" asked Connie.

"Well, it's this way. You praise me for being brave. I am not brave always; I am very frightened sometimes. I am very terribly frightened now, dear Connie."

"Oh Ronald!" said Connie, "if you're frightened hall's hup."

"Let me tell you," said Ronald. He laid his little, thin hand on the girl's arm. "It's about father. Do you think, Connie, that Mammy Warren could have invented that story about him?"

"I dunno," said Connie.

"But what do you think, Connie? Tell me just what you think."

"Tell me what you think, Ronald."

"I am afraid to think," said the child. "At first I believed it, just as though father had spoken himself to me. I thought for sure and certain he'd be waiting for me here. I didn't think for a single moment that he'd be the sort of father that would come and stand outside in the landing and go away again just because I wasn't here. For, you see, I am his own little boy; I am all he has got. I know father so well, I don't believe he could do that kind of thing."

"Oh, but you can't say," answered Connie. "Certain sure, it seemed as though Agnes spoke the truth."

"I thought that too; only father's a very refined sort of man, and he'd never, never chuck Mrs. Warren under the chin."

"Agnes might have invented that part," said poor Connie. But in her heart of hearts she had long ago given up all hope of Ronald's father coming to fetch him.

"She might," said Ronald; "that is quite true; and he might have had to go to the countryperhaps to rescue some one in great danger. He is the sort who are always doing that. That's quite, quite likely, for it would be in keeping with father's way. And he'd like me, of course, to be unselfish, and never to make a fusshe hated boys who made a fuss. Oh yes, I did believe it; and on Saturday night and on Sunday, when Big Ben talked to us, it seemed that it was mother telling me that father would soon be with me. But a whole week has gone and he hasn't come. Why, it's Saturday night again, Connie. I've been back again in this house for a whole week now, and father has never, never come."

"Maybe he'll come to-night," said Connie.

"I don't think so; somehow I'd sort of feel it in my bones if he was coming back."

"What do yer mean by that?" said Connie.

"Oh, I'd be springy-like and jumpy about. But I'm not. I feeloh, so lazy and soso tired! and a little bityes, a greatbitfrightenedterribly frightened."

"You must cheer up, Ronald," said Connie. Then she added, "I wish we could get out o' this. I wish I could pick the lock and get aw'y."

"Oh, I wish you could, Connie," said the child. "Couldn't you try?"

"I'm a'most afeered to go into Mammy Warren's room," said Connie; "for ef she did come back and see me any time, she'd punish me awful; but p'r'aps I might find tools for picking the lock in her room."

"Oh, do let's try!" said Ronald.

Connie half-rose, then sat down again.

"It's me that's the coward now," she said.

"Oh, how so, Connie?"

"'Cos," said Connie, "there's that dark room with no winder'tain't a dream, Ronald."

"I thought it wasn't," said Ronald, turning white.

"Noit's there," said Connie, "and I'm afeered o' it."

Ronald sat very still for a minute then. He was thinking hard. He was only a little boy of ten years old, but he was a very plucky one. He looked at Connie, who although a little older than he, was very slight and small for her age.

"Connie," he said, "if you and I are ever to make our escape we must not be frightened. Even the dark closet won't frighten me now. I am going into Mrs. Warren's room."

"Oh Ronald! Are you? Dare you?"

"Yes, I dare. Father did worse things than thatwhy should I be afraid?"

"You'd win the V. C., Ronald, wouldn't you, now?"

Ronald smiled.

"Not for such a little, little thing. But perhaps some day," he said; and his eyes looked very bright. "Connie, if we can unpick the lock and get the door open, where shall we go?"

"We'll go," said Connie in a brisk voice, "back to Father John as fast as ever we can."

"Father John," said Ronald"who is he?"

"I told you, RonnieI told you about him."

"I forgot for a minute," said Ronald. "You mean the street preacher."

"Yus," said Connie. "'E'll save us. There's no fear o' Mammy Warren getting to us ever again ef he takes us in 'and."

Ronald smiled.

"The only thing I'm afraid of is this," he said"that if it's true about father, he may come here and find me gone."

"Let's leave a note for him," said Connie then. "Let's put it on the table. If Mammy Warren should come back she'll find the note, but that won't do any harm, for she knows Father John, and she's awful afeered of him, 'cos she said as much, so she'd never follow us there."

"The very thing!" said Ronald. "Let's get some paper. Will you write the note, Connie?"

The children poked round in the sitting-room, and found a sheet of very thin paper, and an old pen, and a penny bottle of ink. Ronald dictated, and Connie wrote:

"Dear Father,I've waited here for a week. I am trying to be very brave. Connie's an awful nice girl. We've picked the lock here, father, and we've gone to Father John, in Adam Street. Please come quick, for your little boy is so very hungry for you. Come quick, darling father.Your little waiting boy, Ronald."

"That'll bring him," said Ronald. "We'll put it on the table."

Connie had written her letter badly, and there were several blots; but still a feat was accomplished. Her cheeks were bright with excitement now.

"What shall I put outside?" she asked"on the envelope, I mean."

Ronald thought for a minute; then he said in a slow and impressive voice:

"To Major Harvey, V. C., from Ronald."

"Nobody can mistake who it's meant for," said Ronald.

"Here's a bit of sealing-wax," said Connie. "Let's seal it."

They did so, Connie stamping the seal with a penny thimble which she took out of her pocket.

"And now," said Ronald, pulling himself up, "all is ready, and I am going into Mammy Warren's room to try and find tools for picking the lock."

"I'm a-goin' with yer," said Connie.

"Oh Connie, that is brave of you."

"No," said Connie, "it 'ud be real cowardly to let yer go alone."

Hand in hand the two children crossed the ugly sitting-room, and opened the door which led into that mysterious apartment known as Mammy Warren's room. It certainly was a very strange-looking place. There was no bed to be seen anywhere, which in itself was surprising. But Connie explained to Ronald that the huge wooden wardrobe was doubtless a press-bed which let down at night.

"She'd keep all kinds of things at the back of the bed," said the practical Connie, who had seen several similar arrangements in the houses of the poor.

This room, however, although ugly and darkvery darkseemed to be suspiciously bare. The children had turned on the gasfor evening had already arrivedand they could see with great distinctness.

Mammy Warren owned the upper part of this tenement-house, and no one ever came up the creaking stairs except to visit her. The children therefore knew that if there was a footstep they would be in danger. Connie, however, assured Ronald that she could put out the light and be innocently seated by the fire if Mammy Warren did arrive unexpectedly.

All was silence, however, on the creaking stairs, and they were able to resume their search. The chest of drawers stood with all its drawers open and each one of them empty. No sort of tool could the children find. The yellow and black silk dress had disappeared, but the disreputable old beggar's clothes hung on the peg behind the door. There was also a very ancient bonnet, which was hung by its strings over the dress. Otherwise there was not a scrap of anything whatever in the room except the press bedstead, which the children could not possibly open, and the empty chest of drawers.

"But here," said Connie, "is a door. P'rhaps it's a cupboard door."

"Let's try if it will open," said Ronald.

He turned the handle. The door shot back with a spring, and the boy's face turned pale.

"The dark closet!" said Connie. "The dark, dark room without a winder!"

Ronald caught hold of Connie's hand and squeezed it tightly. After a minute he said in a husky voice:

"Come away."

Connie shut the mysterious closet door. The children turned out the gas in Mammy Warren's bedroom, and went back to the sitting-room. Here they crouched down, pale and trembling, before the fire.

"Don't, Ronniedon't," said Connie.

"Hold me very tight, Connie," said the little boy.

She did so, pressing him to her heart and kissing his little face. After a minute tears came to his eyes, and he said in a sturdy tone:

"Now I am better. It was wrong of me to be so frightened."

"Harkthere's the Woice!" said Connie.

They sat very still while Big Ben proclaimed the hour of nine.

"What does he say?" asked Ronald, turning round and looking at Connie.

"I know," said Connie, a light on her pretty face. "Father John preached on it once. I know wot Big Ben's a-sayin' of to-night."

"Tell me," said Ronald.

"He that shall endure," said Connie. "Yes, Connie," repeated Ronald"'He that shall endure'"

"To the end," said Connie, "shall be saved," she added.

"Oh Connie!" cried the boy. "Do you really, really think so?"

"Father John says it, and Father John couldn't tell a lie," continued the girl. "He says that is one of God's promises, and God never made a mistake. 'He that shall endure to the endshall be saved.'"

"Then," said Ronald, "if we endure we shall be saved."

"Yes," replied Connie.

"You're not frightened, then?"

"Not after that," said Connie.

"How can you tell that was what Big Ben said?"

"'Eard him," said Connie.

She unclasped Ronald's arms from her neck and stood up.

"I'm better," she said; "I'm not frightened no more. Sometimes it's 'ard to endureFather John says it is. But "E that shall endure to the end'to the endhe made a great p'int o' that'shall be saved.'"

"Then we'll be saved," said Ronald.

"Yus," answered Connie.

She looked down at the little boy. The boy was gazing into the fire and smiling. Connie put on some fresh lumps of coal, and the fire broke into a cheerful blaze. It did not matter at all to the good coal whether it burned out its heart in an attic or a palace; wherever it was put to do its duty, it did it. Now54 gay little flames and cheerful bursts of bubbling gas rendered even the hideous room bright.

"W'y, it's long past tea!" said Connie. "I'll put on the kettle and we'll have our tea, Ronald. Maybe Aggie'll be back in a minute, and maybe she'd like a cup o' tea."

Connie put on the kettle, and then went to the cupboard to get out the provisions. These were exceedingly short. There was little more than a heel of very stale bread, and no butter, and only a scrape of jam; but there was a little tea in the bottom of the tea-canister, and a little coarse brown sugar in a cup.

Connie laid the table quite cheerfully.

"We'll toast the bread," she said. "Tea and toast is famous food."

She got an old, bent toasting-fork, and she and Ronald laughed and even joked a little as they browned the stale bread until it was quite crisp and tempting-looking.

"I'd ever so much rather have this tea than a great, big, grand one with Mammy Warren," said Connie.

"Yes, Connie," said the boy; "so would I."

They had no milk with their tea, but that was, after all but a small circumstance. They scraped out the jam-pot and spread its contents on the hot toast, and contrived to enjoy the slender meal to the utmost.

Ronald said nothing about breakfast the next morning; he doubtless did not even give it a thought. But Connie remembered it well, although she took care not to allude to it.

Ten o'clock struck, and still Agnes did not appear. Eleven, twelveand no sign either of Mammy Warren or the girl.

"Shall we go to bed?" said Ronald.

"Let's bring our beds and lay 'em on the floor," said Connie, "in this room. Some'ow I don't think as Mammy Warren 'ull come back to-night. She wouldn't 'ave tuk all her things ef she meant to come; would she, Ronald?"

"I don't know," said Ronald. He was very sleepy, for the hour was terribly late for so young a child to be awake.

After a little reflection Connie decided only to drag his bed into the front room. She could lie on the floor by his side, wrapped up in a blanket. The fire was built up with the last scrap of coal in the hod, and then Ronald lay down without undressing. Connie begged of him to take off his clothes, but he said to her:

"Maybe father'll come in the middle of the night. I somehow feel as if something must happen to-night, and I don't want not to be ready."

Connie therefore only removed his shoes. She tucked the blankets round him, and said, "Good-night, Ronnie."

"What is that verse?" asked Ronald again. "'He that shall endure to the end'"

"'Shall be saved,'" finished Connie.

When she came to these words she noticed that little Ronald was sound asleep. Connie changed her mind about lying55 down. She sat on the floor by the boy's side, laid her head on the pillow close to his, and also dropped asleep.

Big Ben called out the hour but the children slept. Perhaps the Voice spoke to them in their dreams, for they smiled now and then. Doubtless they were far away in those dreams from the dreadful attic, from the influence of a most cruel woman, from hunger and cold. The fire burned to a fine red glow, and then cooled down and grew gray and full of ashes, and eventually went out. For it had burned its heart out trying to help the children; and without a heart, even fire cannot keep alive.

But the two children slept on, although Ronald now stirred uneasily and coughed in his sleep. It seemed to Connie that she also was oppressed by something, as though a great and terrible nightmare were sitting on her chest. Ronald coughed louder and opened his eyes.

"Connie, Conniewhere are we?" he cried.

Connie sat up with a stare.

"I be stiff," she began, "andand cold. Wotever's the hour? Bide a bit, Ronald, and I'll find the matches and turn on the gas."

"What's the matter with the room?" said Ronald.

"I don't know nothing," said Connie.

"My eyes smart," said Ronald, "and I can't breathe."

"I feel queer too," said Connie. "I won't be a second finding out, though. You lie quiet."

She groped about, found a match-box, which still contained a few matches, struck a light, and applied it to the gas, which was at full pressure now, and roared out, making a great flame.

"W'y, the room's full o' smoke," said Connie. "Wottever can it be?"

Ronald sat up in bed, opening his eyes.

"Where does it come from?" he said. "The fire is out."

Just then Big Ben proclaimed the hour of three.

"He that shall endure," thought Connie. "To the end," darted through Ronald's mind; and just then both children heard an unmistakable and awful roar. Was it the roar of human voices or the roar of something elsea devouring and awful element? Connie turned white. Now, if ever, was the time to be brave.

"I'll open the winder and look out," she said.

She sprang towards it and, with a great effort, pushed it half up. The moment she did so, the noise from without came louder, and the noise from within was more deafening.

"Fire! fire!" shouted a multitude of people from below in the street; and "Fire! fire!" cried the frenzied inhabitants of the old tenement-house. Connie and Ronald were on the top story. Connie went back to Ronald.

"The house is on fire, Ronnie!" she said. "But we mustn't be frightened, either of us; we must think of the grand verse, and of what Big Ben said. Big Ben's an angel, you mind; Giles knows all about that."

"Oh yes," said Ronald, his teeth chattering; for the draught from the open window, although it relieved his breathing, made him intensely cold. "It's a beautiful verse, isn't it, Connie?" he continued.

"Yus," said Connie. "Let's get to the winder, Ronnie dear. We'll call out. There are people down in the street. The fire-engines 'ull be on in a minute; we'll be saved, in course."

"Oh, of course," said Ronnie. He staggered to the floor, and put his feet into his shoes. "A good thing I wasn't undressed," he said.

"Yus," said Connie. "Now, let's get to the winder."

The children staggered there. The smoke was getting more dense; the room was filling faster and faster with the horrible, blinding, suffocating thing. But at the window there was relief. Connie put out her head for a minute, and then quickly drew it back.

"There's flames burstin' out o' the winders," she said. "I wish as the firemen 'ud come."

The children clung to one another. Just then, above the roar of the flames and the screams of the people, something else was distinctly audible. The fast approach of horses; the gallant figures of men in brass helmets: the brave firemenmembers of the noblest brigade in the worldwere on the spot.

"It's hall right," said Connie. "They've come. Don't yer be a bit frightened, Ronnie; we'll soon be out o' this. You ax Giles w'en you see him wot 'e thinks o' firemen. 'Es father were one. Oh, there's no fear now that they've come!"

She pressed close to the window and put out her head and shoulders. Ronald did likewise. The men out in the street were acting promptly. The hose were brought to bear on the increasing flames. But all to no purpose; the house was past saving. Was any one within?

"No," said a woman down in the crowd; "hevery soul is out, even to my last bibybless him!"

She gave a hysterical cry, and sat down on a neighboring doorstep.

But the firemen of the London Brigade are very careful to ascertain for themselves whether there is any likelihood of loss of life.

"Has any one come down from the top floor?" asked a tall young man. He had a splendid figurebroad, square shoulders, and a light and athletic framewhich showed at once that he was the very best possible sort of fireman.

Just then the flames burst out more brightly than ever, and Connie, with her fair hair surrounding her little face, and Ronald clinging to her hand, were both distinctly seen.

"My God!" cried the firemen, "there are children up there. Put the escape up at oncedon't lose an instantI am going up to them."

"You can't; it's certain death," said one or two. Several other voices were also raised in expostulation. But if any one in that crowd supposed that they were going to turn George Anderson, the bravest fireman in London, from his purpose, they were mistaken.

"That little angel face, and the face of the boy by her side!" he said once or twice under his breath. And then up and up he wentup and upthe children in the burning room (for the flames had broken out behind them now) watching and watching. His fear was that they might fall from their perilous position. But they had both crept out on to the window-ledge.

"Courage, courage!" he shouted to them. "Hold tightI'll be there in a minute!"

"The window is so hot!" gasped Connie.

"Thinkthink of the Voice," whispered Ronald.

He closed his eyes. In another minute he would have been beyond all earthly succor, and up in those beautiful realms where angels live, and his mother would meet him. But this was not to be.

In less than an instant a firm hand rescued the two children from their perilous position, and they were brought down to the ground uninjured. Ronald fainted in that descent, but Connie kept her consciousness. They were out of Mammy Warren's awful house. She had a queer sense as though she had been delivered from a worse danger even than fire.

People crowded round, and presently the tall fireman came up.

"What is your name?" he said to Connie.

"Connie," she replied.

"Well, Connie," he answered, "it was the sight of your beautiful face in the window that gave me courage to save yer. Now, do you want to have a shelter for yourself and your little brother to-night?'

"Thank you, sir," said Connie. The man pulled a cardit looked just like a gentleman's visiting cardout of his pocket.

"Will you take that," he said, "to No. Carlyle Terrace? It's just round the corner. Take your little brother with you. There are two bells to the house. Look for the one that has the word 'Night' written under it. It used to be a doctor's house, but there's no doctor there now. My mother will understandgive her that card, and tell her what has happened. Good night."

He turned away. It was some time before Connie and Ronald could get rid of the many neighbors who volunteered help, and who regarded the two pretty children as the hero and heroine of the hour. Offers of a shake-down for the night, of a hasty meal, of a warm fire, came to Connie from all sorts of people. But she had made up her mind to follow out the directions of the tall fireman, and saying that she58 had friends at No. Carlyle Terrace, she and Ronald soon started off to go to the address the fireman had given them.

They were both too excited to feel the effects of all they had gone through at first, but when they reached the house, and Connie pressed the button of the bell which had the word "Night" written under it, she was trembling exceedingly.

"Why are we coming here?" asked Ronald.

"I dunno," said Connie. "Seems as though a hangel was with us all the time."

"I expect so," answered Ronald in a very weak voice.

"And," continued Connie, "he's a-leadin' of us 'ere."

They had pressed the bell, and quicklywonderfully quicklythey heard steps running down the stairs; and the door was opened by a tall womanvery tall and very thinwith a beautiful pale face and soft motherly eyes.

"What is it?" she asked. "What is the matter? Oh, my poor little dears! And how you smell of fire! Have you been in a fire?"

"Please, ma'am," said Connie, "be yer the mother o' Mr. George Andersonthe bravest fireman, ma'am? He told me to give yer this card, ma'am."

"I am Mrs. Anderson. Oh, of course, if he's sent you"

"'E saved us from the fire, ma'am," said Connie.

"Come in, you poor little things," said Mrs Anderson. She drew the children in; she shut the door behind them. It seemed to Connie when that door shut that it shut out sorrow and pain and hunger and cold; for within the house there was warmthnot only warmth for frozen little bodies, but for tired souls.

Mrs. Anderson was one of the most motherly women in London; and George, her son, knew what he was about when he sent the children to her.

Soon they were revived with warm baths and with hot port-wine and water, and very soon afterwards they were both lying in beds covered with linen sheets that felt soft and fine as silk. But Mrs. Anderson sat by them both while they slept, for she did not like the look on the boy's face, and felt very much afraid of the shock for him.

"The little girl can stand more," she said to herself. "She's a beautiful little creature, but she's a child of the people. She has been accustomed to hardships all her life; but with the boy it's differenthe's a gentleman by birth. Something very cruel has happened to him, poor little lad! and this seems to be the final straw."

Mrs. Anderson was a very wise woman, and her fears with regard to little Ronald were all too quickly realized. By the morning the boy was in a high state of fever. A doctor was summoned, and Mrs. Anderson herself nursed him day and night. Connie begged to be allowed to remain, and her request was granted.

"For the present you shall stay with me," said Mrs. Anderson. "I don't know your story, nor the story of this little fellow, but I am determined to save his life if I can."

"I can tell yer something," said Connie. "Little Ronald's a real gent'e's the son of a hofficer in 'Is Majesty's harmy, an' the hofficer's name is Major Harvey, V. C."

"What?" cried Mrs. Anderson. She started back in amazement. "Why, I knew him and his wife," she said. "I know he was killed in South Africa, and I know his dear wife died about a year ago. Why, I've been looking for this child. Is your story quite true, little girl?"

"Yus, it's quite true," said Connie. "But tell medo tell meis his father really dead?"

"I fear so. It is true that his death was not absolutely confirmed; but he has been missing for over two years."

"Ma'am," said Connie, "wot do yer mean by his death not bein' confirmed?"

"I mean this, little girl," said Mrs. Anderson"that his body was never found."

"Then he ain't dead," said Connie.

"What do you mean?"

"I feel it in my bones," said Connie, "same as Ronald felt it in his bones. 'E ain't dead."

Mrs. Anderson laid her hand on the girl's pretty hair.

"I am getting in a real trained nurse to look after Ronald Harvey," she said. "If he's the son of my old friend, more than ever is he my care now; and you this evening, little Connie, shall tell me your story."

This Connie did. When she had described all that had occurred to her during the last few weeks, Mrs. Anderson was so amazed that she could hardly speak.

"My poor child!" she said. "You can't guess what terrible dangers you've escaped. That dreadful woman was, without doubt, a member of a large gang of burglars. Several have been arrested within the last day or two, and I have no doubt we shall hear of her soon at the police courts."

"Burglars?" said Connie "burglars? Them be thieves, bean't they?"

"Yes thieves."

"But what could she do with us?" said Connie.

"She used you for her own purposes. While people were looking at you, she was doubtless picking their pockets. Don't think any more about it, dear, only be thankful that you have escaped. And now, don't you feel very anxious about your father and your old friends?"

"Yus," said Connie. "I'd like to go home. I'd like them to know once for all what happened."

"Would you like to go back to-night? You can return to me, you know. I shall be up with Ronald until far into the night."

Connie rose swiftly.

"You're not afraid of the streets, my poor little child?"

"Oh no, ma'am. I'm only quite an ordinary girl. I ha' learnt my lesson," continued Connie. "I were real discontent wid my life at the factory, but I'll be discontent no more."

"You had a sharp lesson," said Mrs. Anderson. "I think God wants you to be a particularly good and a particularly brave woman, or He wouldn't have let you go through so much."

"Yes, ma'am," answered Connie; "and I'll try 'ard to be good and brave."

CHAPTER XIII

PETER HARRIS

While Connie was going through such strange adventures in Mammy Warren's attic room, her father, Giles, and Sue, and dear Father John were nearly distracted about her.

Peter Harris was a rough, fierce, unkempt individual. He was fond of drink. He was not at all easily impressed by good things; but, as has been said before, if he had one tender spot in his heart it was for Connie. When he drank he was dreadfully unkind to his child; but in his sober moments there was nothing he would not do for the pretty, motherless girl.

As day after day passed without his seeing her, he got nearly frantic with anxiety. At first he tried to make nothing of her disappearance, saying that the girl had doubtless gone to visit some friends; but when a few days went by and there were no tidings of her, and Sue assured him that she not only never appeared now at the great warehouse in Cheapside where they used to work together, but also that she had been seen last with Agnes Coppenger, and that Agnes Coppenger had also disappeared from her work at the sewing-machine, he began to fear that something bad had happened.

Father John was consulted, and Father John advised the necessity of at once acquainting the police. But although the police did their best, they could get no trace whatever either of Agnes or of Connie.

Thus the days passed, and Connie's friends were very unhappy about her. Her absence had a bad effect on Peter, who, from his state of grief and uneasiness, had taken more and more consolation out of the gin-palace which he was fond of frequenting. Every night now he came home tipsy, and the neighbors were afraid to go near. Soon he began to abuse Connie, to say unkind things about her, and to fly into a passion with any neighbor who mentioned her name.

Giles shed silent tears for his old playmate, and even the voice of Big Ben hardly comforted him, so much did he miss the genial companionship of pretty Connie. But now at last the girl herself was going home. She had no fear. She was full of a wild and yet terrible delight. How often she had longed for her father! Connie had a great deal of imagination, and during the dreadful time spent at Mother Warren's, and in especial since Ronald had come, she began61 to compare her father with Ronald's, and gradually but surely to forget the cruel and terrible scenes when that father was drunk, and to think of him only in his best moments when he kissed her and petted her and called her his dear little motherless girl.

Oh, he would be glad to see her now! He would rejoice in her company.

Connie quickly found the old house in Adam Street, and ran up the stairs. One or two people recognized her, and said, "Hullo, Con! you back?" but being too busy with their struggle for life, did not show any undue curiosity.

"Is my father in?" asked Connie of one.

The man said, "He be." And then he added, "Yer'd best be careful. He ain't, to say, in his pleasantest mood to-night."

Connie reached the well-known landing. She turned the handle of the door. It was locked. She heard some one moving within. Then a rough voice said:

"Get out o' that!"

"It's me, father!" called Connie back. "It's Connie!"

"Don't want yerget away!" said the voice.

Connie knelt down and called through the keyhole:

"It's meI've 'ad a dreadful timelet me in."

"Go 'waydon't want yerget out o' this!"

"Oh fatherfather!" called Connie. She began to sob. After all her dreams, after all her longings, after all her cruel trialsto be treated like this, and by her father! It seemed to shake her very belief in fathers, even in the great Father of all.

"Pleasepleasel'm jest wanting yer awfu' bad!" she pleaded.

Her gentle and moving voicethat voice for which Peter Harris, when sober and in his right mind, so starved to hear againnow acted upon him in quite the opposite direction. He had not taken enough to make him stupid, only enough to rouse his worst passions. He strode across the room, flung the door wide, and lifting Connie from her knees, said to her:

"Listen. You left me without rhyme or reasonnot even a word or a thought. I sorrowed for yer till I turned to 'ate yer! Now then, get out o' this. I don't want yer, niver no more. Go down them stairs, unless yer want me to push yer down. Go 'wayand be quick!"

There was a scowl on his angry face, a ferocious look in his eyes. Connie turned quite gently, and without any apparent anger went downstairs.

"Ah!" said a man in the street, "thought yer wouldn't stay long."

"He's wery bad," said Connie. She walked slowly, as though her heart were bleeding, down Adam Street until she came to the house where Father John Atkins lived.

It was a little house, much smaller than its neighbors. Father John's room was on the ground floor. She knocked62 at the door. There was no answer. She turned the handle: it yielded to her pressure. She went in, sank down on the nearest chair, and covered her face with both her hands.

She was trembling exceedingly. The shock of her father's treatment was far greater than she could well bear in her present weak and over-excited condition. She had gone throughoh, so muchso very much! That awful time with Mammy Warren; her anxiety with regard to little Ronald; and then that final, awful, never-to-be-forgotten day, that night which was surely like no other night that had ever dawned on the worldthe noise of the gathering flames, the terrific roar they made through the old building; the shouts of the people down below; the heat, the smoke, the pain, the cruel, cruel fear; and then last but not leastthe deliverance!

When that gallant fireman appeared, it seemed to both Connie and Ronald as though the gates of heaven had opened, and they had been taken straight away from the pains of hell into the glories of the blest. But all these things told on the nerves, and when Connie now had been turned away from her father's door, she was absolutely unfit for such treatment.

When she reached Father John's she was as weak and miserable a poor little girl as could found anywhere in London.

"My dear! my dear!" said the kind voicethe sort of voice that always thrilled the hearts of those who listened to him. A hand was laid on the weeping girl's shoulder. "Look up," said the voice again. Then there was a startled cry, an exclamation of the purest pleasure.

"Why Conniemy dear Conniethe good Lord has heard our prayers and has sent you back again!"

"Don't matter," said Connie, sobbing on, quite impervious to the kindness, quite unmoved by the sympathy. "There ain't no Father 'chart 'eaven," she continued. "I don't believe in 'Im no more. There ain't no Father, and no Jesus Christ. Ef there were, my own father wouldn't treat me so bitter cruel."

"Come, Connie," said the preacher, "you know quite well that you don't mean those dreadful words. Sit down now by the cosy fire; sit in my own little chair, and I'll talk to you, my child. Why, Connie, can't you guess that we've been praying for you?"

"Don't matter," whispered Connie again.

The preacher looked at her attentively. He put his kind hand for a minute on her forehead, and then, with that marvellous knowledge which he possessed of the human heart and the human needs, he said nothing for the time being. Connie was not fit to argue, and he knew she was worn-out. He got her to sit in the old arm-chair, and to lay her golden head against a soft cushion, and then he prepared coffeestrong coffeeboth for her and himself.

It was late, and he was deadly tired. He had been up all the night before. It was his custom often to spend his nights in this fashion; for, as he was fond of expressing it, the Divine63 Master seemed to have more work for him to do at night than in the daytime.

"There are plenty of others to help in the daytime," thought Father John, "but in the darkness the sin and the shame are past talking about. If I can lift a burden from one heart, and help one poor suffering soul, surely that is the best night's rest I can attain to."

Last night he had put a drunken woman to bed. He had found her on a doorstep, and had managed, notwithstanding his small stature and slender frame, to drag her upstairs. There her terrified children met him. He managed to get them into a calm state of mind, and then induced them to help him for all they were worth. The great, bulky woman was undressed and put into bed. She slept, and snored loudly, and the children crowded round. He made them also go to bed, and went away, promising to call in the morning.

He did so. The woman was awake, conscious, and bitterly ashamed. He spoke to her as he alone knew how, and, before he left, induced her to go with him to take the pledge. He then gave her a little money out of his slender earnings to get a meal for the children, and spent the rest of the day trying to get fresh employment for her. She had been thrown out of work by her misdemeanors; but Father John was a power, and more than one lady promised to try Mrs. Simpkins once again. The little preacher was, therefore, more tired than his wont. He bent over Connie. She drank her coffee, and, soothed by his presence, became calmer herself.

"Now then," he said, "you will tell me everything. Why did you run away?"

"'Cos I were tired o' machine-work. But, oh, Father John! I niver, niver meant to stay aw'y. I jest thought as I were to get a nice new situation; I niver guessed as it 'ud be a prison." Connie then told her story, with many gaps and pauses.

"You see," said Father John when she had finished, "that when you took the management of your own life into your own hands you did a very dangerous thing. God was guiding you, and you thought you could do without Him. You have been punished."

"Yus," said Connie. "I'll niver be the same again."

"I hope, indeed, that you will not be the same. You have gone through marvellous adventures, and but for God Himself you would not now be in the world. It is not only your pain and misery that you have to consider, but you have also to think of the pain and misery you inflicted on others."

"No," said Connie defiantly, "that I won't do. I thought father 'ud care, but he turned me from 'ome."

"He did care, Connie. I never knew any one so distracted. He cared so terribly, and was so sore about you, that he took to drink to drown his pain. In the morning, when he is sober, you will see what a welcome he will give you."

"No," said Connie, shaking her head.

"But I say he will. He will help you, and he will be a father to you. I will take you to him myself in the morning."

Connie did not say anything more. When she had finished her coffee, the preacher suggested that he should take her to Sue and Giles. The girl looked at him wildly. In telling her story, she had never mentioned the name of the lady who had taken her in, nor the name of the brave fireman who had befriended her. But now Father John boldly asked her for these particulars. Her little face flushed and she looked up defiantly.

"I dunnut want to give 'em," she said.

"But I ask you for them, Connie," said the preacher.

Connie could no more withstand Father John's authoritative tone than she could fly. After a minute's pause she did tell what she knew, and Father John wrote Mrs. Anderson's address down in his note-book.

"Now then, Connie," he said, rising, "you're better. Sue and Giles will be so glad to see you once more! Come, dear; let me take you to them."

Connie stood up. There was a curious, wild light in her eyes; but she avoided looking at the street preacher, and he did not observe it. Had he done so he would have been more careful.

The two went out into the street together. It was now getting really late. The distance between the preacher's room and the humble lodgings where Sue and Giles lived was no great way, but to reach the home of the little Giles they had to pass some very ill-favored courts. At one of these Connie suddenly saw a face she knew. She started, trembling, and would have fled on had not a hand been raised to warning lips. The preacher at that instant was stopped by a man who wanted to ask him a question with regard to a child of his whom Father John was trying to find employment for.

Before he knew what had happened, Connie's hand was dragged from his. The girl uttered a slight cry, and the next minute was enveloped in the darkness of one of the worst courts in the whole of London.

"Quietquiet!" said a voice. "Don't you let out one sound or you'll niver speak no more. It's meAgnes. I won't do yer no 'arm ef ye're quiet. Come along with me now."

Connie went, for she could not do anything else. Her feelings were absolutely confused. She did not know at that fearful moment whether she was glad or sorry to be back with Agnes Coppenger again. She only felt a sense of relief at having slipped away from Father John, and at having, as she thought, parted from her own cruel father.

"Oh Agnes!" she whispered, "hide me; and don'tdon't take me back to Mammy Warren!"

"Bless yer!" said Agnes, "she's coped by the perlice. Mammy Warren's awaiting her trial in the 'Ouse of Detention; yer won't be worried by her no more."

"W'ere are yer taking me, then, Agnes?"

"'Ome to my 'ouse, my dear."

"Yer'll promise to let me go in the morning?"

"Safe an' sure I will—that is, ef yer want to go."

Agnes was now walking so fast that Connie had the utmost difficulty in keeping up with her. She seemed all the time to be dodging, getting into shadows, avoiding lights, turning rapidly round corners, making the most marvellous short cuts, until at last—at last—she reached a very tall house, much taller than the one where Mammy Warren had lived. She made a peculiar whistle when she got there. The door was opened by a boy of about Connie's age.

"'Ere we be, Freckles," said Agnes; "and I ha' got the beautiful and saintly Connie back again."

"Hurrah for saintly Connie!" cried Freckles.

The two girls were dragged in by a pair of strong hands, and Connie found herself in utter darkness, descending some slippery stairs—into what depths she had not the slightest idea.

"These are the cellars," said Agnes when at last a door was flung open, and she found herself in a very poorly lit apartment with scarcely any furniture. "You was in hattics before," continued Agnes; "now ye're in the cellars. Yer didn't greatly take to kind Mammy Warren, but perhaps yer'll like Simeon Stylites better. He's a rare good man is Simeon—wery pious too. He sets afore him a saint o' the olden days, an' tries to live accordin'. He ain't in yet, so yer can set down and take things heasy."

Connie sat down.

"I'm that frightened!" she said. Agnes began to laugh.

"Sakes!" she exclaimed, "you ha' no cause. Simeon's a real feeling man, and he's allers kind to pore gels, more particular ef they 'appen to be purty."

Agnes now proceeded to light a fire in a huge, old-fashioned grate. There seemed to be abundance of coal. She built the fire up high, and when it roared up the chimney she desired Connie to draw near.

"You ain't got over yer fright yet," she began.

"Don't talk of it," said Connie.

"I guess as I won'tyer do look piquey. 'Ow's the other kid?"

"I dunno."

Agnes laughed and winked. After a minute she said,

"Yer needn't tell me. 'E's with Mrs. Anderson, mother o' the fireman. The fireman'e's a real 'andsome manI can tike to that sort myself. The kid's wery bad, he is. Wull, ef he dies it'll be a pity, for he 'ave the makings in 'im of a first-rate perfessional."

"Perfessional?" said Connie.

"Yusef he lives 'e'll be one. Simeon Stylites 'ull see to that. You'll be a perfessional, too. There's no use in these 'ere days bein' anything of an amattur; yer must be a perfessional or yer can't earn yer bread."

"I don't understand," said Connie.

"Sakes! you be stupid. It's good to open yer heyes now. Wot do yer think Mammy Warren wanted yer for?"

"I never could tell, only Mrs. Anderson said"

"Yustell us wot she said. She's a torflet's get 'er idees on the subjeck."

"I won't tell yer," said Connie.

"Ohthat's yer little gime! WullI don't keerI'll tell yer from my p'int o' view. Mammy Warren wanted yernot for lovedon't think no sech thingbut jest 'cos she could make you a sort o' decoy-duck. W'ile she was pickin' up many a good harvest, folks was a-starin' at you; an' w'en the little boy were there too, w'y, they stared all the more. She 'ad the boy first, and he were a fine draw. But he tuk ill, an' then she had to get some sort, an' I told her 'bout you, and 'ow purty you were, an' wot golden 'air you 'ad. 'Her golden 'air was 'angin' down her back,' I sung to her, an' she were tuk with the picter. Then I got yer for heryou knows 'ow. Wull, pore Mammy Warren! she's in quad for the present. But she'll come out agin none the worse; bless yer! they feeds 'em fine in quad now. Many a one as I know goes in reg'lar for the cold weather. You see, we'n yer gets yer lodgin' an' yer food at Government expense, it don't cost yer nothing, an' yer come out none the worse. That's wot Mammy Warren 'ull do. But Simeon Stylites-'e's a man 'oo prides himself on niver 'avin' been tuk yet. He'll teach yer 'ow to be a perfessional. Now thenyer ain't frightened, be yer?"

"No," said Connie. Once again she was the old Connie. She had got over her anguish of despair and grief about her father's conduct. She must get out of this, and the only chance was to let Agnes think that she didn't mind.

"Yer'll make a beautiful perfessional!" said Agnes, looking at her with admiration now. "I couldI could grovel at yer feetpore me, so plain as I ham an' hall, an' you so wery genteel. There now, 'oo's that a-knockin' at the door?"

Agnes went to the door. She opened it about an inch, and had a long colloquy with some one outside.

"All right, Freckles," she said, "you can go to bed."

She then came back to Connie.

"Simeon ain't returning afore to-morrer," she said. "We'll tike to our beds. Come along with me, Connie."

CHAPTER XIV

THE SEARCH

When Connie had been suddenly dragged with extreme force from the preacher's side, he had darted after her, and would have been knocked down himself, and perhaps killed, if the neighbor who had accosted him had not also gone a67 step or two into the dark alley and dragged him back by main force.

"You don't go down there, Father John," he said"not without two or three big men, as big as myself. That you don'tI'll keep you back, Father John by all the strength in my body; for if you go down you'll be killed, and then what use will yer be to the poor little gel?"

Father John acknowledged the justice of this. A crowd of men and women had gathered round, as they always did in those parts at the slightest disturbance. Father John recognized many of them, and soon formed a little body of strong men and women. The policemen also came to their aid. They searched the blind alley, going into every house. In short, they did not leave a stone unturned to recover poor Connie; but, alas! all in vain.

Father John was at least glad that he had not gone to visit Sue and Giles. He could not bear to bring them such terrible tidings as that poor Connie had come home and had been kidnapped again.

"We'll get her," said the policeman. "There are lots of thieves about here; but as we've unearthed that dreadful character, Mother Warren, we'll quickly get the rest of the gang. Don't you be afraid, Father John; the child will be in your hands before the day is out."

Nevertheless, Father John spent a sleepless night, and earlyvery earlyin the morning he started off to visit Peter Harris. Peter had slept all night. In the morning he awoke with a headache, and with a queer feeling that something very bad had happened.

When Father John entered his room he gazed at him with bloodshot eyes.

"Wottever is it?" he said. "I had a dreamI must be mistook, of course, but I thought Connie had come back."

"Well," said Father John very gravely, "and so she did come back."

"Wot?" asked the father. He sat up on the bed where he had thrown himself, and pushed back his rough hair.

"I have some very sad news for you, Harris. Will you wash first and have a bit of breakfast, or shall I tell you now?"

"Get out with you!" said the man. "Will I wash and have a bit o' breakfast? Tell me about my child, an' be quick!"

All the latent tenderness in that fierce heart had reawakened.

"Connie back?" said the man. "Purty little Connie? You don't niver say so! But where be she? Wherever is my little gel?"

"You ask God where she is," said the preacher in a very solemn voice. "She's nowhere to be found. She came here, and you—you turned her away, Peter Harris."

"I did wot?" said Harris.

"You turned her off—yes, she came to me, poor child. You had taken too much and didn't know what you were doing."

The man's face was ghastly pale.

"What do yer mean?" he said.

"You took too much, and you were cruel to your child. She came to me in bitter grief. I did what I could to soothe her; I assured her that I know you well, and that you'd be all right and quite ready to welcome her home in the morning."

"Well, and so I be. Welcome my lass home? There ain't naught I wouldn't do for her; the best that can be got is for my Connie. Oh, my dear, sweet little gel! It's the fatted calf she'll 'ave—the Prodigal didn't have a bigger welcome."

"But she is no prodigal. She was sinned against; she didn't sin. Doubtless she did wrong to be discontented. She was never very strong, perhaps, either in mind or body, and she got under bad influence. She was often afraid to go home, Peter Harris, because of you; for you were so savage to her when you took, as you call it, a drop too much. I'll tell you another time her story, for there is not a moment now to spare; you must get up and help to find her."

Peter Harris sprang to his feet just as though an electric force had pulled him to that position.

"Find her?" he said. "But she were herehere! Where be she? Wot did yer do with her, Father John?"

"I didn't dare to bring her back here last night, and she could not stay with me. I was taking her to Giles and Sue when"

"Manspeak!"

Harris had caught the preacher by his shoulder. Father John staggered for a minute, and then spoke gently,

"As we were passing a blind alley some one snatched her from me, right into the pitch darkness. I followed, but was pulled back myself. As soon as possible we formed a party and went to search for her, aided by the police; but she has vanished. It is your duty now to help to find her. The police have great hopes that they have got a clue, but nothing is certain. Beyond doubt the child is in danger. Wake up, Harris. Think no more of that horrible poison that is killing you, body and soul, and do your utmost to find your lost child."

"God in heaven help me!" said the miserable man. "Lostyou say? And she come 'ereand I turned her off? Oh, my little Connie!"

"Keep up your courage, man; there's not a minute of time to spend in vain regrets. You must help the police. You know nearly all the byways and blind alleys of this part of London. You can give valuable information; come at once."

A minute or two later the two men went out together.

CHAPTER XV

CONCENTRATION OF PURPOSE

While these dreadful things were happening to Connie, Sue rose with the dawn, rubbed her sleepy eyes until they opened broad and wide, and went with all youthful vigor and goodwill about her daily tasks.

First she had to light the fire and prepare Giles's breakfast; then to eat her own and tidy up the room; then, having kissed Giles, who still slept, and left all in readiness for him when he awoke, she started for her long walk from Westminster to St. Paul's Churchyard. She must be at her place of employment by eight o'clock, and Sue was never known to be late. With her bright face, smooth, well-kept hair, and neat clothes, she made a pleasing contrast to most of the girls who worked at Messrs. Cheadle's cheap sewing.

Sue possessed in her character two elements of success in life. She had directness of aim and concentration of purpose.

No one thought the little workgirl's aims very high; no one ever paused to consider her purpose either high or noble; but Sue swerved not from aim or purpose, either to the right hand or to the left.

She was the bread-winner in the small family. That was her present manifest duty. And some day she would take Giles away to live in the country. That was her ambition. Every thought she had to spare from her machine-work and her many heavy duties went to this far-off, grand result. At night she pictured it; as she walked to and from her place of work she dwelt upon it.

Some day she and Giles would have a cottage in the country together. Very vague were Sue's ideas of what country life was like. She had never once been in the country; she had never seen green fields, nor smelt, as they grow fresh in the hedges, wild flowers. She imagined that flowers grew either in bunches, as they were sold in Convent Garden, or singly in pots. It never entered into her wildest dreams that the ground could be carpeted with the soft sheen of bluebells or the summer snow of wood anemones, or that the hedge banks could hold great clusters of starry primroses. No, Sue had never seen the place where she and Giles would live together when they were old. She pictured it like the town, only cleanvery cleanwith the possibility of procuring eggs really fresh and milk really pure, and of perhaps now and then getting a bunch of flowers for Giles without spending many pence on them.

People would have called it a poor dream, for Sue had no knowledge to guide her, and absolutely no imagination to fill in details; but, all the same, it was golden in its influence on the young girl, imparting resolution to her face and purpose70 to her eyes, and encircling her round, in her young and defenseless womanhood, as a guardian angel spreading his wings about her.

She walked along to-day brightly as usual. The day was a cold one, but Sue was in good spirits.

She was in good time at her place, and sat down instantly to her work.

A girl sat by her side. Her name was Mary Jones. She was a weakly girl, who coughed long and often as she worked.

"I must soon give up, Sue," she panted between slight pauses in her work. "This 'ere big machine seems to tear me hall to bits, like; and then I gets so hot, and when we is turned out in the middle o' the day the cold seems to strike so dreadful bitter yere;" and she pressed her hand to her sunken chest.

"'Tis goin' to snow, too, sure as sure, to-day," answered Sue. "Don't you think as you could jest keep back to-day, Mary Jones? Maybe you mightn't be seen, and I'd try hard to fetch you in something hot when we comes back."

"Ye're real good, and I'll just mak' shift to stay in," replied Mary Jones. But then the manager came round, and the girls could say no more for the present.

At twelve o'clock, be the weather what it might, all had to turn out for half an hour. This, which seemed a hardship, was absolutely necessary for the proper ventilation of the room; but the delicate girls felt the hardship terribly, and as many of them could not afford to go to a restaurant, there was nothing for them but to wander about the streets. At the hour of release to-day it still snowed fast, but Sue with considerable cleverness, had managed to hide Mary Jones in the warm room, and now ran fast through the blinding and bitter cold to see where she could get something hot and nourishing to bring back to her. Her own dinner, consisting of a hunch of dry bread and dripping, could be eaten in the pauses of her work. Her object now was to provide for the sick girl.

She ran fast, for she knew a shop where delicious penny pies were to be had, and it was quite possible to demolish penny pies unnoticed in the large workroom. The shop, however, in question was some way off, and Sue had no time to spare. She had nearly reached it, and had already in imagination clasped the warm pies in her cold hands, when, suddenly turning a corner, she came face to face with Harris. Harris was walking along moodily, apparently lost in thought. When he saw Sue, however, he started, and took hold of her arm roughly.

"Sue," he said, "does you know as Connie came back last night?"

"Connie?" cried Sue. Her face turned pale and then red again in eagerness. "Then God 'ave heard our prayers!" she exclaimed with great fervor. "Oh! won't my little Giles be glad?"

"You listen to the end," said the man. He still kept his hand on her shoulder, not caring whether it hurt her or not.

"She come back, my purty, purty little gel, but I 'ad tuk too much, and I were rough on her and I bid her be gone, and she went. She went to Father John; 'e were kind to her, and 'e were taking her to you, w'en some willainI don't know 'oocaught her by the arm and pulled her down a dark alley, and she ain't been seen since. Wottever is to be done? I'm near mad about hermy pore little gel. And to think that II should ha' turned her aw'y!"

Sue listened with great consternation to this terrible tale. She forgot all about poor Mary Jones and the penny pie which she hoped to smuggle into the workroom for her dinner. She forgot everything in all the world but the fact that Connie had come and gone again, and that Peter Harris was full of the most awful despair and agony about her.

"I'm fit to die o' grief," said the man. "I dunno wot to do. The perlice is lookin' for her 'igh an' low, and Oh Sue, I am near off my 'ead!"

Sue thought for a minute.

"Is Father John looking for her too?" she said.

"W'y, yusof course he be. I'm to meet the perlice again this afternoon, an' we'llwe'll make a rare fuss."

"Yer'll find her, in course," said Sue. "W'y, there ain't a doubt," she continued.

"Wot do yer mean by that?"

"There couldn't be a doubt," continued the girl; "for God, who brought her back to us all, 'ull help yer if yer ax 'Im."

"Do yer believe that, Sue?"

"Sartin sure I doI couldn't live if I didn't."

"You're a queer un," said Harris, he felt a strange sort of comfort in the rough little girl's presence. It seemed to him in a sort of fashion that there was truth in her words. She was very wisewiser than most. He had always respected her.

"You're a queer, sensible gel," he said then"not like most. I am inclined to believe yer. I'm glad I met yer; you were always Connie's friend."

"Oh yus," said Sue; "I love her jest as though she were my real sister."

"An' yer do think as she'll come back again?"

"I'm sartin sure of it."

"Turn and walk with me a bit, Sue. I were near mad w'en I met yer, but somehow you ha' given me a scrap o' hope."

"Mr. Harris," said Sue, all of a sudden, "you were cruel to Connie last night; but w'en she comes back again you'll be different, won't yer?"

"I tuk the pledge this morning," said Harris in a gloomy voice.

"Then in course you'll be different. It were w'en yer tuk too much that you were queer. W'en you're like you are now you're a wery kind man."

"Be I, Sue?" said Harris. He looked down at the small girl. "No one else, unless it be pore Connie, iver called me a kind man."

"And I tell yer wot," continued Sue"ef ye're sure she'll come backas sure as I amshe"

"Then I am sure," said Harris. "I'm as sure as there's a sky above us. There now!"

"And a God above us," said Sue.

The man was silent.

"In that case," continued Sue, "let's do our wery best. Let's 'ave iverything nice w'en she comes 'ome. Let's 'ave a feast for her, an' let me 'elp yer."

"Yer mean that yer'll come along to my room an' put things in order?" said Harris.

"Yes; and oh, Mr. Harris! couldn't yer take her a little bit of a present?"

"Right you are, wench," he said. Harris's whole face lit up. "That be a good thought!" He clapped Sue with violence on the shoulder. "Right you be! An' I know wot she've set 'er silly little 'eart onw'y, a ringa purty ring with a stone in it; and 'ere's a shopthe wery kind for our purpose. Let's come inyou an' meand get her one this wery instant minute."

The two entered the shop. A drawer of rings was brought for Harris to select from. He presently chose a little ring, very fine, and with a tiny turquoise as decoration. He felt sure that this would fit Connie's finger, and laying down his only sovereign on the counter, waited for the change. Sue had gone a little away from him, to gaze in open-eyed wonder at the many trinkets exhibited for sale. Notwithstanding her excitement about Connie, she was too completely a woman not to be attracted by finery of all sorts; and here were scarves and laces and brooches and earringsin short, that miscellaneous array of female decorations so fascinating to the taste of girls like Sue. In this absorbing moment she forgot even Connie.

In the meantime, in this brief instant while Sue was so occupied, the man who served turned his back to get his change from another drawer. He did this leaving the box with the rings on the counter. In the corner of this same box, hidden partly away under some cotton-wool, lay two lockets, one of great value, being gold, set with brilliants. In this instant, quick as thought, Harris put in his hand, and taking the diamond locket, slipped it into his pocket. He then received his change, and he and Sue left the shop together.

He noticed, however, as he walked out that the shopman was missing the locket. His theft could not remain undiscovered. Another instant and he would be arrested and the locket found on his person. He had scarcely time for the most rapid thoughtcertainly no time for any sense of justice to visit his not too fine conscience. The only instinct alive in him in that brief and trying moment was that of73 self-preservation. He must preserve himself, and the means lay close at hand. He gave Sue a little push as though he had stumbled against her, and then, while the girl's attention was otherwise occupied, he transferred the locket from his own pocket to hers, and with a hasty nod, dashed down a side-street which lay close by.

Rather wondering at his sudden exit, Sue went on. Until now she had forgotten Mary Jones. She remembered her with compunction. She also knew that she had scarcely time to get the penny pies and go back to Cheapside within the half-hour. If she ran, however, she might accomplish this feat. Sue was very strong, and could run as fast as any girl;

she put wings to her feet, and went panting down the street. In the midst of this headlong career, however, she was violently arrested. She heard the cry of "Stop thief!" behind her, and glancing back, saw two men, accompanied by some boys, in full pursuit. Too astonished and frightened to consider the improbability of their pursuing her, she ran harder than ever. She felt horrified, and dreaded their rudeness should they reach her. Down side-streets and across byways she dashed, the crowd in pursuit increasing each moment. At last she found that she had run full-tilt into the arms of a policeman, who spread them out to detain her.

"What's the matter, girl? Who are you running away from?"

"Oh, hide mehide me!" said poor Sue. "They are calling out 'Stop thief!' and running after me so hard."

Before the policeman could even reply, the owner of the pawnshop had come up.

"You may arrest that girl, policeman," he said roughly. "She and a man were in my shop just now, and one or other of 'em stole a valuable diamond locket from me."

"What a shame! I didn't touch it!" said Sue. "I never touched a thing as worn't my own in hall my life!"

"No doubt, my dear," said the policeman; "but of course you won't object to be searched?"

"No, of course," said Sue; "you may search me as much as you likeyou won't get no stolen goods 'bout me;" and she raised her head fearlessly and proudly. The crowd who had now thickly collected, and who, as all crowds do, admired pluck, were beginning to applaud, and no doubt the tide was turning in Sue's favor, when the policeman, putting his hand into her pocket, drew out the diamond locket. An instant's breathless silence followed this discovery, followed quickly by some groans and hisses from the bystanders.

"Oh, but ain't she a hardened one!" two or three remarked; and all pressed close to watch the result.

Sue had turned very whiteso white that the policeman put his hand on her shoulder, thinking she was going to faint.

"She is innocent," said in his heart of hearts this experienced functionary; but he further added, "It will go hard for her to prove itpoor lass!"

Aloud he said:

"I've got to take you to the lock-up, my girl; for you must say how you 'appened to come by that 'ere little trinket. The quieter you come, and the less you talk, the easier it 'ull go wid you."

"I have nothink to say," answered Sue. "I can'tcan't see it at all. But I'll go wid yer," she added. She did not asseverate any more, nor even say she was innocent. She walked away by the policeman's side, the crowd still following, and the owner of the pawnshophaving recovered his property, and given his address to the policemanreturned to his place of business.

Sue walked on, feeling stunned; her thought just now was how very much poor Mary Jones would miss her penny pies.

CHAPTER XVI

PICKLES

The lock-up to which the policeman wanted to convey Sue was at some little distance. With his hand on her shoulder, they walked along, the crowd still following. They turned down more than one by-street, and chose all the short cuts that Constable Z could remember. One of these happened to be a very narrow passage, and a place of decidedly ill repute. The policeman, however, still holding his terrified charge, walked down it, and the crowd followed after. In the very middle of this passagefor it was little morethey were met by a mob even greater than themselves. These people were shouting, vociferating, waving frantic hands, and all pointing upwards. The policeman raised his eyes and saw that the cause of this uproar was a house on fire. It was a very tall, narrow house, and all the top of it was completely enveloped in flames. From one window, from which escape seemed impossiblefor the flames almost surrounded ita man leaned out, imploring some one to save him. The height from the ground was too great for him to jump down, and no fire-escape was yet in sight.

Policeman Z was as kind-hearted a man as ever lived. In the excitement of such a moment he absolutely forgot Sue. He rushed into the crowd, scattering them right and left, and sent those who had not absolutely lost their heads flying for the fire-escape and the engines. They all arrived soon after, and the man, who was the only person in the burning part of the house, was brought in safety to the ground.

In the midst of the shouting, eager crowd Sue stood, forgetting herself, as perhaps every one else there did also, in such intense excitement. Scarcely, however, had the rescued man reached the ground when she felt herself violently pulled from behindindeed, not only pulled, but dragged so strongly that75 she almost lost her feet. She attempted to scream, but a hand was instantly placed over her mouth, and she found herself running helplessly, and against her will, down a narrow passage which flanked one side of the burning house; beyond this into a small backyard; then through another house into another yard; and so on until she entered a small, very dirty room. This room was full of unknown condiments in jars and pots, some queer stuffed figures in fancy-dresses, some wigs and curls of false hair, and several masks, false noses, etc., etc. Sue, entering this room, was pushed instantly into a large arm-chair, whereupon her captor came and stood before her. He was a lad of about her own size, and perhaps a year or two younger. He had a round, freckled face, the lightest blue eyes, and the reddest, most upright shock of hair she had ever seen. He put his arms akimbo and gazed hard at Sue, and so motionless became his perfectly round orbs that Sue thought he had been turned into stone. Suddenly, however, he winked, and said in a shrill, cheerful tone:

"Well, then, plucky 'un, 'ow does yer find yerself now?"

Not any number of shocks could quite deprive Sue of her common-sense. She had not an idea of what had become of her. Was this another and a rougher way of taking her to the lock-up? Was this queer boy friend or foe?

"Be yer agen me, boy?" she said.

"Agen yer! Well, the ingratitude! Ha'n't I jest rescued yer from the hands o' that 'ere nipper?"

"Oh!" exclaimed Sue; and the relieved tension of her poor, terrified little heart found vent in two big tears which rose to her eyes.

The red-haired boy balanced himself on one toe in order to survey those tears more carefully.

"Well," he said at length, in a tone in which there was a ludicrous mingling of wonder and contempt"well, ye're a queer un fur a plucky una wery queer un. Crying! My eyes! Ain't yer hin luck not to be in prison, and ain't that a subject for rejoicing? I don't cry when I'm in luck; but then, thank goodness! I'm not a gel. Lor'! they're queer cattle, gels arewery queer, the best o' 'em. But they're as they're made, poor things! We can't expect much from such weakness. But now look you here, you gellook up at me, full and solemn in the face, and say if ye're hinnercent in the matter o' that 'ere locket. If yer can say quite solemn and straightforward as yer his innercent, why, I'll help yer; but if yer is guiltyand, mark me, I can tell by yer heyes ef ye're talking the truthI can do naught, fur I'm never the party to harbor guilty folks. Now speak the truth, full and solemn; be yer hinnercent?"

Here the red-haired boy got down on his knees and brought his eyes within a few inches of Sue's eyes.

"Be yer hinnercent?" he repeated.

"Yes," answered Sue, "I'm quite, quite hinnercent; yer can believe me or not as yer pleases. I'm quite hinnercent, and I76 won't cry no more ef yer dislikes it. I wor never reckoned a cry-baby."

"Good!" said the boy; "I b'lieves yer. And now jest tell me the whole story. I come hup jest when the perleeceman and the pawnbroker were a-gripping yer. Lor'! I could a' twisted out o' their hands heasy enough; but then, to be thankful agen, I ain't a gel."

"There's no good twitting me wid being a gel," interrupted Sue; "gels have their use in creation same as boys, and I guess as they're often the pluckier o' the two."

"Gels pluckier! Well, I like that. However, I will say as you stood game. I guessed as you wor hinnercent then. And now jest tell me the story."

"It wor this way," began Sue, whose color and courage were beginning to return. Then she told her tale, suppressing carefully all tears, for she was anxious to propitiate the red-haired boy. She could not, however, keep back the indignation from her innocent young voice; and this indignation, being a sure sign in his mind of pluckiness, greatly delighted her companion.

"'Tis the jolliest shame I ever heard tell on in all my life," he said in conclusion; but though he said this he chuckled, and seemed to enjoy himself immensely. "Now then," he added, "there's no doubt at all as ye're hinnercent. I know that as clearI feels as sartin on that p'intas tho' I wor reading the secrets of my own heart. But 'tis jest equal sartin as a magistrate 'ud bring you hin guilty. He'd sayand think hisself mighty wise, too'You had the locket, so in course yer tuk the locket, and so yer must be punished.' Then you'd be tuk from the lock-up to the House o' Correction, where you'd 'ave solitary confinement, most like, to teach you never to do so no more."

"'Ow long 'ud they keep me there?" asked Sue. "'Ow long 'ud they be wicked enough to keep me there fur what I never did?"

"Well, as it wor a first offence, and you but young, they might make it a matter of no longer than a year, or maybe eighteen months. But then, agen, they'd 'ave to consider as it wor diamonds as you tuk. They gems is so waluable that in course you must be punished according. Yes, considerin' as it wor diamonds, Sue, I would say as you got off cheap wid two years."

"You talk jest as tho' I had done it," said Sue angrily, "when you know perfect well as I'm quite hinnercent."

"Well, don't be touchy. I'm only considerin' what the judge 'ud say. I ain't the judge. Yes, you'd 'ave two years. But, lor'! it don't much matter wot time you 'ad, for you'd never be no good arter."

"Wot do you mean now?" asked Sue.

"I mean as you'd never get no 'ployment, nor be able to hold up yer head. Who, I'd like to know, 'ud employ a prison lassand what else 'ud you be?"

Here Sue, disregarding her companion's dislike to tears, broke down utterly, and exclaimed through her sobs:

"Oh! poor Gilespoor, poor Giles! It 'ull kill my little Giles. Oh! I didn't think as Lord Jesus could give me sech big stones to walk hover."

"Now ye're gettin' complicated," exclaimed the red-haired boy. "I make 'lowance fur yer tearsye're but a gel, and I allow as the picture's darkbut who hever is Giles? And where are the stones? Ye're setting still this 'ere minute, and I guess as the arm-chair in which I placed yer, though none o' the newest, be better than a stone."

"Giles is my brother," said Sue; "and the stoneswell, the stones is 'phorical, ef yer knows wot that means."

"Bless us, no! I'm sure I don't. But tell about Giles."

So Sue wiped her eyes again and went back a little further in her life-story.

"It is complicated," said her companion when she paused"a lame brother, poor chap, and you the support. Well, well! the more reason as you should keep out o' prison. Now, Sue, this is wot I calls deep; jest keep still fur a bit, and let me put on my considerin' cap."

The red-haired boy seated himself on the floor, thrust his two hands into his shock of hair, and stared very hard and very straight before him. In this position he was perfectly motionless for about the space of half a minute; then, jumping up, he came again very close to Sue.

"Be yer willin' to take the adwice of a person a deal wiser nor yourself? Look me full in the heyes and answer clear on that p'int."

"Yes, I'm sure I am," said Sue, in as humble a spirit as the most exalted teacher could desire.

"Good!" said the red-haired boy, giving his thigh a great clap. "Then you've got to hearken to me. Sue, there's nothink in life fur you but to hide."

"To hide!" said Sue.

"Yes. You must on no 'count whatever let the perleece find yer. We must get to discover the guilty party, and the guilty party must confess; but in the meanwhile yer must hide. There must be no smell o' the prison 'bout yer, Sue."

"Oh! butbutboyI don't know yer name."

"Pickles," said the red-haired boy, giving his head a bob. "Pickles, at yer sarvice."

"Well, then, Pickles," continued Sue, "if I go and hide, what 'ull become o' Giles?"

"And what 'ull come o' him ef yer go ter prisonyer goose? Now, jest yer listen to the words o' wisdom. You mustn't go back to Giles, fur as sure as you do the perleece 'ull have you. That would break that little tender brother's heart. No, no, leave Giles ter me; you must hide, Sue."

"But where, and fur how long?" asked Sue.

"Ah! now ye're comin' sensible, and axin' refreshin' questions. Where? Leave the where to me. How long? Leave the how long ter me."

"Oh Pickles! ye're real good," sobbed Sue; "and ef yer'll only promise as Giles won't die, and that he won't break his heart wid frettin', why, I'll leave it ter youI'll leave it all ter you."

"And yer couldn'tsearch the world overleave it to a safer person," said Pickles. "So now that's a bargainI'll take care on Giles."

CHAPTER XVII

CINDERELLA

"The first thing to be considered, Sue," said Pickles, as he seated himself on the floor by her side, "is the disguise. The disguise must be wot I consider deep."

"Wot hever does yer mean now?" asked Sue.

"Why, yer Silly, yer don't s'pose as yer can go hout and about as you are now? Why, the perleece 'ud have yer. Don't yer s'pose as yer'll be advertised?"

"I dunno heven wot that his," said Sue.

"Oh! my heyes, ain't yer green! Well, it 'ull be, say, like this. There'll be by hall the perleece-stations placards hup, all writ hout in big print: 'Gel missingplain gel, rayther stout, rayther short, wid round moon-shaped face, heyes small, mouth big, hair"

"There! you needn't go on," said Sue, who, though by no means vain, scarcely relished this description. "I know wot yer mean, and I don't want ter be twitted with not being beautiful. I'd rayther be beautiful by a long way. I s'pose, as the disguise is ter change me, will it make me beautiful? I'd like that."

Pickles roared. "Well, I never!" he said. "We'll try. Let me see; I must study yer fur a bit. Hair wot's called sandy nowchanged ter black. Heyebrows; no heyebrows in 'ticlarmark 'em hout strong. Mouth: couldn't sew hup the mouth in the corners. No, Sue, I'm feared as I never can't make no pictur' of yer. But now to be serious. We must set to work, and we has no time ter spare, fur hold Fryin-pan 'ull come home, and there'll be the mischief to pay ef he finds us yere."

"Who's he?" asked Sue.

"Who? Why, the owner of this yer shop. I'm in his employ. I'm wot's called his steady right-hand man. See, Sue, yere's a pair o' scissors; get yer hair down and clip away, and I'll get ready the dye."

Pickles now set to work in earnest, and proved himself by no means an unskilled workman. In a wonderfully short space of time Sue's long, neutral-tinted hair was changed to a very short crop of the darkest hue. Her eyebrows were also touched up, and as her eyelashes happened to be dark, the effect was not quite so inharmonious as might have been feared. Pickles was in ecstasies, and declared that "Not a policeman in

London 'ud know her." He then dived into an inner room in the funny little shop, and returned with an old blue petticoat and a faded red jersey. These Sue had to exchange for her own neat but sober frock.

"Ye're perfect," said Pickles, dancing round her. "Yer looks hangelic. Now fur the name."

"The name?" said Sue. "Must I 'ave a new name too?"

"In course yer must; nothink must let the name o' Sue pass yer lips. Now, mind, that slip o' the tongue might prove fatal."

"Wery well," said Sue in a resigned voice of great trouble.

"Yer needn't be so down on yer luck. I don't myself think anythink o' the name o' Sue; 'tis what I considers low and common. Now, wot's yer favorite character? Say in acting, now."

"There's no character hin all the world as I hadmires like Cinderella," said Sue.

"Oh, my heyes, Cinderella, of hall people! Worn't Cinderella wot might 'ave bin called beautiful? Dressed shabby, no doubt, and wid hard-hearted sistersbut hadn't she small feet, now? Well, Sue, I don't say as ye're remarkable fur them special features b'in' small, nor is yer looks wery uncommon; but still, ef yer have a fancy for the name, so be it. It will be fun thinkin' of the beautiful, small-footed Cinderella and looking at you. But so much the better, so come along, Cinderella, fur Fryin'-pan 'ull catch us ef we don't make haste."

"Where are we to go?" asked the poor little newly made Cinderella, with a piteous face.

"Now, yer needn't look like that. None but cheerful folks goes down wid me. Where are yer to go to? Why, to mother, of coursewhere else?"

"Oh, have you got a mother?" asked Sue.

"Well, wot next? 'Ow did I happen ter be born? Yes, I has a mother, and the wery best little woman in the worldso come along."

CHAPTER XVIII

THE METROPOLITAN FIRE BRIGADE

Pickles and Sue had to go a long way before they reached the destination of "the best little woman in the world." They walked along by-streets and all kinds of queer places, and presently reached a part of London where Sue had never been before. They passed whole streets of warehouses, and came then to poor-looking dwelling-houses, but all of an immense height, and very old and dirty. It was the back slums of Westminster over again, but it was a Westminster severed as far as one pole is from another to Sue.

"We does a roaring trade yere," said Pickles, looking around him with the air of a proprietor well satisfied with his property.

"Wot in?" asked Sue.

"Wot hin? Well, that may surprise yer. Hin fire, of course."

"Wot do yer mean?" asked Sue.

"Wot does I mean? I mean as we deals in that 'ere rampagious helement. We belongs to the great London Fire Brigade. That his, my brother Will does; and I have a cousin wot thinks hisself no end of a swell, and he's beginning his drill. Do you suppose, you goose, as I'd have acted as I did, wid that 'ere remarkable coolness jest now, when the fire wor burning, and the man wor on the wery brink of destruction, ef fire had not bin, so to speak, my native hair? But now, here we are at last, so come along hup to mother!"

Taking Sue's hand, Pickles dragged her up flight after flight of stairs, until they reached the top of one of the very tall, dirty houses. Here he suddenly flung open a door, and pushing Sue in, sang out:

"Mother, yere I be! And let me introduce to you Cinderella. Her sisters have bin that unkind and mean as cannot be told, and she have taken refuge wid us until the Prince comes to tie on the glass slipper."

No doubt Pickles' mother was thoroughly accustomed to him, for she did not smile at all, but coming gravely forward, took Sue's two hands in hers, and looking into her face, and seeing something of the great trouble there, said in a soft, kind tone:

"Sit down, my dearsit down. If I can help you I will."

"Oh, you can help her real fine, mother!" said Pickles, beginning to dance a hornpipe round them both. "And I said as you were the wery best little 'oman in all the world, and that you would do hall you could."

"So I will, my lad; only now do let the poor dear speak for herself."

But Sue did not. There are limits beyond which fortitude will not go, and those limits were most suddenly reached by the poor child. Her morning's early rising, her long walk to her place of business, her hard work when she got there; then her hurried run for the sick girl's lunch, her cruel betrayal, her very startling capture by Pickles; the fact that her hair had been cut off, her clothes changed, her very name altered, until she herself felt that she must really be somebody else, and not the Sue whom Giles loved.

All these things she had borne with tolerable calmness; but now (for Sue was really starving) the warm room, the bright fireabove all, the kind face that bent over her, the gentle voice that asked to hear her taleproved too much. She put up her toil-worn hands to her face and burst into such sobs as strong people give way to in agony.

Mrs. Price beckoned to Pickles to go away, and then, sitting81 down by Sue's side, she waited until the overloaded heart should have become a little quieted; then she said:

"And now, my dear, you will tell me the story."

Sue did tell ittold it allMrs. Price sitting by and holding her hands, and absolutely not speaking a single word.

"You believes me, marm?" said Sue at last.

Mrs. Price looked in the girl's eyes and answered simply:

"Yes, poor lamb, I quite believe you. And now I am going to get you some supper."

She made Sue lie back in the easy-chair by the fire, and drawing out a little round table, laid a white cloth upon it.

Sue's mind, by this time partly relieved of its load, was able to take in its novel surroundings. The house might be very tall and very dirty, but this room at least was clean. Floor, walls, furnitureall reflected a due and most judicious use of soap and water; and the woman moving about with gentle, deft fingers, arranging now this and now that, was quite different from any woman Sue had ever seen before. She was a widow, and wore a widow's cap and a perfectly plain black dress, but she had a white handkerchief pinned neatly over her shoulders, so that she looked half-widow, half-nun.

She was tall and slender, with very beautiful dark eyes. Sue did not know whether to think her the very gravest person she had ever seen or the very brightest. Her face was thoughtful and sweet; perhaps when in repose it was sad, but she never looked at a human being without a certain expression coming into her eyes which said louder and plainer than words, "I love you."

This expression gave the hungry and poor who came in contact with her glance many a heart-thrill, and it is not too much to say they were seldom disappointed of the sympathy which the look in those dark and lovely eyes gave them reason to hope for.

Mrs. Price now laid the tea-things, giving the poor little shorn and transformed Cinderella sitting by the hearth so many expressive glances that she began to feel quite a heavenly peace stealing over her. "Worn't Jesus real good to bring me yere?" was her mental comment. She had scarcely made it before two young men came in.

These young men were dressed in the uniform of the London Fire Brigade. They looked dusty, and the taller of the two was covered with smoke and dirt.

"Mother," he said as he tossed his helmet on the table. "I've been worked almost to death. You have supper ready, I hope."

"Yes, yes, my lada nice little piece of boiled pork, smoking hot, and pease-pudding and potatoes. I am glad you've brought George with you. He is kindly welcome, as he knows."

"As he knows very well," answered George, with a smile.

He touched the woman's shoulder for an instant with his82 big hand. Then the two young men went into the next room to have a wash before supper.

"William is coming on fine," said George, when they returned, looking at the other fireman"though you did disobey orders, William, and are safe to get a reprimand.Fancy, Mrs. Price! this brave son of yours, returning from his day's drill, must needs see a fire and rush into it, all against ordersay, and save a poor chap's lifebefore any one could prevent him."

It may be as well to explain here that each man who wishes to join the Metropolitan Fire Brigade must first have served some time at sea; also, before a man is allowed to attend a fire he must be thoroughly trainedin other words, he must attend drill. There's a drill class belonging to each station. It is under the charge of an instructor and two assistant instructors. Each man, on appointment, joins this class, and learns the use of all the different appliances required for the extinction of fire.

William Price had not quite completed his eight weeks' drill.

"Yes, it was a ticklish piece of work," continued Anderson. "The poor chap he rescued was surrounded by flames. Then, too, the street was so narrow and the crowd so great that the whole matter is simply wonderful; but that policeman who kept order was a fine fellow."

"Why, it worn't never the fire as we come from jest now!" here burst from Sue.

"Hushhush, Cinderella!" said Pickles, who had come back, giving her a push under the table. "It 'ud be more suitable to yer present sitiwation ef yer didn't talk. In course it wor that same fire. Why, it wor that deed o' bravery done by my own nearest o' kin as incited me to hact as I did by you."

"Whoever is the girl?" said Price, noticing poor Sue for the first time.

"Cinderella's the name of this 'ere misfortunate maiden," replied Pickles; "an' yer ax no more questions, Bill, an' yer'll get no stories told."

"I must go, Mrs. Price," said Anderson; "but I'll be back again as soon as possible."

"Tell me first, George," said the widow, "how your mother is."

"I haven't been to see her for a few days, but she wrote to say that both the children who were rescued from the fire a few days back are doing fairly well. The boy was bad at first, but is now recovering."

"Ah! that was a brave deed," said Price in a voice of the greatest admiration.

"And did she tell you the names of the poor little critters?"

"She did. Connie was the name of one"

"Connie?" cried Sue, springing to her feet.

"Sit down, Cinderella, and keep yourself quiet," cried Pickles.

George Anderson gave the queer little girl who went by this name a puzzled glance.

"Yes," he said briefly, "Connie was the name of one, and Ronald the name of the other. I never saw a more beautiful little creature in all the world than Connie."

"That's 'er!" broke from Sue's irrepressible lips.

CHAPTER XIX

A SAINTLY LADY

When so many strange things were happening, we may be sure that Father John was not idle. He had hoped much from Peter Harris's knowledge of the byways and dens and alleys of Westminster. But although Peter was accompanied by the sharpest detectives that Scotland Yard could provide, not the slightest clue to Connie's whereabouts could be obtained. The man was to meet more detectives again that same afternoon, and meanwhile a sudden gleam of hope darted through Father John's brain.

What a fool he had been not to think of it before! How glad he was now that he had insisted on getting the name and address of the brave fireman deliverer from Connie on the previous night!

He went straight now to the house in Carlyle Terrace. He stopped at No. . There he rang the bell and inquired if Mrs. Anderson were within.

Mrs. Anderson was the last woman in the world to refuse to see any one, whether rich or poor, who called upon her. Even impostors had a kindly greeting from this saintly lady; for, as she was fond of saying to herself, "If I can't give help, I can at least bestow pity."

Mrs. Anderson was no fool, however, and she could generally read in their faces the true story of a man or woman who came to her. More often than not the story was a sad one, and the chance visitor was in need of help and sympathy. When this was not the case, she was able to explain very fully to the person who had called upon her what she thought of deceit and dishonest means of gaining a livelihood; and that person, as a rule, went away very much ashamed, and in some cases determined to turn over a new leaf. When this really happened Mrs. Anderson was the first to help to get the individual who had come to her into respectable employment.

She was by no means rich, but nearly every penny of her money was spent on others; her own wants were of the simplest. The house she lived in belonged to her son, who, although a gentleman by birth, had long ago selected his professionthat of a fireman in the London Fire Brigade. He had a passion for his calling, and would not change it for the richest and most luxurious life in the world.

Now Mrs. Anderson came downstairs to interview Father John. Father John stood up, holding his hat in his hand. He always wore a black frock-coat; his hair hung long over his shoulders; his forehead was lofty; his expressive and marvelously beautiful gray eyes lit up his rugged and otherwise plain face. It was but to look at this man to know that he was absolutely impervious to flattery, and did not mind in the least what others thought about him. His very slight but perceptible deformity gave to his eyes that pathetic look which deformed people so often possess.

The moment Mrs. Anderson entered the room she recognized him.

"Why," she said in a joyful tone, "is it true that I have the honor of speaking to the great street preacher?"

"Not great, madam," said Father John"quite a simple individual; but my blessed Father in heaven has given me strength to deliver now and then a message to poor and sorrowful people."

"Sit down, won't you?" said Mrs. Anderson.

Father John did immediately take a chair. Mrs. Anderson did likewise.

"Now," said the widow, "what can I do for you?"

"I will tell you, madam. Her father and I are in great trouble about the child"

"What child?" asked Mrs. Anderson. "You surely don't mean little Connie Harris? I have been nervous at her not reappearing to-day. At her own express wish, she went to visit her father last night. I would have sent some one with her, but she wouldn't hear of it, assuring me that she had been about by herself in the London streets as long as she could remember; but she has not returned."

"No, madam?"

Over Father John's face there passed a quick emotion. Then this last hope must be given up.

"You have news of her?" said Mrs. Anderson.

"I have, and very bad news."

Father John then related his story.

"Oh, whywhy did I let her go?" said Mrs. Anderson.

"Don't blame yourself dear lady; the person to blame is the miserable father who would not receive his lost child when she returned to him."

"Oh, poor little girl!" said Mrs. Anderson. "Such a sweet child, too, and so very beautiful!"

"Her beauty is her danger," said Father John.

"What do you mean?"

"She told me her story, as doubtless she has told it to you."

"She has," said Mrs. Anderson.

"There is not the least doubt," continued the street preacher, "that that notorious thief, Mrs. Warren, used the child to attract people from herself when she was stealing their goods. Mrs. Warren is one of the most noted pickpockets in London. She has been captured, but I greatly fear that85 some other members of the gang have kidnapped the child once more."

"What can be done?" said Mrs. Anderson. "I wish my son were here. I know he would help."

"Ah, madam," said Father John, "how proud you must be of such a son! I think I would rather belong to his profession than any other in all the worldyes, I believe I would rather belong to it than to my own; for when you can rescue the body of a man from the cruel and tormenting flames, you have a rare chance of getting at his soul."

"My son is a Christian as well as a gentleman," said Mrs. Anderson. "He would feel with you in every word you have uttered, Father John. I will send him a message and ask him if he can meet you here later on to-night."

"I shall be very pleased to come; and I will if I can," said Father John. "But," he added, "my time is scarcely ever my ownI am the servant of my people."

"Your congregation?" said Mrs. Anderson.

"Yes, madam; all sorts and conditions of men. I have no parish; still, I consider myself God's priest to deliver His message to sorrowful people who might not receive it from an ordained clergyman."

Mrs. Anderson was silent. Father John's eyes seemed to glow. He was looking back on many experiences. After a minute he said:

"The consolation is this: 'He that shall endure to the endshall be saved.'"

"How very strange that you should speak of that!" said Mrs. Anderson.

"Why so, madam? Don't you believe it?"

"Oh, indeed I do! But I'll tell you why I think it strange. There is a little boythe child who was also rescued from the firein my house. He was very ill at first; he is now better, but not well enough to leave his bedroom. I was anxious about him for a time, but he is, I thank God, recovering. Now, this child went on murmuring that text during his deliriuma strange one to fall from the lips of so young a child."

"Indeed, yes, madam. I am most deeply interested. I am glad you have mentioned the little boy. Connie told me about him last night. I am sorry that in my anxiety for her I forgot him."

"You could never forget little Ronald if you were to see him," said Mrs. Anderson. "I don't think I ever saw quite so sweet a child. His patience, his courage, and I think I ought to add his faith, are marvelous."

"He cannot be nicer or better than a little boy of the name of Giles who lives in a very poor attic near my own room," said the preacher.

"I wonder," said Mrs. Anderson after a pause, "if you could spare time to come up and see little Ronald with me."

"I should be only too glad," said Father John.

So Mrs. Anderson took the preacher upstairs, and very softly opened the door, beyond which stood a screen. She entered, followed by the preacher, into a pretty room, which had lovely photographs hanging on the walls, that bore on childhood in different aspects. There was the summer childthe child of happinessplaying in the summer meadows, chasing butterflies and gathering flowers. And there also was the winter childthe child of extreme desolationshivering on a doorstep in one of London's streets. There were other children, toosaintly childrenSt. Agnes and her lamb, St. Elizabeth, St. Ursula; and, above all, there were photographs of the famous pictures of the Child of all children, the Child of Bethlehem.

The windows of the room were shaded by soft curtains of pale blue. A cheerful fire burned in the grate, and a child lay, half-sitting up, in a bed covered by a silken eiderdown.

The child looked quite content in his little bed, and a trained nurse who was in the room went softly out by another door as Mrs. Anderson and the preacher entered.

"Hasn't Connie come back?" asked Ronald.

"No, dear," said Mrs. Anderson; "she's not able to do so just yet."

"I want her," said Ronald, suppressing a sigh.

"I have brought this gentleman to see you, Ronald."

"What?"

The boy cast a quick glance at the somewhat ungainly figure of Father John. Another disappointmentnot the father he was waiting for. But the luminous eyes of the preacher seemed to pierce into the boy's soul. When he looked once, he looked again. When he looked twice, it seemed to him that he wanted to look forever.

"I am glad," he said; and a smile broke over his little face.

Father John sat down at once by the bedside, and Mrs. Anderson went softly out of the room.

"Waiting for something, little man?" said the street preacher.

"How can you tell?" asked Ronald.

"I see it in your eyes," said the preacher.

"It's father," said Ronald.

"Which father?" asked the preacher.

"My own," said Ronald"my soldier fatherthe V. C. man, you know."

"Yes," said Father John.

"I want him," said Ronald.

"Of course you do."

"Is he likely to come soon?" asked Ronald.

"If I could tell you that, Ronald," said the street preacher, "I should be a wiser man than my Father in heaven means me to be. There is only one Person who can tell you when your earthly father will come."

"You mean Lord Christ," said Ronald.

"I mean Christ and our Father in heaven."

Ronald shut his eyes for a minute. Then he opened them.

"I want my father," he said. "I'm sort o' starving for him."

"Well," said Father John, "you have a father, you knowyou have two fathers. If you can't get your earthly father down here, you're certain safe to get him up there. A boy with two fathers needn't feel starved about the heart, need he, now?"

"I suppose not," said Ronald.

"He need not, of course," said Father John. "I'll say a bit of a prayer for you to the Heavenly Father, and I know that sore feeling will go out of your heart. I know it, Ronald; for He has promised to answer the prayers of those who trust in Him. But now I want to talk to you about something else. I guess, somehow, that the next best person to your father to come to see you now is your little friend Connie."

"Yes, yes!" said Ronald. "I've missed her dreadful. Mrs. Anderson is sweet, and Nurse Charlotte very kind, and I'm beginning not to be quite so nervous about fire and smoke and danger. It's awful to be frightened. I'll have to tell my father when he comes back how bad I've been and how unlike him. But if I can't get him just nowand I'm not going to be unpatientI want Connie, 'cos she understands."

"Of course she understands," said the preacher. "I will try and get her for you."

"But why can't she come back?"

"She can't."

"But why—why?"

"That is another thing I can't tell you."

"And I am not to be unpatient," said Ronald.

"You're to be patient—it's a big lesson—it mostly takes a lifetime to get it well learned. But somehow, when it is learned, then there's nothing else left to learn."

Ronald's eyes were so bright and so dark that the preacher felt he had said enough for the present. He bent down over the boy.

"The God above bless thee, child," he said; "and if you have power and strength to say a little prayer for Connie, do. She will come back when the Heavenly Father wills it. Good-bye, Ronald."

CHAPTER XX

CAUGHT AGAIN

When Connie awoke the next morning, it was to see the ugly face of Agnes bending over her.

"Stylites is to 'ome," she said briefly. "Yer'd best look nippy and come into the kitchen and 'ave yer brekfus'."

"Oh!" said Connie.

"You'll admire Stylites," continued Agnes; "he's a wery fine man. Now come alongbut don't yer keep him waiting."

Connie had not undressed. Agnes poured a little water into a cracked basin for her to wash her face and hands, and88 showed her a comb, by no means specially inviting, with which she could comb out her pretty hair. Then, again enjoining her to "look slippy," she left the room.

In the kitchen a big breakfast was going on. A quantity of bacon was frizzling in a pan over a great fire; and Freckles, the boy who had let Connie and Agnes in the night before, was attending to it. Two men with rough facesone of them went by the name of Corkscrew, and the other was known as Nutmegwere standing also within the region of the warm and generous fire. But the man on whom Connie fixed her pretty eyes, when she softly opened the door and in all fear made her appearance, was of a totally different order of being.

He was a tall man, quite young, not more than thirty years of age, and remarkably handsome. He had that curious combination of rather fair hair and very dark eyes and brows. His face was clean-shaven, and the features were refined and delicate without being in the least effeminate; for the cruel strength of the lower jaw and firmly shut lips showed at a glance that this man had a will of iron. His voice was exceedingly smooth and gentle, however, in intonation.

When he saw Connie he stepped up to her side and, giving her a gracious bow, said:

"Welcome to the kitchen, young lady."

"It's Stylitesbob yer curtsy," whispered Agnes in Connie's ear.

So Connie bobbed her curtsy. Was this the man she was to be so dreadfully afraid of? Her whole charming little face broke into a smile.

"I'm so glad as you're Stylites!" she said.

The compliment, the absolutely unexpected words, the charm of the smile, had a visible effect upon the man. He looked again at Connie as though he would read her through and through; then, taking her hand, he led her to the breakfast-table.

"Freckles," he said, "put a clean plate and knife on the table. That plate isn't fit for a young lady to eat off."

Freckles grinned from ear to ear, showing rows of yellow teeth. He rushed off to wash the plate in question, and returned with it hot and shining to lay again before Connie's place. Simeon Stylites himself helped the little girl to the choicest pieces of bacon, to delicate slices of white bread, and to any other good things which were on the table. As he did this he did not speak once, but his eyes seemed to be everywhere. No one dared do a thing on the sly. The rough-looking men, Corkscrew and Nutmeg, were desired in a peremptory tone to take their mugs of tea to another table at the farther end of the great room. One of them ventured to grumble, and both cast angry glances at Connie. Stylites, however, said, "Shut that!" and they were instantly mute as mice.

The boy Freckles also took his breakfast to the other table; but Agnes sat boldly down, and pushing her ill-favored face forward, addressed Simeon in familiar style:

"I nabbed heryer see."

"Shut that!" said Stylites.

Agnes flushed an angry red, gave Connie a vindictive look, but did not dare to utter another word. Connie ate her breakfast with wonderful calm, and almost contentment. During the night which had passed she had gone through terrible dreams, in which Simeon Stylites had figured largely. He had appeared to her in those dreams as an ogrea monster too awful to live. But here was a gracious gentleman, very goodly to look upon, very kind to her, although rude and even fierce to the rest of the party.

"He'll let me go 'ome," thought Connie; "he 'ave a kind 'eart."

The meal came to an end. When it did so Corkscrew came up and inquired if the young "amattur" were "goin' to 'ave her first lesson in perfessional work."

"Shut that!" said Stylites again. "You go into cellar No. and attend to the silver, Corkscrew.Nutmeg, you'll have the other jewelry to put in order this morning. Is the furnace in proper order?"

"Yus, sir."

"Get off both of you and do your business. We're going out this evening."

"When, sir?"

"Ten o'clocksharp's the word."

"On wot, sir?"

"No. 's the job," said Simeon Stylites.

"And wot am I to do?" said Agnes.

"Stay indoors and mend your clothes."

"In this room, sir?"

"No; your bedroom."

"Please, Simeon Stylites, yer ain't thanked me yet for bringin' Connie along."

For answer Stylites put his hand into his pocket, produced half-a-crown, and tossed it to Agnes.

"Get into your room, and be quick about it," he said.

"May I take Connie along, please, sir?"

"Leave the girl alone. Go!"

Agnes went.

"Come and sit in this warm chair by the fire, dear," said Stylites.

Connie did so. The smile round her lips kept coming and going, going and coming. She was touched; she was soothed; she had not a scrap of fear; this great, strong, kind man would certainly save her. He was so different from dreadful Mammy Warren.

"Freckles," said the chief, "wash the breakfast things; put them in order; take them all into the pantry. When you have done, go out by the back door, being careful to put on the old man's disguise to-day. Fasten the wig firmly on, and put a patch over your eye. Here's five shillings; get food for the day, and be here by twelve o'clock sharp. Now go."

"Yus, sir."

Freckles had an exceedingly cheerful manner. He knew very little fear. The strange life he led gave him a sort of wild pleasure. He winked at Connie.

"Somethin' wery strange be goin' to 'appen," he said to himself. "A hamattur like this a-brought in by private horders, an' no perfessional lesson to be tuk." He thought how he himself would enjoy teaching this pretty child some of the tricks of the trade. Oh, of course, she was absolutely invaluable. He didn't wonder that Mammy had brought in such spoil when Connie was there. But even Freckles had to depart, and Connie presently found herself alone with the chief.

He stood by the hearth, looking taller and more exactly like a fine gentleman, and Connie was more and more reassured about him.

"Please, sir" she began.

"Stop!" he interrupted.

"Mayn't I speak, sir?"

"Nonot now. For God's sake don't plead with me; I can't stand that."

"Why, sir?"

But Connie, as she looked up, saw an expression about that mouth and that jaw which frightened her, and frightened her so badly that all the agony she had undergone in Mammy Warren's house seemed as nothing in comparison. The next minute, however, the cruel look had departed. Simeon Stylites drew a chair forward, dropped into it, bent low, and looked into Connie's eyes.

"Allow me," he said; and he put his hand very gently under her chin, and raised her little face and looked at it.

"Who's your father?" he asked.

"Peter Harris."

"Trade?"

"Blacksmith, sir."

"Where do you live?"

"Adam Street, sir; and"

"Hush! Only answer my questions."

Stylites removed his hand from under the girl's chin, and Connie felt a blush of pain sweeping over her face.

"How long were you with that woman Warren?"

"Dunno, sir."

"What do you mean by answering me like that?"

"Can't 'elp it, sir. Tuk a fright therebad firecan't remember, please, sir."

"Never mind; it doesn't matter. Stand up; I want to look at your hair."

Connie did so. Simeon took great masses of the golden, beautiful hair between his slender fingers. He allowed it to ripple through them. He felt its weight and examined its quality.

"Sit down again," he said.

"Yus, sir."

"You're exactly the young girl I want for my profession."

"Please, sir"

"Hush!"

"Yus, sir."

"I repeatand I wish you to listenthat in my profession you would rise to eminence. You haven't an idea what it is like, have you?"

"NoI mean I'm not sure"

"You had better keep in ignorance, for it won't be really necessary for you to understand."

"Oh, sir."

"Not really necessary."

Connie looked up into the stern and very strange face.

"But you miss a good deal," said Stylites"yes, a very great deal. Tell me, for instance, how you employed your time before you entered Mrs. Warren's establishment."

"I did machine-work, sir."

"I guessed as muchor perhaps Coppenger told me. Machine-workattic work?Shop?"

"Yus, sirin Cheapside, sira workshop for cheap clothing, sir."

"Did you like it?"

"No, sir."

"I should think not. Let me look at your hand."

He took one of Connie's hands and examined it carefully.

"Little, tapering fingers," he said, "spoiled by work. They could be made very white, very soft and beautiful. Have you ever considered what a truly fascinating thing a girl's hand is?"

Connie shook her head.

"You'd know it if you stayed with me. I should dress you in silk and satins, and give you big hats with feathers, and lovely silk stockings and charming shoes."

"To wear in this 'ere kitchen, sir?"

"Oh no, you wouldn't live in this kitchen; you would be in a beautiful house with other ladies and gentlemen. You would like that, wouldn't you?"

"Yus, siref I might 'ave Ronald and Giles and father and Father John, and p'rhaps Mrs. Anderson and Mr. George Anderson, along o' me."

"But in that beautiful house you wouldn't have Mr. and Mrs. Anderson, nor your father, nor that canting street preacher, nor the children you've just mentioned. It's just possible you might have the boy Ronald, but even that is problematicalyou'd have to give up the rest."

"Then, sir," said Connie, "I rayther not go, please."

"Do you think that matters?" said Stylites.

"Wot, sir?"

"That you'd rather not go?"

"I dunno, sir."

"It doesn't matter one whit. Children who come here92 aren't asked what they'd rather or rather not do, girlthey've got to do what I order."

The voice came out, not loud, but sharp and incisive, as though a knife were cutting something.

"Yus, siryus, sir."

"Connie"the man's whole tone altered"what will you give me if I let you go?" "Oh, sir"

"I want you to give me something very big, I've taken great trouble to secure you. You're the sort of little girl I want; you would be very useful to me. You have come in hereit is true you haven't the least idea where this house isbut you've come in, and you've seen me, and you've discovered the name which these low people call me. Of course, you can understand that my real name is not Simeon Stylites—I have a very different name; and my home isn't here—I have a very different home. I would take you there, and treat you well, and afterwards perhaps send you to another home. You should never know want, and no one would be unkind to you. You would be as a daughter to me, and I am a lonely man."

"Oh, sir—sir!" said poor Connie, "I—I like you, sir—I'm not afeered—no, not much afeered—but if you 'ud only let the others come—"

"That I cannot do, girl. If you choose to belong to me you must give up the others."

"Ef I choose, sir—may I choose?"

"Yes—on a condition."

The man who called himself Simeon Stylites looked at the girl with a queer, hungry expression in his eyes.

"I wanted you very badly indeed," he said; "and I was not in the least prepared to be sentimental. But I had a little sister like you. She died when she was rather younger than you. I loved her, and she loved me. I was quite a good man then, and a gentleman—"

"Oh, sir—ye're that now."

"No, girl—I am not. There are things that a gentleman would do which I would not do, and there are things which no gentleman would do which I do. I have passed the line; nevertheless, the outward tokens remain; and I live—well, child, I want for nothing. My profession is very lucrative—very."

Connie did not understand half the words of this strange, queer man, with a terribly stern and yet terribly pathetic voice.

"When I saw you this morning," said Stylites, "I knew at once it was no go. You were like the little Eleanor whom alone in all the world I ever truly loved. You are too young to be told my story, or I would tell it to you."

"Oh, sir," said Connie, "I'd real like to comfort yer."

"You can't do that, and I won't spoil the life of any child with such a look of my little Eleanor. I am going to give you back your liberty—on a condition."

"Wot's that?" said Connie.

"That you never breathe to mortal what happened to you from the time you left your friend, the street preacher, last night, until the time when you found yourself at liberty and outside that same court. Wild horses mustn't drag it from you; detectives must do their utmost in vain. I am willing to do a good deal for you, girl, solely and entirely because of that chance likeness. But I won't have my profession and my chances in life imperilled. Do you promise?"

"Sir, I'll niver, niver tell."

"You must promise more strongly than that the others must be witnesses."

"Oh, sir oh, sir! you must trust me. Don't call the others in; let me promise to you, yer lone self, an' I will keep my word."

The strange man with the strange eyes looked long for a full minute into Connie's face.

"I could have been good to you," he said, "and what I had to offer was not altogether contemptible. But it somehow wouldn't have fitted in with my memory of Eleanor, who went back to God at eleven years of age, very pure in heart, and just like a little child. 'Of such is the Kingdom of Heaven.' Those are the words which mark her little grave in a distant part of the country. If you will follow in her steps, and be pure and good in heart and life, you may meet my Eleanor in another world. And perhaps you may be able to tell her that I a man given over to extreme wickedness did one kind deed for her sake when I gave you back to your friends."

"Sir"

"Not another word. I am a man of moods, and I might recant what I have just said."

Simeon Stylites sounded a little gong on the table. Agnes came hurriedly in.

"Fetch this child's hat and jacket," said the great man imperatively.

Agnes brought them.

"Be I to take her out, sir?" she said.

"No. And listen. This child isn't for us; let her alone in future. Are you ready, Connie?"

"Yus, sir."

Simeon Stylites put on the most gentlemanly overcoat and a well-brushed silk hat, and he took a neat stick in his hand and went boldly out of the house. As soon as ever he got outside he saw a hansom, and beckoned the driver. He and Connie got in.

They went for a long drive, and Stylites dismissed the hansom in a distant part of the town.

"You wouldn't know your way back again?" he said to the girl.

"No, sir; an' ef I knew I wouldn't tell."

"Well, thengood-bye."

"Good-bye, sir."

"Yes, good-bye. Walk down this street till you come to the end. Here's a shillingyou'll get a hansom; ask a policeman to put you in. From there go home again, and forget that you ever saw or heard of Simeon Stylites."

CHAPTER XXI

SAFE HOME AT LAST

When Harris parted from Sue he ran quickly in his cowardly flight. He did not stay his fleet steps until he had gained a very quiet street. Then, knowing that he was now quite safe, he exchanged his running for a rapid walk. He suddenly remembered that he was to meet the detectives, who were moving heaven and earth to get Connie back for him, not later than three o'clock.

They were to meet by appointment in a certain street, and the hour of rendezvous was quickly approaching. He got there in good time; but what was his amazement to see, not only the two detectivesordinary-looking men in plain clothesbut also the street preacher?

The street preacher came up to him eagerly. The detectives also followed close.

"Harris," said Atkins, "you can thank God on your kneesyour child is safe at home."

"Wot?" said Harris.

In that instant something sharp as a sword went through his heart. Oh, what a mean, terrible, horrible wretch he was! What a cowardly deed he had just committed! And yet God was kind, and had given him back his child.

"Connie is in your room, waiting for you," said Atkins. "I went in not an hour ago, hoping to find you, and there she was."

"It's very queer," said Detective Z. "You should have been there also, and have questioned the girl. There isn't the least doubt that she could give the most valuable information, but she won't utter a wordnot a word."

"Won't she, now?" said Harris. "Perhaps not to you, but she wull, quick enough, to her own father."

The entire party then turned in the direction of Harris's rooms. They went up the stairs, and Harris flung the door wide. A little, slight girl, in the identical same dark-blue dress which Harris had bought for her with such pride not many weeks ago, was standing near the fire. Already her womanly influences had been at work.

The fire burned brightly. The room was tidy. The girl herself was waitingexpectation, fear, longing, all expressed in her sensitive face.

"Father!" she cried as Harrisbrutal, red of face, self-reproachful, at once the most miserable and the gladdest man on earthalmost staggered into the room.

He took the slim little creature into his arms, gave her a few fierce, passionate kisses; then saying, "It is good to have yer back, wench," pushed her from him with unnecessary violence. He sank into a seat, trembling all over. The two detectives marked his agitation and were full of compassion for him. How deeply he loved his child, they felt. But Father John read deeper below the surface.

The man was in a very queer state. Had anything happened? He knew Harris well. At such a moment as this, if all were right, he would not be so overcome.

The detectives began to question Connie.

"We want to ask you a few questions, my dear," said Constable Z. "Who dragged you into that court last night?"

"I won't say," answered Connie.

"You won't say? But you know."

"I won't say nothing," said Connie.

"That is blamed nonsense!" cried Harris, suddenly rousing himself. "Yer've got to sayyer've got to make a clean breast of it. Wot's up? Speak!"

"I wouldn't be here, father," said Connie, "'ef I'd not promised most faithfully not iver to tell, and I won't iver, iver, iver tell, not to anybody in all the world."

There was a decidedly new quality in the girl's voice.

"I wouldn't do it for nobody," continued Connie. She drew herself up, and looked taller; her eyes were shining. The detectives glanced at each other.

"If you was put in the witness-box, missy," said one, "yer'd have to break that promise o' yourn, whoever you made it to, or you'ud know what contempt of the law meant."

"But I am not in the witness-box," said Connie, her tone suddenly becoming gay. "It was awful kind of people to look for me, but they might ha' looked for ever and niver found me again. I'm 'ere now quite safe, and nothing 'as 'appened at all, and I'm niver goin' to tell. Please, Father John, you won't ask me?"

"No, my child," said Father John. "You have made a promise, perhaps a rash one, but I should be the last to counsel you to break it."

Nothing more could be gained from Connie at present; and by-and-by Father John and the two detectives left her alone with Harris. When the door closed behind the three men a timid expression came into Connie's gentle eyes. Beyond doubt her father was sober, but he looked very queerfearfully red in the face, nervous, trembling, bad in his temper. Connie had seen him in many moods, but this particular mood she had never witnessed in him before. He must really love her. He knew nothing about that terrible time last night when he had turned her away. Then he did not know what he was doing.

Connie was the last to bear him malice for whatlike many other little girls of her classshe considered he could not help. Most of the children in the courts and streets96 around had fathers who drank. It seemed to Connie and to the other children that this was a necessary part of fathersthat they all took what was not good for them, and were exceedingly unpleasant under its influence.

She stood now by the window, and Harris sank into a chair. Then he got up restlessly.

"I be goin' out for a bit, lass," he said. "You stay 'ere."

"Oh, please, father," said Connie, "ef you be goin' out, may I go 'long and pay Giles a wisit? I want so much to have a real good talk with him."

When Connie mentioned the word Giles, Harris gave quite a perceptible start. Something very like an oath came from his lips; then he crushed back his emotion.

"Hall right," he said; "but don't stay too long there. And plait up that 'air o' yourn, and put it tight round yer 'ead; I don't want no more kidnappin' o' my wench."

There was a slight break in the rough man's voice, and Connie's little sensitive heart throbbed to the tone of love. A minute later Harris had gone out, and Connie, perceiving that it was past four o'clock, and that it would not be so very long before Sue was back from Cheapside, prepared to set off in quite gay spirits to see little Giles.

She went into her tiny bedroom. It was a very shabby room, nothing like as well furnished as the one she had occupied at Mammy Warren's. But oh, how glad she was to be back again! How sweet the homely furniture looked! How dear was that cracked and handleless jug! How nice to behold again the wooden box in which she kept her clothes!

The little girl now quickly plaited her long, thick hair, arranged it tightly round her head, and putting on a shabby frock and jacket, and laying the dark blue, which had seen such evil days, in the little trunk, she hastily left the room.

She was not long in making her appearance in Giles's very humble attic. Her heart beat as she mounted the well-worn stairs. How oftenoh, how often she had though of Giles and Sue! How she had longed for them! The next minute she had burst into the room where the boy was lying, as usual, flat on his back.

"Giles," she said, "I've come back."

"Connie!" answered Giles. He turned quickly to look at her. His face turned first red, then very pale; but the next minute he held up his hand to restrain further words.

"Don't say anything for half a minute, Connie, for 'e's goin' to speak."

"Big Ben? Oh!" said Connie.

She remembered what Big Ben had been to her and to Ronald in Mammy Warren's dreadful rooms. She too listened, half-arrested in her progress across the room. Then, above the din and roar of London, the sweet chimes pealed, and the hour of five o'clock was solemnly proclaimed.

"There!" said Giles. "Did yer 'ear wot he said now?"

"Tell usdo tell us!" said Connie.

"'The peace of God which passeth all understanding.'" said Giles. "Ain't it fine?"

"Oh yus," said Connie"yus! Gileslittle Giles'ow I ha' missed yer! Oh Giles, Giles! this is the peace o' God come back to me again."

Giles did not answer, and Connie had time to watch him. It was some weeks now since she had seen himweeks so full of events that they were like a lifetime to the child; and in those weeks a change had come over little Giles. That pure, small, angel face of his looked smaller, thinner, and more angelic than ever. It seemed as if a breath might blow him away. His sweet voice itself was thin and weak.

"I did miss yer, Connie," he said at last. "But then, I were never frightened; Sue wereover and over."

"And w'y weren't yer frightened, Giles?" said Connie. "You 'ad a reason to be, if yer did but know."

"I did know," said Giles, "and that were why I didn't fret. I knew as you were safeI knew for sartin sure that Big Ben 'ud talk to yer'e'd bring yer a message, same as 'e brings to me."

"Ohhe didhe did!" said Connie. "I might ha' guessed that you'd think that, for the message were so wery strong. It were indeed as though a Woice uttered the words. But oh, GilesI 'ave a lot to tell yer!"

"Well," said Giles, "and I am ready to listen. Poke up the fire a bit, and then set near me. Yer must stop talking w'en 'e speaks, but otherwise you talk and I listen."

"Afore I do anything," said Connie"'ave you 'ad your tea?"

"No. I didn't want it. I'll 'ave it w'en Sue comes 'ome."

"Poor Sue!" said Connie. "I'm that longin' to see her! I 'ope she won't be hangry."

"Oh, no," said Giles. "We're both on us too glad to be angry. We missed yer sore, both on us."

While Giles was speaking Connie had put on the kettle to boil. She had soon made a cup of tea, which she brought to the boy, who, although he had said he did not want it, drank it off with dry and thirsty lips.

"Dear Connie!" he said when he gave her the cup to put down.

"Now you're better," said Connie, "and I'll speak."

She began to tell her story, which quickly absorbed Giles, bringing color into his cheeks and brightness into his eyes, so that he looked by no means so frail and ill as he had done when Connie first saw him. She cheered up when she noticed this, and reflected that doubtless Giles was no worse. It was only because she had not seen him for so long that she was really frightened.

When her story was finished Giles spoke:

"You're back, and you're safeand it were the good Lord as did it. Yer'll tell me 'bout the fire over agin another day; and yer'll tell me 'bout that little Ronald, wot 'ave so brave a father, another day. But I'm tired now a bit. It's wonnerful, all the same, wot brave fathers do for their children. W'en I think o' mine, an' wot 'e wor, an' 'ow 'e died, givin' up his life for others, I'm that proud o' him, an' comforted by him, an' rejoiced to think as I'll see 'im agin, as is almost past talkin' on. But there! you'd best go 'ome now; you're quite safe, for 'E wot gives Big Ben 'is message 'ull regard yer."

"But why mayn't I wait for Sue?" said Connie.

"No," said Giles in a faint tone; "I'm too tiredI'm sort o' done up, Conniean' I can't listen, even to dear Sue axin' yer dozens and dozens o' questions. You go 'ome now, an' come back ef yer like later on, w'en Sue 'ull be 'ome and I'll ha' broke the news to her. She knows she must be very quiet in the room with me, Connie."

So Connie agreed to this; first of all, however, placing a glass with a little milk in it by Giles's side. She then returned to her own room, hoping that she might find her father there before her.

He was not there; his place was empty. Connie, however, was not alarmed, only it had struck her with a pang that if he really loved her half as much as she loved him he would have come on that first evening after her return. She spent a little time examining the room and putting it into ship-shape order, and then suddenly remembered that she herself was both faint and hungry.

She set the kettle on, therefore, to boil, and made herself some tea. There was a hunch of bread and a piece of cold bacon in the great cupboard, which in Connie's time was generally stored with provisions. She said to herself:

"I must ax father for money to buy wittles w'en he comes in." And then she made a meal off some of the bacon and bread, and drank the sugarless and milkless tea as though it were nectar. She felt very tired from all she had undergone; and as the time sped by, and Big Ben proclaimed the hours of seven, eight, and nine, she resolved to wait no longer for her father. She hoped indeed, he would not be tipsy to-night but she resolved if such were the case, and he again refused to receive her, to go to Mrs. Anderson and beg for a night's lodging.

First of all, however, she would visit Giles and Sue. Giles would have told Sue the most exciting part of the story, and Sue would be calm and practical and matter-of-fact; but of course, at the same time, very, very glad to see her. Connie thought how lovely it would be to get one of Sue's hearty smacks on her cheek, and to hear Sue's confident voice saying:

"You were a silly. Well, now ye're safe 'ome, you'll see as yer stays there."

Connie thought no words would be quite so cheerful and stimulating to hear as those matter-of-fact words of Sue's. She soon reached the attic. She opened the door softly, and yet with a flutter at her heart.

"Sue," she said. But there was no Sue in the room; only Giles, whose face was very, very white, and whose gentle eyes were full of distress.

"Come right over 'ere, Connie," he said. She went and knelt by him.

"Ye're not well," she said. "Wot ails yer?"

"Sue ain't come 'ome," he answered"neither Sue nor any tidin's of her. No, I ain't frightened, but I'mI'm lonesome, like."

"In course ye're not frightened," said Connie, who, in the new rôle of comforter for Giles, forgot herself.

"I'll set with yer," she said, "till Sue comes 'ome. W'y, Giles, anythink might ha' kep' her."

"No," said Giles, "not anythink, for she were comin' 'ome earlier than usual to-night, an' we was to plan out 'ow best to get me a new night-shirt, an' Sue herself were goin' to 'ave a evenin' patchin' her old brown frock. She were comin' 'omeshe 'ad made me a promise; nothin' in all the world would make her break itthat is, ef she could 'elp herself."

"Well, I s'pose she couldn't 'elp herself," said Connie. "It's jest this way. They keep her in over hoursthey often do that at Cheadle's."

"They 'aven't kep' 'er in to-night," said Giles.

"Then wot 'ave come to her?" "I dunno; only Big Ben"

"Giles dear, wot do yer mean?"

"I know," said Giles, with a catch in his voice, "as that blessed Woice comforts me; but there! I must take the rough with the smooth. 'E said w'en last 'e spoke, 'In all their affliction 'E were afflicted.' There now! why did those words sound through the room unless there is trouble about Sue?"

Connie argued and talked, and tried to cheer the poor little fellow. She saw, however, that he was painfully weak, and when ten o'clock struck from the great clock, and the boyhis nerves now all on edgecaught Connie's hand, and buried his face against it, murmuring, "The Woice has said them words agin," she thought it quite time to fetch a doctor.

"You mustn't go on like this, Giles," she said, "or yer'll be real ill. I'm goin' away, and I'll be back in a minute or two."

She ran downstairs, found a certain Mrs. Nelson who knew both Sue and Giles very well, described the state of the child, and begged of Mrs. Nelson to get the doctor in.

"Wull, now," said that good woman, "ef that ain't wonnerful! Why, Dr. Deane is in the 'ouse this very blessed minute attending on Hannah Blake, wot broke her leg. I'll send him straight up to Giles, Connie, ef yer'll wait there till he comes. Lor, now!" continued Mrs. Nelson, "w'y hever should Sue be so lateand this night, of all nights?"

Connie, very glad to feel that the doctor was within reach, returned to the boy, who now lay with closed eyes, breathing fast. Dr. Deane was a remarkably kind young man. He knew the sorrows of the poor, and they all loved him, and when he saw Giles he bent down over the little fellow and made a careful examination. He then cheered up the boy as best he could, and told him that he would send him a strengthening medicine, also a bottle of port-wine, of which he was to drink some at intervals, and other articles of food.

"Wen 'ull Sue come back?" asked Giles of the doctor.

"Can't tell you that, my dear boy. Your sister may walk in at any minute, but I am sure this little friend will stay with you for the night."

"Yus, if I may let father know," said Connie.

"You mustn't fret, Giles; that would be very wrong," said the doctor. He then motioned Connie on to the landing outside. "The boy is ill," he said, "and terribly weakhe is half-starved. That poor, brave little sister of his does what she can for him, but it is impossible for her to earn sufficient money to give him the food he requires. I am exceedingly sorry for the boy, and will send him over a basket of good things."

"But," said Connie, her voice trembling, "is he wery, wery ill?"

"Yes," said the doctor"so ill that he'll soon be better. In his case, that is the best sort of illness, is it not? Oh, my child, don't cry!"

"Do yer mean that Giles is goin'goin' right aw'y?" whispered Connie.

"Right awayand before very long. It's the very best thing that could happen to him. If he lived he would suffer all his life. He won't suffer any more soon. Now go back to him, and cheer him all you can."

Connie did go back. Where had she learnt such wonderful self-controlshe who, until all her recent trials, had been rather a selfish little girl, thinking a good deal of her pretty face and beautiful hair, and rebelling when trouble came to her? She had chosen her own way, and very terrible trials had been hers in consequence. She had learned a lesson, partly from Ronald, partly from Big Ben, partly from the words of her little Giles, whom she had loved all her life. For Giles's sake she would not give way now.

"Set you down, Connieright here," said Giles.

She sat down, and he looked at her.

"Wot do doctor say?" said Giles.

"Oh, that ye're a bit weakly, Giles. He's goin' to send yer a basket o' good wittles."

Giles smiled. Then he held out his shadowy little hand and touched Connie.

"Niver mind," he said softly; "I know wot doctor said."

A heavenly smile flitted over his face, and he closed his eyes.

"It won't be jest yet," he said. "There'll be plenty o' time. Connie, wull yer sing to me?"

"Yus," said Connie, swallowing a lump in her throat.

"Sing "Ere we suffer."'"

Connie began. How full and rich her voice had grown! She remembered that time when, out in the snow, she had sunglittle Ronald keeping her company:

"Here we suffer grief and pain,
Here we meet to part again,
In Heaven we part no more.
Oh! that will be joyful,
When we meet to part no more."
The words of the hymn were sung to the very end, Giles listening in an ecstasy of happiness.

"Now, 'Happy Land,'" he said.

Connie sang:

"There is a Happy Land,
Far, far away,
Where saints in glory stand,
Bright, bright as day."
The second hymn was interrupted by the arrival of a messenger, who brought a bottle of medicine and a large basket. The contents of the basket were laid on the tablea little crisp loaf of new bread, a pat of fresh butter, half a pound of tea, a small can of milk, a pound of sugar, half-a-dozen new-laid eggs, and a chicken roasted whole, also a bottle of port-wine.

"Now then," said Connie, "look, Gileslook!"

The messenger took away the basket. Even Giles was roused to the semblance of appetite by the sight of the tempting food. Connie quickly made tea, boiled an egg, and brought them with fresh bread-and-butter to the child. He ate a little; then he looked up at her.

"You must eat, too, Connie. Why, you be white and tired!"

Connie did not refuse. She made a small meal, and then, opening the bottle of wine with a little corkscrew which had also been sent, kept the precious liquid in readiness to give to Giles should he feel faint.

Eleven o'clock rang out in Big Ben's great and solemn voice. Connie was very much startled when she heard the great notes; but, to her surprise, Giles did not take any notice. He lay happy, with an expression on his face which showed that his thoughts were far away.

"Connie," he said after a minute, "be yer really meanin' to spend the night with me?"

"Oh yus," said Connie, "ef yer'll 'ave me."

"You've to think of your father, Conniehe may come102 back. He may miss yer. Yer ought to go back and see him, and leave him a message."

"I were thinking that," said Connie; "and I won't be long. I'll come straight over here the very minute I can, and ef Sue has returned"

"Sue won't come backnot yet," said Giles.

"Why, Gileshow do you know?"

"Jesus Christ told me jest now through the Woice o' Big Ben," said the boy.

"Oh Gileswot?"

"'E said, 'Castin' all your care on God, for He careth for you.' I ha' done it, and I'm not frettin' no more. Sue's all right; God's a-takin' care of her. I don't fret for Sue now, no more than I fretted for you. But run along and tell your father, and come back." Connie went.

At this hour of night the slums of Westminster are not the nicest place in the world for so pretty a girl to be out. Connie, too, was known by several people, and although in her old clothes, and with her hair fastened round her head, she did not look nearly so striking as when Mammy Warren had used her as a decoy-duck in order to pursue her pickpocket propensities, yet still her little face was altogether on a different plane from the ordinary slum children.

"W'y, Connie," said a rough woman, "come along into my den an' tell us yer story."

"Is it Connie Harris?" screamed another. "W'y, gel, w'ere hever were yer hall this time? A nice hue and cry yer made! Stop 'ere this minute and tell us w'ere yer ha' been."

"I can't," said Connie. "Giles is bad, and Sue ain't come 'ome. I want jest to see father, and then to go back to Giles. Don't keep me, neighbors."

Now, these rough peoplethe roughest and the worst, perhaps, in the landhad some gleams of good in them; and little Giles was a person whom every one had a soft word for.

"A pore little cripple!" said the woman who had first spoken."Get you along at once, Connie; he's in."

"I be sorry as the cripple's bad, and Sue not returned," cried another. "I 'ope Sue's not kidnapped too. It's awful w'en folks come to kidnappin' one's kids."

While the women were talking Connie made her escape, and soon entered her father's room. She gave a start at once of pleasure and apprehension when she saw him there. Was he drunk? Would he again turn her out into the street? She didn't knowshe feared. Peter Harris, however, was sober. That had happened in one short day which, it seemed to him, made it quite impossible for him ever to drink again.

He looked at Connie with a strange nervousness.

"Wull," he said, "you be late! And 'ow's Giles?"

He did not dare to ask for Sue. His hopefor he had a hopewas that Sue had come back without ever discovering the locket which he had transferred to her pocket. In that case he might somehow manage to get it away again without103 her knowing anything whatever with regard to his vile conduct. If God was good enough for that, why, then indeed He was a good God, and Harris would follow Him to his dying day. He would go to the preacher and tell him that henceforth he meant to be a religious, church-going man, and that never again would a drop of drink pass his lips. He had spent an afternoon and evening in the most frightful remorse, but up to the present he had not the most remote intention of saving Sue at his own expense. If only she had escaped unsuspected, then indeed he would be good; but if it were otherwise he felt that the very devils of hell might enter into his heart.

"'Ow's Giles? 'Ow did he take yer comin' 'ome again, wench?"

"Oh father," said Connie, panting slightly, and causing the man to gaze at her with wide-open, bloodshot eyes, "Giles is wery, wery badI 'ad to send for the doctor. 'E come, and 'e saidah! 'e said as 'ow little Giles 'ud soon be leavin' us. I can'tcan't speak on it!"

Connie sat down and covered her face with her hands. Harris drew a breath at once of relief and suspicion. He was sorry, of course, for little Giles; but then, the kid couldn't live, and he had nothing to do with his death. It was Sue he was thinking about. Of course Sue was there, or Connie would have mentioned the fact of her not having returned home.

Connie wept on, overcome by the strange emotions and experiences through which she had so lately passed.

"Connie," said her father at last, when he could bear the suspense no longer, "Sue must be in great takin'poor Sue!"

"But, father," said Connie, suddenly suppressing her tears, "that's the most dreadful part of allSue ain't there!"

"Not there? Not to 'ome?" thundered Harris.

"No, fathershe ha' niver come back. It's goin' on for twelve o'clockan' Giles expected her soon arter six! She ain't come back, 'ave Sue. Wottever is to be done, father?"

Harris walked to the fire and poked it into a fierce blaze. Then he turned his back on Connie, and began to fumble with his neck-tie, tightening it and putting it in order.

"Father," said Connie.

"Wull?"

"Wot are we to do 'bout Sue?"

"She'll be back come mornin'."

"Father," said Connie again, "may I go and spend the night 'long o' Giles? He's too weakly to be left."

"No," said Harris; "I won't leave yer out o' my sight. Ef there's kidnappin' about an' it looks uncommon like ityou stay safe within these four walls."

"But GilesGiles?" said Connie.

"I'll fetch Giles 'ere."

"Father! So late?"

"Yuswhy not? Ef there's kidnappin' about, there's niver104 any sayin' w'en Sue may be back. I'll go and fetch him now, and you can get that sofy ready for him; he can sleep on it. ThereI'm off! SueGod knows wot's come o' Sue; but Giles, e' sha'n't want."

Harris opened the door, went out, and shut it again with a bang. Connie waited within the room. She was trembling with a strange mixture of fear and joy. How strange her father wasand yet he was good too! He was not drunk to-night. That was wonderful. It was sweet of him to think of bringing Giles to Connie's home, where Connie could look after him and give him the best food, and perhaps save his life. Children as inexperienced as Connie are apt to take a cheerful view even when things are at their lowest. Connie instantly imagined that Giles in his new and far more luxurious surroundings would quickly recover.

She began eagerly to prepare a place for him. She dragged a mattress from her own bed, and managed to put it on the sofa; then she unlocked a trunk which always stood in the sitting-room; she knew where to find the key. This trunk had belonged to her mother, and contained some of that mother's clothing, and also other things.

Connie selected from its depths a pair of thin and very fine linen sheets. These she aired by the fire, and laid them over the mattress when they were quite warm. There was a blanket, white and light and very warm, which was also placed over the linen sheets; and a down pillow was found which Connie covered with a frilled pillow-case; and finally she took out the most precious thing of alla large crimson and gold shawl, made of fine, fine silk, which her mother used to wear, and which Connie dimly remembered as thinking too beautiful for this world. But nothing was too beautiful for little Giles; and the couch with its crimson covering was all ready for him when Harris reappeared, bearing the boy in his arms.

"I kivered him up with his own blanket," he said, turning to Connie. "Ain't that sofy comfor'ble to look at? You lie on the sofa, sonny, an' then yer'll know wot it be to be well tended."

Little Giles was placed there, and Connie prepared a hot bottle to put to his feet, while Harris returned to the empty room to fetch away the medicine and get the things which Dr. Deane had ordered. He left a message, too, with Mrs. Nelson, telling her what had become of the boy, and asking Dr. Deane to call at his house in the future.

"You be a good man," said Mrs. Nelson in a tone of great admiration. "My word, now! and ain't it lucky for the kid? You be a man o' money, Mr. Harrishe'll want for nothing with you."

"He'll want for nothing no more to the longest day he lives," answered Harris.

"Ah, sir," said Mrs. Nelson, "hehe won't live long; he'll want for nothing any more, sir, in the Paradise of God."

"Shut up!" said Harris roughly. "Ye're all with yer grumblin's and moans jest like other women."

"And what message am I to give to Suepoor girlwhen she comes 'ome?" called Mrs. Nelson after him.

But Harris made no reply to this; only his steps rang out hard and firm and cruel on the frosty ground.

CHAPTER XXII

NEWS OF SUE

The next morning, when Connie awoke, she remembered all the dreadful things that had happened. She was home again. That strange, mysterious man, Simeon Stylites, had let her go. How awful would have been her fate but for him!

"He were a wery kind man," thought Connie. "And now I must try to forget him. I must never mention his name, nor think of him no more for ever. That's the way I can serve him bestpore Mr. Simeon! He had a very genteel face, and w'en he spoke about his little sister it were real touching. But I mustn't think of him, for, ef I do, some day I might let his name slip, an' that 'ud do him a hurt."

Connie's thoughts, therefore, quickly left Simeon Stylites, Agnes Coppenger, Freckles, Nutmeg, and Corkscrew, and returned to the exciting fact that Sue was now missing, and that Giles was under her own father's roof.

She sprang out of bed, and quickly dressing herself, entered the general sitting-room. She was surprised to find that her father had taken his breakfast and had gone; that Giles was sitting up, looking very pretty, with his little head against the white pillow, and the crimson and gold shawl covering his couch.

"Why, Connie," he said, the minute he saw her, "wot a silly chap I wor yesterday! It's all as plain now as plain can beI know everything now."

"Wottever do you mean?" said Connie. "But don't talk too much, Giles, till I ha' got yer yer breakfast."

"Bless yer!" said Giles, with a weak laugh, "I ha' had my breakfast an hour and a half agoyer father guv it to me. He be a wery kind man."

"My father guv you your breakfast?" said Connie.

She felt that wonders would never cease. Never before had Harris been known to think of any one but himself.

"Set down by me, Connie; you can't do naught for your breakfast until the kettle boils. I'll tell yer now w'ere Sue is."

"Where?" asked Connie. "Oh Giles! have yer heard of her?"

"Course I 'aveI mean, it's all as clear as clear can be. It's only that Sue 'ave more money than she told me 'bout, and that she's a-tryin' to give me my 'eart's desire."

"Your 'eart's desire, Giles?"

"Yusher an' me 'ave always 'ad our dream; and dear Sueshe's a-makin' it come to pass, that's all. It's as plain as plain can be. She's a-gone to the country."

"To the country? Oh no, Giles; I don't think so. Wottever 'ud take her to the country at this time o' year?"

"It's there she be," said Giles. "She knew as I wanted dreadful to 'ear wot it were like, an' she 'ave gone. Oh Connie, you went to the country; but she didn't guess that. She ha' gonedear Sue 'aveto find out all for herself; an' she thought it 'ud be a rare bit of a s'prise for me. I must make the most of it w'en I see her, and ax her about the flowers and everything. She's sartin to be back to-day. Maybe, too, she could get work at plain sewin' in the country; an' she an' me could live in a little cottage, an' see the sun in the sky, and 'ear the birds a singin'. It's a'most like 'eaven to think of the countryain't it, Connie?"

"Yus," said Connie, "the country's beautiful; but wicked people come out o' Lunnon to it, an' then it's sad. An' there's no flowers a-growin' in the fields and 'edges in the winter, Gilesan' there's no birds a-singin'."

"Oh! but that 'ull come back," said Giles. "You can eat yer breakfast now, Connie, an' then arter that we'll talk more about the country. You ain't goin' to work to-daybe you, Connie?"

"Oh no," said Connie; "I ha' lost that place, an' I dunno w'ere to find another. But there's no hurry," she added, "and I like best now to be along o' you."

Connie then ate her breakfast, and Giles lay with his eyes closed and a smile of contentment on his face.

In the course of the morning there came an unlooked-for visitor.

A funny-looking, red-haired boy entered the room. Seeing Giles asleep, he held up his finger warningly to Connie, and stealing on tiptoe until he got opposite to her, he sat down on the floor.

"Wull, an' wottever do yer want?" asked Connie.

"Hush!" said the red-haired boy.

He pointed to Giles. This action on the part of a total stranger seemed so absurd to Connie that she burst out laughing. The red-haired boy never smiled. He continued to fix his round, light-blue eyes on her face with imperturbable gravity.

"Wull," he exclaimed under his breath, "ef she ain't more of a Cinderella than t' other! Oh, wouldn't the Prince give her the glass slipper! Poor, poor Cinderella at 'ome! you've no chance now. Ain't she jest lovely! I call her hangelic! My word! I could stare at that 'ere beauteous face for hiver."

As these thoughts crept up to the fertile brain of Pickles his lips moved and he nodded his head, so that Connie really began to think he was bewitched.

"Wottever do you want?" she whispered; and, fortunately107 for them both, at that juncture Giles stirred and opened his eyes.

"That's right!" cried Pickles. "Now I can let off the safety-valve!"

He gave a sigh of relief.

"Whoever's he?" asked Giles, looking from the red-faced boy to Connie. But before she had time to reply, Pickles sprang to his feet, made a somersault up and down the room, then stood with his arms akimbo just in front of Giles.

"I'm glad as you hintroduced the word 'he,' young un; hotherwise, from the looks of yer both, you seems to liken me to a monster. Yer want to know who's he? He's a boya full-grown human boysomething like yerself, only not so flabby by a long chalk."

"But wot did you want? and wot's yer name, boy?" said Connie, who could not help laughing again.

"Ah!" said Pickles, "now ye're comin' to the p'int o' bein' sensible, young 'oman. I thought at first you could only drop hangelic speeches, an' that you 'ailed from the hangel spheres; but now I see ye're a geloh, quite the very purtiest I hiver laid heyes on. Now, as I've spoke my true mind, I'll hanswer yer questions in a discreet an' pious manner. My name is PicklesPickles, at yer sarvice."

"I never heered such a name in all my life," said Connie.

"Wery like not. I were christened by the proper name o' James; but no James as ever walked 'ud hold meit didn't fit no w'y; an' Pickles did. So Pickles I am, an' Pickles I'll be to the end o' the chapter. Now, as to wot I wantsw'y; I wants a talk with that mealy-faced chap wot looks as if I'd heat him up alive."

"No, I don't," said Giles. "I were only thinking as you 'ad the wery reddest 'air I iver see'd in my life."

"Personal remarks air considered ill-mannered, young man. And let me tell yer as my hair's my special glory. But now to business. You can't know, I guess, wot I wants yer for."

"No, I can't," said Giles.

"That's rum; and I to tike the trouble not only to wisit yer own most respectable mansion, but to foller yer 'ere in the true sperrit of kindness."

"Ye're wery good; but I can't guess wot ye're up to," answered Giles.

"Dear, dear! the silliness o' folks! Now, w'en a stranger seeks yer hout, isn't it safe to s'pose as he brings news?"

"Wull, yes."

"Next clueshall I 'elp yer a bit? You 'asn't, so to speak, lost something latelythimble, or a pair of scissors, or something o' that sort?"

"Oh, it's Sue! It's my darling Sue;" exclaimed Giles, a light breaking all over his face. "'As yer brought news of Sue, boy?"

"Be Sue a thimble, scissors, or a gel?"

"Oh! a gel, in coursemy own dear, dear, only sister."

"A little, fat, podgy kind o' woman-gel, wid a fine crop o' freckles and sandy hair?"

"Yes, yes; that's she. I have bin waiting fur her hall night. Where is she? Please, please, Pickles, where is she?"

"Well, can't yer guess? Where 'ud she be likely ter be? She worn't a wandering sort o' gel, as neglected her home duties, wor she?"

"Oh no! she never stayed out in hall her life afore."

"She worn't, so to speak, a gel as wor given to pilfer, and might be tuk to cool herself in the lock-up."

"Nevernever! Sue 'ud sooner die than take wot worn't her own; and I wish I wor strong enough to punch yer head fur thinkin' sech a thing," said Giles, his face now crimson with indignation.

"Well, softly, softly, young un; I didn't say as she did pilfer. I think that 'ere podgy gel as honest as the day. But now, can't yer guess where she his?"

"Oh yes! I can guess wery well," answered Giles, his face softening down. "I guessed long agodidn't I, Connie?"

"Well, now, wot hever did yer guess?" asked Pickles, in some amazement.

"Oh! there wor but one thing to guess. There were one dream as Sue and I were halways dreaming, and she have gone off widout me at last, to see wot it wor like. She'll be back hany moment, arter she have seen and found hout hall she could. Sue have gone to the country, Pickles."

"Oh, my heyes! to the country!" exclaimed Pickles. His face grew crimson, and he was obliged to leave his seat and walk to the window, where he remained with his back to the others for nearly a minute, and where he indulged in some smothered mirth.

When he turned round, however, he was as grave as a judge.

"You are clever," he said to Giles.

"I'm right, ain't I?" asked Giles.

"In course; you're always as right as a trivet."

"Oh, I'm so glad! And does she find it wery beautiful?"

"Scrumptious! fairy-like! scrumptious!"

"Oh, how happy I am! And when 'ull she be back?"

"Well, that's the part as may moderate your raptures; she can't exactly tell when. She sent me to tell yer as she don't exactly know. It may be to-morrow; or, agen, it mayn't be fur a week, or even more. She's hever so sorry, and she sends yer a whole pocketful o' love, but she can't tell when she'll get back."

"But what is she stayin fur?"

"Oh! my heyes! wot is she staying fur? You wants ter live in a cottage in the country, don't yer?"

"Why, yes, that's hour dream."

"Well, ha'n't she to find hout wot the price o' them are? Ha'n't she, stoo-pid?"

"I s'pose so. Is that what she's staying fur?"

Pickles nodded.

"You don't never tell no lies, do you, boy?"

"I! Wot do yer take me fur? You can b'lieve me or not as yer pleases."

"Oh! I do b'lieve yer. Will yer take a message back to Sue?"

"Why, in course."

"Tell her to have two rooms in the cottage, and plenty o' flowers hall round, and a big winder where I can look hout at the stars when I can't sleep o' nights."

"Yes, I'll tell her faithful. Hanythink else?"

"Tell her as I love to think as she's in the country, but to come back as fast as she can; and givegive her my wery best love. And you wouldn't like to give her a kiss fur me?"

"Oh! my heye! yere's a rum go. Fancy me a-kissing CindI means Sue. No, young un, I hasn't the wery least hobjection in life. I'll give her two resounding smacks the wery minute as I sees her. Lor'! it will be fine fun. Now, good-bye. I'll come and see yer soon agen.Good-bye, my beauty. I only wishes as it wor you I wor axed ter kiss.Good-bye, Giles. I'll remember wot yer said 'bout that 'ere cottage."

"Be sure as the winders is big enough fur me to see the stars," called out Giles after him.

CHAPTER XXIII

AMATEUR DETECTIVE

Mrs. Price had been blessed by nature with two sons, each as different in manners, disposition, appearance, and tastes as the poles. William, aged twenty, was dark, quiet-looking, with a grave and kind face. In disposition he was as fine a fellow as ever breathed, thoughtful for others, good to all, doing his duty because he loved and feared both God and his mother. He was very reserved, and seldom spoke, but when he did give utterance to his thoughts they were to the point and worth listening to. Mrs. Price was often heard to say that the mere presence of her elder son in the room gave her a sense of repose, that she felt that she had some one to lean onwhich in truth she had.

James, her second and younger son, had not one of his brother's characteristics; he had no gentle courtesies, no quiet ways. Except when asleep, he was never known to be still for a moment. One glance at his fiery head, at his comical face, would show plainly that he was a very imp of mischief. He was kind-heartedhe would not willingly injure the smallest living thingbut his wild, ungovernable spirit, his sense of the ludicrous in all and every circumstance, made him sometimes do unintentional harm, and his mother had some difficulty in getting him out of the scrapes into which110 he was always putting himself. No work he had ever done had so delighted the boyish heart of James Price, alias Pickles, as the capture of Sue from the hands of the police. The whole story had a certain flavor about it which would be sure to captivate such a nature as his. Sue was innocent; he was quite certain of that. But then, as certainly some one else was guilty. Here, then, was a work after his own heart; he would find out who the guilty party was. He had a great deal of the detective about him; indeed, he had almost resolved to join that body when he was grown-up.

He had brought Sue to his mother; and his mother, too, believing in the girl's innocence, was yet much puzzled how to advise her or what to do with her. Sue, being thoroughly drilled and frightened into such a course by Pickles, had declared that nothing would induce her to go home; for that if she did she would certainly be taken to prison, and found guilty of a crime of which she was quite innocent. Mrs. Price, too, felt that she could not counsel Sue to go back, though the agony of the poor girl, when she thought of Giles waiting and longing for her, was sad to witness.

To comfort her a little, Pickles went to see Giles, being warned by Sue on no account to tell him the truth, which would, she said, absolutely and at once break his heart.

Pickles, winking profoundly, told her to leave it to him. He went, and Giles himself supplied him with an idea on which he was not slow to work. Giles was fully persuaded that Sue was in the country, and might not return for some days. He seemed more pleased than otherwise that she should be so employed. Pickles was so delighted with his own success that he danced a kind of hornpipe all the way home.

He found Sue by herself and very disconsolate, for Mrs. Price had gone out on some errands.

The first thing he did was to go up to her and give her two very fierce salutes, one on her brow, the other on the point of her chin.

"There, now," he said; "that 'ere little tender brother sent yer them."

"Oh Pickles! how is he? Is he wery cut up?" asked poor Cinderella, raising a tearful face.

"Cut up? Not a bit o' him! Why, he's quite perky; he think as you has gone to the country."

"Oh Pickles! how hever could he?"

"Well, listen, and I'll tell yer."

Pickles here related his whole interview, not forgetting to reproduce in full all his own clever speeches, and his intense admiration for Connie.

"I'd do a great deal fur you, Cinderella," he said in conclusion; "fur though ye're as ordinary a woman as I hiver met, yet still yer belongs to the species, and I has a weakness fur the species; but oh, lor'! ef it had been that 'ere Connie, why, I'd have a'most spilt my life-blood fur that hangelic creature."

"Well, yer see, it wor only me," said Sue, not a little piqued.

"Yes, it wor only you. But now, wot do you think of it all?"

"Oh! I'm wery glad and thankful that Giles is wid Connie. He wor halways fond of Connie, and I'm real pleased as he thinks as I'm gone to the countrythat 'ull satisfy him ef hanythink will, fur he have sech a longing fur it, poor feller! But oh, Pickles! I do hope as you didn't tell him no lies, to make him so keen upon it."

"Nonot I. I only nodded and made-believe as he wor clever. No, I wor careful o' the utterances o' the tongue, which is an unruly member."

"Well, I'm glad," said Sue. "I only hope as it ain't wrong to deceive him."

"No, it ain't a bit wrong; don't you go a fussing about nothink. But now you have got to listen to me, fur I have got something most serious to talk over."

"I'll listen," replied Sue.

"Good! And wot little bit o' brain you have you may stick inter the listening, too, fur you will presently have to think a deal."

"Wery well," answered Sue, who had long ago come to consider Pickles the greatest oracle she had ever seen.

Pickles planted himself on his knees in front of her, and having placed one hand firmly on each leg, bent forward until he brought himself into what he considered a telling position with regard to her face.

"Ef yer want to unearth a secret, stare 'em well right inter the heyes," was one of his detective principles.

"Now, Cinderella," he began, "you say as ye're hinnercent o' that 'ere theft?"

"You know I am," answered Sue.

"And yet that 'ere wauluable trinket wor found in yer pocket."

"Well, I can't help that."

"I'm afraid yer can't, Cinderella; and a wery ugly business it is fur yer; it 'ud bring yer in guilty in hany court wot hiver."

"I know that, PicklesI know that only too well; that's why I'm here."

"An' you must stay yere until ye're proved hinnercent."

"Yes."

"Well, that may be awkwardnot fur us, but fur poor, little tender Giles. He thinks as ye're gone to the country, and I give him to understand as yer would not be back fur maybe a day or two. But he's hall on a quiver fur yer to come back now; he's hall on a tremble to know wot the country is like. He says ye're to get a cottage as have a big winder in it, fur he wants to see the stars o' nights. Now, I think by the looks o' Giles as he'll fade away wery quick ef yer don't come back soon."

"Oh, I know itI know it!" said Sue. "What shall I do? Ef I do go back I shall be tuk ter prison. Oh! oh! oh!" and she began to weep.

"Don't cry, you silly! Cryin' never mended no broken bones. You dry your eyes and listen when the oracle speaks."

"I will," said Sue, endeavoring to check her sobs.

"Well then, yer hinnercence must be proved. The way to prove yer hinnercence is to find hout who put that 'ere trinket in yer pocket."

"Oh Pickles! I don'tI don't think hany one could be so wicked."

"Bless yer, gel! yer hasn't gone about and seen life like me. 'Tis a wicked world, Cinderella. Some one put that locket in yer pocket; ef it worn't yerself, it wor another."

"I don't know why hany one should do it," said Sue.

"You leave that to me. The reason is a mystery; the person wot did it is a mystery; it remains fur this yere child"giving his breast a great slap"to unravel them both. Now, Cinderella, wot kind o' man wor that 'ere Peter Harris wot went wid yer to the shop?"

"He wor a wery rough kind o' man," said Sue, "and he often drank. He wor in trouble jest then 'bout Connie. Connie is his daughter. She wor away fur a bit, and had come back, and he wanted to give her a ring, and, as I telled yer, we went inter the shop to buy her one."

"And had that 'ere Harris much money?"

"He didn't say as he hadn't; he gave a sovereign to pay fur the ring."

"Don't yer think, Cinderella, as it wor he put the locket in your pocket?"

"Indeed I don't," answered Sue, in great indignation. "He wor a bit rough, and used to drink a good deal, but I never heerd mortal say as he worn't as honest a man as ever stepped. Besides, Pickles, he wor a friend to me, and I wor a friend to Connie, and even ef he wished to do something so desperate wicked he couldn't, fur I wor at the other side o' the shop a'most."

"All the same," replied Pickles, shaking his fiery head, "I believe as he did it. 'Tis a desperate big mystery, but I means to clear it hup, so you leave it ter me, Cinderella."

CHAPTER XXIV

MOTHER AND SON

That night Mrs. Price and her younger son had a conversation.

"I do not want to send her away, Jamie," she said when they had discoursed with much interest for some time. "She shall and must stay here for the present; but it cannot go on always, for what would the poor little brother do? If Cinderella is the bread-winner, and Cinderella can earn no bread, the poor little fellow will starve."

James Price, alias Pickles, was looking very sober, even thoughtful.

"It tuk a deal o' time to save hup, and 'tis rare and comforting to reflect on having itbut there's my half-crown," he said.

"Bless you, my laddie! it will help a trifle, but half-a-crown won't feed the smallest eater for long."

"Then, mother, you know I allow no one ter dictate ter me but you. Wot's to be done? Ere we to betray the hinnercent?"

"No, my ladno. I confess I am sorely puzzled."

"But I ain't," said Pickles, who had knowingly brought his mother round to make this confession. "I ain't puzzled the least bit in life, fur I know who is the real thief."

"Now, Jamie, what do you mean?"

"Mother, it were the man as went with Cinderella inter the shop; it wor he wot stole the locket and then put it inter her pocket. I don't know how he did it, nor why he did it, but I do know that did do it."

"Oh! my dear boy, in your love of mystery you are allowing your imagination to run away with you. I do not think any one would be so wicked."

"Never you mind, mother; take it on trust as there's that much wickedness in this yer world. Be thankful ye're hout o' the way o' hearing o' what's disgusting to dwell on, but this yere is a mystery as must be cleared hup. How do you s'pose, mother, as the locket did get inter Cinderella's pocket?"

"It may have slipped in as she stood by the counter."

"Oh, come, mother! that 'ud go down wid no jury as hiver walked. No, no; b'lieve me as 'tis as I say; and wot's more, 'tis my business to prove the truth o' my thoughts. There's a mystery, but James Price, alias Pickles, 'ull unravel it. You keep Cinderella fur a week yere, mother, and I'll engage as the guilty party confesses by the end o' that time."

"I will keep the little girl as long as is necessary, Pickles. But do be careful. Do not allow your vivid imagination to make you unjust to others."

"You leave it ter me, mother. You jest promise faithful to keep Cinderella fur a bit, and I'll do the rest."

"Yes, Jamie," said Mrs. Price, "I certainly will make that promise."

"That's a brick o' a mother. And now I'm off to bed, fur there's nothing like sleep when the brain is much exercised, as mine is at present."

CHAPTER XXV

ABOUT RONALD

While poor Harris was trying to soothe the agonies of his conscience by being specially and extra good to Giles, and while Giles, who under Connie's care was recovering a certain114 measure of strength, and poor little Sue was still acting the part of Cinderella with Pickles as her champion, another child who plays an important part in this story was gradually recovering health and strength.

When Ronald was well enough, to come downstairs, and then to walk across Mrs. Anderson's pretty little parlor, and on a certain fine day to go out with her for a walk, the good lady thought it was full time to make inquiries with regard to his relations.

She questioned her son George on the subject, and this gallant young fireman gave her what advice he could.

"No, don't employ detectives, mother," said George. "Somehow I hate the whole lot of them. Keep Ronald as long as you want to; he's a dear little chap, and a gentleman by birth, and he loves you too."

"I want to keep him, George; the child is the greatest delight and comfort to me. He is very unlike other childrenvery sensitive and delicate. But I do think that if he has relations they ought to know of his whereabouts."

"You have questioned him, of course, on the matter," said George Anderson.

"Nonot much; he hasn't been strong enough. I think, too, the severe illness he has undergone, and the terrible frights he has been subject to, have to a certain extent affected his mind; and beyond the fact that he is always looking for his father, and hoping that his father may walk in, he never talks about the old days."

"Well, mother," said George, "I must be off now; duty time is close at hand." As he spoke he rose from the seat by the fire which he had been enjoying in his mother's room.

"Of course, there is little doubt that Major Harvey is dead; but you could call at the War Office and inquire, mother, couldn't you?"

"Yes, I could and will; and I won't employ detectives, my boy. You may be certain of one thingthat I don't want to part with the child."

The next day after breakfast, Mrs. Anderson felt that it was time to question Ronald with regard to his past life.

"You are quite well now, Ronald," she said.

"Yes," said Ronald, "ever so strong. I feel brave, too," he added; "it would take a very great deal to frighten me now. A soldier's boy should be brave," he continued, that pleading, pathetic look coming into his dark eyes, which gave such a special charm to his little face.

"This soldier's boy is very brave," said Mrs. Anderson, patting his little hand, as the child stood close to her.

"My father was a V. C., ma'am," remarked Ronald in a soft tone.

"You're very proud of that, Ronaldyou have good reason to be," said his friend. "But now, dear, I seriously want to ask you a few questions. You have told me about Connie, and about some of your dreadful life with Mammy Warren. I am115 anxious that you should try to forget all these terrible things as much as possible."

"Oh! but, please, I never could forget dear Connie."

"I don't want you to forget her. I have been planning a delightful surprise for you with regard to her. But other things you can forget."

"There's another person I don't want to forget," said Ronald; "that is the good woman in the country who gave me delicious new-laid eggs and chops and chicken. Mrs. Cricket was her name. I used to think of The Cricket on the Hearth often when I was looking at her. She was very like one, you knowsuch a cosy, purring sort of woman."

"How long were you with her, Ronald?"

"I don't remember going to her," said Ronald, shaking his head; "but perhaps I was too ill. But I do remember being with her, and the little path in the wood, and how I gradually got better, and how she petted me. And I remember Connie coming down the path looking like an angel; but Connie was the only bright thing for me to think about that dreadful day. But oh, pleaseplease, Mrs. Anderson! poor Mrs. Cricket! Father hasn't come back, you knowhe is coming, of course, but he hasn't come yetand no one has paid Mrs. Cricket!"

"No one has paid her, dear?"

"Nobody at all. Mammy Warren said to her that father would pay her, but I know now it must have been all a lie."

"I am very much afraid it was," said Mrs. Anderson. "That Mammy Warren was a dreadful woman. Well, Ronald, I must try and get Mrs. Cricket's address, and we'll send her some money; and some day perhapsthere's no saying whenyou may be able to go back to her. Would you like to see her again?"

"Very, very much," said the child, "if Mammy Warren doesn't come to fetch me."

"Very well: I will endeavor to get her address. Perhaps Connie could tell me."

"Oh! perhaps she could," said Ronald; "for I couldn't. I haven't a notion where she lived, except that it was far in the country, and the cottage was teenyjust two rooms, you knowand there was a pretty wood outside, and the horse-chestnuts lying on the ground."

"But now, Ronald, I want you to go farther back. Tell me of things that happened whenwhen your mother was alive."

"II'll try," said the boy.

"Go on, deartell me all you can."

"It's very difficult," said Ronald. "I remember little bits, and then I forget little bits."

"I don't want you to worry yourself, dear; but can you recall anybody ever calling to see your motheranybody who might be a relation of yours?"

"There was the old gentleman, of course," said Ronald.

"Who, dear?"

"He was very old, and he wore glasses, and his hair was116 white. He most times made mother cry, so II used to be sorry when he came."

"Can you recall his name?"

"Mother used to call him Uncle Stephen; but he was not her relationhe was father's. I think he always scolded mother; she used to look dreadfully bad after he was gone. I don't want to see him again."

"But he may have had a kind heart."

"Oh, I don't know," said Ronald. "I don't want to see him again."

"Do you think, by chance, that his name was Harvey?"

"I don't know. I think he in a sort of way belonged to father."

"Then," said Mrs. Anderson, "I guess that his name was Harvey. Now, I won't question you any more, Ronald. You may sit up and play with your bricks."

Ronald played happily enough, and Mrs. Anderson, after thinking for a few minutes, wrote out an advertisement. The advertisement ran as follows:

"If a gentleman who was called Uncle Stephen by a little boy, son of the late Major Harvey, who was supposed to have been killed in action at Ladysmith on , would wish to know anything of the same boy, he can get full particulars from Mrs. Anderson, Carlyle Terrace, Westminster."

This advertisement was put into the Times, the Standard, the Telegraph, and in fact, into all the daily newspapers. It appeared once, and Mrs. Anderson satas she expressed itwith her heart in her mouth for a whole day. But nothing happened: nobody came to inquire; there was no letter on the subject of the little son of brave Major Harvey. On the second day of the advertisement Mrs. Anderson felt a great relief in her heart.

"After I have advertised for a whole week," she said to herself, "I shall, I think, have done my duty, and perhaps I shall be allowed to keep the dear child."

She had looked, and felt, very sad on the first day of the advertisement, but on the second day she was more cheerful, and suggested to Ronald that Connie should come and have tea with him.

Ronald was delighted, and clapped his hands in glee. Mrs. Anderson wrote a little note to Connie, slightly blaming her for not coming to see her, but begging her to call that afternoon and have tea with Ronald. Connie was greatly delighted when she got the letter.

"May I go, Giles? Do yer mind?" she asked.

"In course not," answered Giles. "Why should I mind? Yer'll dress yerself in yer wery best, Connie, and I'll like well to look at yer afore yer goes out, an' w'en yer comes back."

So Connie put on her dark-blue costume once more, and brushed out her mane of golden hair and let it hang down her back; for she knew that Ronald would scarcely recognize her deprived of this ornament. Then, having left his tea all117 ready for Giles, she ran quickly in the direction of Mrs. Anderson's house.

She arrived there at four o'clock in the afternoon, to see a little face pressed up close to the pane of glass, and eager eyes watching for her. When she appeared on the steps little hands began to clap, and there was an eager rush of footsteps and then Ronald himself opened the door.

"Oh Connie, Connie!" he said, "come indo, do come in!"

"How be yer, Ronald?" asked Connie.

"I'm as well as well can be, and I'm happy, too. Mrs. Anderson is just a beautiful old lady, and so very good to me! But come and tell me all about yourself. You and I are to have tea all alone in this room. We will have fun. Why, Connie dear, how lovely you look!"

Connie told Ronald that he also looked lovely, and the two children sat down side by side, while Ronald related the little bit of his story which had transpired since Connie saw him last.

"I was very ill," he said, "for a bit, and silly, andand cowardly. But a wonderful man came to see me, and he talkedoh, so beautifully!and then I got better; and Mrs. Anderson has been more than good to meno one was ever so good to me before except father. She tells me, Connie, that I must not keep looking out for father; for if he can come he will, and if he can't I've just got to wait with patience. The street preacher, too, talked about patience. It's a little bit hard to be very patient, isn't it, Connie?"

"Yus," said Connie.

"Oh! and, Connie, some day perhaps you and I may go and stay with Mrs. Cricket in the country, and Mrs. Anderson is going to send her money for the chickens and fresh eggs and things. But I can't remember where the country iscan you, Connie?"

"We got out at a plice called Eastborough, an' the cottage wor a ivy cottage down a lane."

"Ivy Cottage—of course!" said Ronald. "How stupid of me to have forgotten! Now it's all right, and dear Mrs. Cricket will get her money."

When Ronald had told all his story Connie told all hers. In especial she told about Giles, and about poor Sue, who had vanished just as suddenly and completely as she (Connie) and Ronald himself on a certain day had disappeared from their friends.

"It's very, very queer," said Ronald. "Connie," he added, "I want to see that little boy. Can't you take me back to him now—can't you?"

"Yus," said Connie, "I could; but would it be right?"

"We'll ask Mrs. Anderson," said Ronald, "I'm certain sure she won't mind. You know the way there; you won't let yourself be kidnapped any more, will you, Connie?"

"No," said Connie.

Then tea was brought in, and the children enjoyed it. But118 Ronald could think of nothing but Giles and his earnest desire to see him. Once again he begged and implored of Connie to take him, just to sit for a few minutes by the little cripple's side, and Connie again said that Mrs. Anderson ought to know.

It was just at that moment that a cab drew up at the door, and out of the cab there stepped a white-headed old man, who came ponderously up the steps, leaning on a gold-headed stick. He rang the bell with a loud peal. Ronald began to listen.

"Who can it be?" he said. He ran to the window, and looking out, saw the cab waiting; but he missed the sight of the old gentleman, whom doubtless he would have recognized; and the neat little parlor-maid went to open the door, and then the labored steps were heard in the hall, and the drawing-room door was opened and shut, and there was silence.

"A visitor for my dear new aunty," said Ronald. "I always call her my aunty, and she likes it very much. Oh Connie, do take me just to see Giles! I know it isn't wrong, and I should be quite safe with you."

"First of all," said Connie, "we'll ring the bell and ask if we may speak to Mrs. Anderson for a minute."

"Very well," said Ronald; "only I 'spect she's busy with the person who has called."

Anne came to answer the children's summons, and told them that her mistress was particularly engaged and could not be disturbed.

"That's all right," answered Ronald; "you can go away now, please. You needn't take the tea-things just for a bit. You can go away, please, Anne."

Anne, who was devoted to Ronald, thought that the children wanted to play together, and left them alone in the little parlor. The light was growing dim, and Connie poked the fire into a blaze.

"I ought to be goin' back," she said. "Giles 'ull want me. I'll come another day, Ronald, and Mrs. Anderson'll let me bring yer back to Giles then."

"No, noto-day," said Ronald"to-dayto-nightthis minute. It isn't wrong. I must see him. You'll take me to see him, and then you'll bring me back, won't you, Connie?"

"W'y, yus," said Connie. "I s'pose it ain't wrong; but you can't do more nor set down in the room for about five minutes, Ronald, for yer'll 'ave to get back 'ere quite early, you know."

Ronald, delighted at any sort of consent on the part of his little friend, rushed upstairs to fetch his velvet cap and his little overcoat. But he forgot, and so did Connie, all about the thin house-shoes he was wearing. Soon he had slipped into the coat, and cramming the cap on his head and looking up at Connie with a gay laugh, said:

"Now we'll come."

They were in the hall, and had just opened the hall door, when suddenly that of the drawing-room was opened, and the old man, who helped himself along with a stick, came out. Ronald looked back and caught sight of him; but Ronald himself being in shadow, the old man did not notice him. The old man then spoke in a loud voice:

"It is all settled, then, and I will call to-morrow morning at ten o'clock to fetch back the boy. Have him ready. And now, good-day to you, madam."

But the old gentleman suddenly stopped as he uttered these words, for the hall door was slammed by some one else with violence, and Ronald turned a white face up to Connie.

"It's himselfit's Uncle Stephen. He made mother cry and cry. I won't go back to him. I won't be his boy. Hide mehide me, Connie!"

Connie herself felt very much frightened.

"Come along 'ome with me," she said. "He can't get yer at my 'ome. Don't shrink like that, Ronald. Be a man, dear Ronald."

The children got back to Connie's rooms without any special adventure. There Giles was waiting with that peaceful look on his face which seemed more or less to quiet every one who came in his way. He smiled all over his little face when he saw Connie, and then his eyes grew big and surprised as he noticed the small boy who kept her company.

"Why are yer back so soon, Connie?" he said. "I warn't not one little bit lonesome. And 'oo's he?" said Giles.

"This is my dear little friend Ronald," said Connie.

"And I wanted to see you awful bad," said Ronald, running up to Giles, flinging his cap on the floor, and kneeling down by him. "I have thought of youoh, so much! It was you, you know, who taught me to endure to the end. Did Connie tell you about that?"

"Yes," said Giles, "she told me."

Ronald looked up at Connie. Giles watched the two, and then he held out his little hand and touched Ronald's.

"You're wery brave," he said. "You had a brave father."

"He is a V. C. man. He's coming to see me one day," said Ronald.

"I know," said Giles. "It's real supporting to 'ave a brave father. I have one too."

"Have you?" said Ronald. "And is he coming to see you one day?"

"NoI'm goin' to 'im. Don't let's talk about it now."

Ronald sat down on the side of Giles's crimson and gold bed, and glanced round the room. Connie lit a paraffin lamp and put it on the table. In his first excitement at seeing Giles, Ronald forgot the mad terror which had awakened in him at the sound of Uncle Stephen's voice. But now he remembered.

"I have come to stay," he remarked emphatically.

"Oh no, Ronald, you can't," exclaimed Connie.

"I am not going back," exclaimed Ronald. "Giles, I needn't, need I? There's a dreadful man coming to-morrow, and he's120 going to take me away from my darling aunty. I won't go. I'll hide here with you, Giles."

"Will yer?" said Giles. "That 'ull be real pain to yer aunty, won't it?"

"Real pain?" said Ronald. "But Connie can tell her. Connie needn't say where I am. She can just tell that I heard Uncle Stephen's voice, and that I am hiding. I can't go back, can I, Gilescan I?"

"Dunno," said Giles; but a wistful expression came into his face.

"Why do you look like that?" asked Ronald.

"Sometimes one 'as to do things one can't do," was Giles's next rather difficult remark.

"But this is really silly," said Ronald, "for we can do the things we can do."

"Course notnot by ourselves," said Giles. "But if we're to endure to the end, why, 'E'll help."

"You remind me of that awful fire," said Ronald.

He jumped up and walked across the room. His eyes were dim; his heart was beating with great rapidity, for he was still weak and had gone through much. Oh, that cruel, cruel old man who had made his mother cry so often! He thought upon him with a growing terror.

Connie looked at Ronald, and then she glanced at Giles and her eyes said to Giles:

"Help me all you can about Ronald." Then Giles called her to him.

"Leave Ronald with me for a bit," he said. "Go back and tell Mrs. Anderson; but leave little Ronald with me."

Connie immediately went out; but Ronald was so absorbed in trying to quiet his beating heart, and in trying to recover his courage, that he did not even know when she closed the door after her.

Connie ran as quickly as she could all the way to Carlyle Terrace. There she rang a loud peal at the front door. It was Mrs. Anderson herself who opened it to her.

"Oh Connie!" said the widow, "thank God! Have you brought news of Ronald? What has happened, Conniewhat has happened?"

Connie immediately entered the house.

"May I speak to yer, ma'am?" she said.

"Certainly; but where is the boy?"

"He's quite safe, ma'amhe's with Giles."

"Why did he go out? He did very wrong."

"I did wrong too," said Connie. "I tuk him. He's frightened, ma'am. Ronnie's rare and frightened. He heered wot the old gentleman said."

"How could he hear?" said Mrs. Anderson.

Connie told.

"'Tain't true, ma'am, is it?" said Connie. "Yer wouldn't niver, niver, let little Ronald go away?"

"Yes, but I must. I am very sad. I wish I needn't send121 him; but the gentleman who called to-day is his father's uncle, and his nearest relation in the world. Connie, you must bring Ronald home. I will go with you myself to fetch him."

"Oh, ma'am," said Connie, beginning to sob, "it 'ull break his 'eart."

"No, Connie," answered Mrs. Anderson. "Hearts like Ronald'sbrave and true and faithfuldon't break; they endure. Besides that, the old gentlemanMr. Harveywill not be unkind to him; I am certain of that."

So Connie and Mrs. Anderson returned side by side to the house where Giles and Ronald were waiting for them.

When they entered they saw a picture which Mrs. Anderson could never forget: the dying boy, with his radiant face, lying on the bed half-supported by pillows, the crimson and gold coverlet making a wonderful patch of color; and Ronald, the tears still wet on his cheeks, but his eyes very bright, his lips firm, his whole attitude that of a soldier's child.

The moment he saw Mrs. Anderson he went up to her.

"I am ashamed," he said. "Giles has told me the son of a V. C. man should not be a coward. It is all rightI am going back."

Mrs. Anderson pressed the boy's hand.

"I knew you wouldn't disappoint me, Ronald," she said. Then she turned and talked a little longer to Giles. She saw how weak the child was, and knew, with a woman's perception, what a very little time longer he had to live in this old world.

"My sister's in the country, ma'am," said Giles in his brightest manner. "She's looking for a little house for her an' metwo winders in our roomthat's wot Sue an' me thought we 'ud likeand iverythink wery purty. Sue may be back any day. She's takin' a good bit of a time a-lookin' for the 'ouse; but she'll find it, an' then I'll go there."

"But are you strong enough to be moved, Giles?" inquired Mrs. Anderson.

"Yus," said Giles in his confident tone, "quite strong enough. I want to see the country, and to live in it for a spell, afore I go right 'ome to the best Country of all. Sue's lookin' out; she'll be backoh, any day, for she knows the time's short."

"Giles," said Connie, "you're too tired to talk any more."

She gave the boy some of his restorative medicine, and Ronald went up and kissed him. "Don't forget," said Giles, "brave fathers"

"Not me!" answered Ronald. "Brave fathers for ever!" Then Ronald went away.

Mrs. Anderson took his hand and led him back to the house. She did not scold him for going out with Connie. She did not mean to reproach him at all; he had made a great victory; she felt proud of him. When supper had come to an end she called the boy to her:

"Ronald dear, I wish to say something. If you were a coward to-day, so was I."

"Youmy aunt?" said Ronald. "Oh nono!"

"Yes. I didn't want to part with you."

Ronald shivered.

"Won't you ever see me any more?"

"I hope so. Mr. Harvey was very kind."

"Is his name Harveysame as mine?"

"Yes, darling; he is your father's uncle, and your father lived with him in his old place in Somersetshire when he was a boy. He loved your father. He'll tell you lots of stories about him."

"About when does he expect father home?" asked Ronald.

"He doesn't know. Perhaps, Ronaldperhapsnever."

But here Ronald gave himself a little shake.

"I know father's coming back," he said"feel it in my bones."

There was silence then between the woman and the boy. After a long time Ronald spoke:

"He made mother cry, all the same."

"He told me about that. He wasn't really unkind to her. I, on the whole, like him, Ronald, and I think you can do a lot for himI think your father would wish it."

"Would he?" said Ronald, his eyes sparkling.

"I think so. I expect God wants you to help him. He's a hard old man because he has no one to love him, but he did care for your father."

Ronald flung his arms round Mrs. Anderson's neck and kissed her.

That night it must be owned that he slept badly; and earlyvery earlyin the morning he awoke.

"Times is pretty bad," thought the boy to himself; "and there's lots o' battles round. But oh, Giles! brave fathers for ever! You and me won't disgrace our fathers, will we, Giles?"

Then he got up and dressed himself, and went downstairs and waited until Mrs. Anderson arrived. As soon as she entered the room he said one word to her"When?"

"Ten o'clock," said Mrs. Anderson. It was eight o'clock then.

"Two hours more," said Ronald.

During those two hours he was very busy. He packed his bricks, and helped Mrs. Anderson to put his very scanty wardrobe into a very tiny trunk. The time went by. Ten o'clock struck, and, sharp to the minute, a cab drew up at the door.

Out of the cab the old gentleman stepped. He entered the hall. He was a very fussy old man, and did not want a young child to live in the house with him. He expected, too, that Mrs. Harvey's boyhe had undoubtedly a great contempt for poor young Harveywould be a miserable, dwindled, wretched sort of creature. But, lo and behold! a little chap123 with head well thrown back, his eyes bright and lips brave, stepped up to him.

"Here I am, Uncle Stephen. I am Ronald. How do you do?"

"Bless my soul!" said the old man. "Let me look at you."

He drew the boy round so as to get the light on his face.

"'Pon my word!" he said, "you are not the sort of little chap I expected. You're uncommon like your father."

Ronald flushed with pride. Mr. Harvey came into the parlor and had a little talk with Mrs. Anderson.

"I am indeed indebted to you, madam," he said. "This boy is so surprisingly like my nephew that I could almost fancy the years had gone back and I was teaching the little chap to take his first gallop.Your father was game on a horse, my lad."

"Yes, sir," said Ronald, nodding his head. "'Spect so, sir," he added. The old gentleman chucked him under the chin and uttered a laugh.

"Well, boy, we must be going," he said. "We mustn't keep your kind friend. You will let me know, madam, for what I am indebted to you."

"For nothing, sir," said Mrs. Anderson. A crimson color rushed into her face. "It has been a labor of love to help this dear little fellow. I could take no money; you mustn't even mention it, sir."

"Well, madamwellI respect your proper pride, and anything I can do By the wayeh, Ronald?there's no saying, but I might invite your friend down to the country.Do you know Somersetshire, madam?"

"I used to know it very well when I was a girl. My people lived in Somersetshire."

"Then perhaps you will come and pay us a visit, and see Ronald after he has learned the full use of the saddle and bridleeh, Ronald?"

"Ohaunty! Will you come?" said Ronald.

"I will, darling.I should like it very much indeed, Mr. Harvey; it is most kind of you to ask me."

"But pleaseplease," said Ronald, who had suddenly lost all his fear, "may Connie come, too?"

"Who's Connie?"

"My special friend and sister."

"Ho, ho!" said the old man. "I must hear more about her. Can make no rash promises. But all right, little chap; I'll do what I can for you. Now, if you had taken after Well, never mindI won't say anything to hurt you."

"And, please," said Ronald suddenly, "of course you wouldn't pay my aunty, for the things she did can't be paid for. But poor Mrs. Cricketaunty, I know her address. The place in the country is called Eastborough; and it's Ivy Cottage, aunty; andshe was good to me"

"Yes," said Mrs. Anderson, "you'll let me explain, please, Mr. Harvey. This dear little boy spent a month at Mrs. Cricket's, and she was never paid a penny."

"She ought to be paid," said Ronald. "Course, when father returns he'll pay you back again. But she ought to get it, for there was real new-laid eggs, and the chickens were so tender."

"'Pon my word," said the old gentleman, "you're a queer boy! I guess you've got the true Harvey blood in you. Never neglect a friendeh? And never owe a penny. Well now, madam, will you see to this? And what amount of money ought I to give you for the woman?"

Mrs. Anderson named what she thought would be a correct sum, and immediately afterwards the old gentleman produced the money from his waistcoat pocket.

It was a hard moment for Ronald when he said good-bye, but after he got into the cab he could not help feeling both surprised and elated. He could not help staring and staring at the old gentleman.

"Was it your photograph," he said at last, "that my father kept in his dressing-room?"

"I expect so," said the old gentleman.

"It's surprising," said Ronald, "how I forget. But now I remember. He loved youhe used to talk to me about you. He said it was you taught him first to be brave."

"Bless himbless him!" said the old gentleman.

His voice got a little raspy; it is certain that his eyes were a little dim.

"Perhaps," said Ronaldhe had a marvelous way of comprehending the situation"but for you he would not have been a V. C. man."

"God bless you! It was in himselfhe had the noblest heart, the grandest nature! There, boy! don't upset me. 'Pon my word! I hated the thought of having you And I hated going to you," said Ronald; "but"

The old face looked into the young face, and the young face looked into the old face, and then they both laughed.

Before they reached the old gentleman's hotel Ronald had so far advanced to a friendly footing that he had peered into the contents of the old man's pocket, had pulled out his watch, had applied it to his ear, and had even gone the amazing length of demanding one for himself.

CHAPTER XXVI

TWO CUPS OF COFFEE

When Harris parted from Giles and Connieon the very same day that Connie had gone to tea with Ronald, on the very same day that Ronald had visited Gileshe was as troubled and miserable as man could be. There was but one brave thing for him to dohe ought to confess his sin.

Where Sue could be he had not the faintest idea. Why was125 she absent? It was days now since she had left her homeSue, of all peopleSue, with a little delicate brother like Giles. It was unlike her to go. There could be but one reason. Harris had taken means to ascertain whether poor Sue had been up before the magistrates. He knew enough about the law, and about crime generally, to know that she would be taken up for theft to Bow Street; but beyond doubt she had never gone there. Where in all the world could she be? Harris was by no means sufficiently sorry to give himself up for conscience's sake; but he was in a state of nervousness and great distress of mind.

As he walked down a side-street, his hands in his pockets, his rough fur capwhich he generally wore slouchedwell off his eyes, he was suddenly accosted by a red-haired boy, who looked at him with a very innocent face and inquired meekly "ef he were lookin' for a job."

"None o' yer sauce, youngster," said Harris, passing on.

"I don't mean the least sauce in life, master," said the red-haired boy, still in the most humble and gentle tone. "I only thought ef we were goin' in the same direction we might p'rhaps cheer each other up."

"You're a likely youngster, you ere," he said, looking down at him with the grimmest of smiles.

"Yus, my mother says as I'm well grown for my hage," replied Pickles; and then, keeping pace with the tall man, he began to whistle softly.

Harris returned to his interrupted thoughts, and soon forgot the small boy, who had to run to keep up with his long strides. Suddenly the little boy exclaimed in a shrill, eager treble:

"I say, mister!"

"Wot now, young 'un?"

"You ain't of a wery obleeging turn, be yer? You couldn't help me, now, ter find a guilty party?"

"You seems a wery rum chap," said Harris rather crossly.

"I don't know nothink 'bout yer guilty parties. There, be off, can't yer!"

"I'll be off in a twinkle, master. I ain't rum a bit; my mother allers said as I wor a real quiet boy; but when my heart is full to bustin' it seems a relief to talk to a body, and you, tho' yer puts on bein' fierce, have a kind nature."

"Now, what hever do yer mean by that?"

"Master, you must furgive a wery timid and heasily repulsed boy; but it ain't possible, even fur one so known to be frightened as me, to be feared of yer. I reads yer kindness in yer heyes, master, and so I makes bold to tell my tale o' woe."

"Well, tell away," said Harris, who could not help laughing and looking a little less gruff than before.

"You wouldn't be inclined, now, that we should have hour talk hover a pint of hot coffee? There's a heatin-house where the young man have took down the shutters and is dusting away in a manner as his real appetizing. I has fourpence in126 my pocket. You wouldn't mind my treating yer, jest fer once, would yer?"

"Not in the least, youngster. I think it'll be a wery sensible use to put yer money to, and a deal more prudent than spending it in marbles or street plays."

"Master, my mother don't allow me to play at marbles, or to hindulge in street wanities, so I has the money and can afford ter be generous. Now let's enter. I smells the coffee a-grinding hup fur hour breakfasts halready."

So Harris and Pickles went in to the eating-house, where in a moment or two, over two steaming cups of excellent coffee, Pickles proceeded to unburden himself of his story.

"It is only a few days agone, master, as the occurrence as distresses me happened. I wor walking along a certain street wot shall be nameless. I wor walking along bravely, as is my wont, and thinking of my mother, when I see'd a young gel a-flying past me. She wor a wery short, stout gel, and her legs they quite waggled as she ran. I never see'd a gel run so wery hard afore, and I pricked hup my senses to guess wot it hall meant. Soon wor the mystery explained. I heerd ahind of her the cry of 'Stop thief!' and a number of men and boys were a-giving of her chase. I thought as I'd run wid 'em and see what it hall meant.

"Presently we shall come up wid the gel. There she wor in the arms of a policeman. He wor a-clutching of her, and trying to find hout wot wor the matter; but she wor so blown she couldn't speak fur a good bit. Then hup comes a man wot said as he had a pawnshop, and that inter the pawnshop had come a man and a gel ter buy a ring, and when they come hout there wor a diamond locket missing. He said as either the gel or the man 'ad tuk the locket; and as the man could not be found, he must get the policeman to search the gel. The poor fat gel, she looked quite scared, and said as she hadn't done it; but the nipper said as she must be searched, and he put in his hand inter her pocket and drew hout the diamond locket. She said as she had never put it there. But, in course, it worn't ter be expected as they'd believe her, so she were tuk orf ter prison. She wor tuk orf ter prisonI see'd her myself."

Here Pickles paused. Nothing could have been more refined and delicate than the use he had made of his eyes during this narrative; only very quick and fleeting glances did he bestow upon his companion.

When Harris at the commencement of his tale started and changed color, Pickles dropped a piece of bread, and stayed under the table looking for it until the man had quite recovered his composure. When his short story had come to an end he paused; then he said, still without bestowing more than the swiftest side-glance on Harris, "The poor fat gel were tuk orf to the lock-hup. But 'tis borne bin on me, master'tis borne him on me, and I can't get no rest day nor nightas that yer gel were hinnercent. I believe as she never tuk the locket, and I think that ef ye're as kind-hearted as yer looks yer'll help me ter find that other guilty party."

Harris rose to his feet.

"Don't be a fool, lad," he said angrily. "I have no time ter give ter sech nonsense. I'm soory fur the gel, but ef she had the locket, of course she tuk the locket. There! I can waste no time. I'll pay fur my hown coffee. Good-morning."

"Good-morning, master, and thank yer. I'm glad as ye're sorry fur the gel; she have a lame brother as must miss her, and her case 'ull go heavy, I fear. It seems as it might be a good work ter find the guilty party. I think as it wor the man as went with her inter the shop. I mean ter attend the trial, and I'll mention, ef permitted, my suspicions. But I won't keep yer longer. Sorry again as yer won't oblige me, I'll go home now and consult my mother."

All the way back to Great Anvill Street, where Mrs. Price lived, Pickles danced a hornpipe.

"I've nailed him at last," he said, chuckling and laughing and dancing all in one breath. "Now to put on the torture screw until he confesses! Oh Pickles, my boy, wot a treasure you'll prove yerself in Scotland Yard!"

CHAPTER XXVII

DELAYED TRIAL

It is quite true that Pickles had put on the torture screw. Harris felt exceedingly uncomfortable as he walked home. It was a fact, then, that Sue had been caught and put in prison. That disagreeable boy had seen it all; he had witnessed her rapid flight; he had heard her protestations of innocence; he had seen her carried off to prison. Sue, so good and brave and honest, would be convicted of theft and would have to bear the penalty of theftof another's theft, not her own. What a foolish girl she had been to run away! Of course, it made her guilt seem all the plainer. There was not a loophole of escape for her. She was certain to be found guilty; probably to-day she would be brought before the magistrate and sentence pronounced upon her. He wondered what magistrate would try her; how long her punishment would last. Had he dared he would have attended her trial. But he did not dare. That red-haired boythat most unpleasant, impudent boywould probably be there. There was no saying what things he might say. He would probably appear as a witness, and nothing would keep that giddy tongue of his quiet. What a very queer boy he was, and how strange were his suspicions! When any one else in all the world would have accepted Sue's guilt as beyond doubt or question, he persisted in declaring her innocent. Nay, more than that, he had even declared that the man who had gone with her into the shop was the guilty person. Harris knew there was no proof against the man. No one had seen him take the locket; no one had witnessed its transfer into Sue's pocket. The man was safe enough. No one living could bring his guilt home to him.

But stay a moment! A horrible fear came over him. Why did that boy speak like that? He saw Sue running away. Perhaps he had seen more than that. Perhaps he had come on the platform of events earlier in the narrative. Harris felt the cold sweat starting to his forehead as it occurred to him that that awful boy had reason for his talkthat he knew to whom he was speaking. When Harris took the locket he might have been flattening his nose against the window-pane at the pawnbroker's; he might have seen all that was taking place. What was to be done? He could not confess, and yet if he didn't he was in horrible danger; his present state was worse than any state he had been in before. Suppose Connie ever found out his meanness, his wickedness.

Harris was very fond of Connie just then. He had suffered during her absence. His home was pleasant to himas pleasant as his guilty conscience would permit during those days, for little Giles was like no one else. Oh, could the awful moment ever come when Giles would look at him with reproachful eyeswhen Giles would turn away from him? The miserable man felt that were such a time to arrive it would be almost as bad as the knowledge that God Himself could not forgive him. He was distracted, miserable; he must find a refuge from his guilty thoughts.

A public-house stood handy. He had not really taken too much for a long time nownot since that terrible night when, owing to drink, he had turned his child from his door. But he would forget his misery now in drink.

"That dreadful boy!" he muttered"that dreadful, dreadful boy, with hair like a flame, and eyes that peered into you like gimlets!"

Harris passed through the great swing-doors. His good angel must almost have disappeared at that moment.

Meanwhile Connie and Giles watched and waited in vain for Sue. She was coming to-dayshe was coming to-morrow. But the weary hours went by and no Sue arrived; there was no message from her. Harris went oftener and oftener to the public-house, and brought less and less of his wages home, and Giles faded and faded, and Connie also looked very sad and weary.

Once Connie said to Giles, when nearly a month had gone by:

"Yer'll 'ave to give up that notion 'bout the country, Giles, for 'tain't true."

"Yus, I believe I must give it up," said Giles.

"Ain't yer anxious now 'bout dear Sue?" asked Connie.

"Not wery," said Giles. "Ef she ain't in the country, the good Lord 'ave her safe somewhere elsethat's wot I'm a-thinkin' of. Father John said to me we'en he come last as trials of this sort are good for me."

"You 'ave nothing but trials, poor Giles!" said Connie.

"Oh no," answered Giles; "I ha' lots o' blessingsyou and Big Ben, the beautiful Woice, you know. Connie, some'ow I think as my wings is growin' wery fast. I think w'en they're full-grown"

"Wot then?" asked Connie.

"Why, I'll fly away. I can't 'ardly believe as a poor little lame boy like me could fly up higher than the stars, but that's wot 'ull 'appen. I picter it wery oftenme no longer tied down to my bed, but with wings, flyin' about as strong as the angels. Only Father John says I'll be higher than the angels, for I'll be one o' the ransomed o' the Lord. I'll see Father John, too, an' you'll come after a bit, an' Sue 'ull come. I can't fret no, I can't."

After this Connie went for the doctor, and the doctor said that the boy was very illthat he might linger a few weeks more, but his sufferings were growing less, and that Connie's kind care was effecting wonders for him.

The weeks went by. Harris grew accustomed to his sense of guilt, and Sue to her captivity. Pickles was anxiously looking forward to a crisis. Harris, after giving way to drink for several days, refrained again and worked steadily. He brought in, in consequence, good wages, and Connie and Giles wanted for nothing. It was the one salve to his conscience, this making of Giles comfortable; otherwise, notwithstanding the manifest amendment of his ways, he was scarcely happy. Indeed, Pickles took care that he should not be so. In the most unlikely and unexpected places this dreadful boy would dart upon him, and more and more certain was Harris that he not only knew his secret, but had witnessed his guilt. Harris would have fled miles from the boy, but the boy would not be fled from. He acted as a perpetual blister on the man's already sore conscience, and Harris almost hated him.

His first resolve to confide in Pickles and bribe him into silence had long ago died away. He dared not even offer to bribe him; the perfectly fearless and uncorrupt spirit which looked out of the eyes of the boy would be, he knew, proof against all that he could do in the matter of either rewards or punishments. No; all that Harris could do was to maintain as imperturbable a spirit as possible while Pickles expatiated upon the cruel fate of Sue. As far as he could dare question him, he learned from Pickles that Sue had not been yet tried even before the magistrate. He wondered greatly at this delay, and Pickles, who read his wonder in his eyes, remarked lightly that the reason of this long postponement was because the police were busy looking for the guilty party.

"Whether they finds him or not," concluded Pickles, "it must come off soon now, fur I'm told that the expense of keeping Sue is breaking that 'ere lock-hup. I 'spect as it 'ull be the finest bit o' a trial as have been fur many a day. I means to be there. And you'll come, won't yer, Mr. Harris?"

"I'm sick o' the subject," said Harris.

"Oh no, you ain't, Mr. Harris; you 'ave a wery quiet manner, as his only wot his right and becoming, but I can see yer hinterest in yer heyes. You can't keep that good-natured, human look out o' yer heyes, Mr. Harris; nor can yer help a-starting when yer sees me a-coming. Oh no, yer may say wot yer likes, but ye're real interested in that pore, misfort'nit Sue, I knows; so you will come to her shameful trial, won't yer?"

In despair, and fearing any other reply, Harris promised.

CHAPTER XXVIII

CINDERELLA WOULD SHIELD THE REAL THIEF

After one of these interviews Pickles went home and consulted Sue.

"Cinderella," he said, "am I to act as yer prince or not?"

"I dunno wot hever yer means, Pickles."

"Well, my beauty, 'tis jest thisthe Prince rescued Cinderella from her cruel sisters, and I want ter rescue you from the arms of justice. You has a wery shameful accusation hanging over you, Cinderella; you is, in short, hiding from the law. I can set yer free. Shall I?"

Sue's plump face had grown quite thin during the anxieties of the past month, and now it scarcely lighted up as she answered Pickles:

"I want ter be set free, but I don't want ter be set free in your way."

"'Tis the only way, Cinderella. The man, Peter Harris, is the guilty party. He tuk that 'ere locket; he put it in yer pocket. I don't know how he did it, nor why he did it, but I do know that no one else did it. I have jest come from him, and lor' bless yer! I have had him on the torture hooks. I made-b'lieve as you were to be tried next week, and I axed him to come to the trial. I could a'most see him shivering at the bare thought, but fur hall that he did not dare but say he'd come. Now, Cinderella, ef you were to allow me to manage it, and I wer to get you and he face to face, why, he'd jest have to confess. I'd have a couple o' witnesses handy, and we'd write it down wot he said, and you'd be set free. I'd manage so to terrify him aforehand that he'd have ter confess"

"And then he'd be put in prison?" said Sue.

"Why, in course; and well he'd deserve it. He's the right party to go, fur he's guilty. Yes, shameful guilty, too."

"He couldn't manage to run away and escape afterwards?"

Pickles laughed. "You think as I'd help him, maybe. Not a bit o' me! I don't harbor no guilty parties, Cinderella, as I ha' told yer heaps and heaps o' times. No, he's guilty, and he goes ter prison; there ain't nothink hard in sending him ter prison."

"It ha' seemed ter me often lately, Pickles, as it must be harder to lie in prison guilty than not guiltyyou ha'nt, nothink ter trouble yer mind ef yer ain't guilty."

"Well then, I s'pose, in that case, as yer'll give yerself hup."

"I'd a deal rayther be in hiding with yer, Pickles; but I don't feel as ef I could put Mr. Harris in prison."

"Then you must go yerself, fur this thing can't go on fur ever."

Sue looked frightened, and her commonplace gray eyes fell to the ground. She took up the poker and began to trace a pattern on the floor: it was as intricate as her own fate just now. She was a little heroine, however, and her noble thoughts redeemed all plainness from her face when at last she spoke:

"Once, Pickles, arter mother died we was brought down wery low. I had a dreadful influenzy, and I couldn't nohow go to the machining, and we were near starving. Mr. Harris lent me a shilling that time, and we pulled through. Another time I couldn't meet the rent, and Connie, she begged of her father, and he give me the money; and when I offerd it him back again he wouldn't take it. He wor a rough man, but he had a kind heart. When I were last at home he wor in a real dreadful trouble about Connieand I loved Connie better nor any one in hall the world, arter Giles. Pickles, it 'ud break Connie's heart fur her father to be tuk to prison. I don't know why he did thatef he really did do itbut I can't furget those two times as he wor good ter me, and hever since I have come yere he have done heverything fur Giles. No, I couldn't send Mr. Harris to prison. I couldn't rest heasy ef I thought o' him sent there by me. I'd rayther lie there myself."

"Wery well, Cinderella; in course you've got ter choose, fur one or other of yer must go to prison, as it is against hall common-sense as you could stay hiding here fur ever. I hadmires yer rare consideration fur that hardened man, Peter Harris. I can't understand itno, not the least bit in the worldbut I hadmires it as I hadmires the top o' the big mountain wot I could never climb, but jest contemplate solemnly from below. I can understand better yer repugnance not to break the heart o' that purty Connie. Most plain women is hard on their more lucky sisters, and I hadmires you, Cinderella, fur rising superior to the wices of yer sex; but wot I can't hunderstandwot puzzles meis yer sad failure in sisterly love. There's that little brother; why, heven now he's pining hal to nothing to see yer. Don't yer think as it 'ull break his heart ef yer is tuk ter prison? Why, ef yer could have seen him when he heerd me even hint at sech a thing! He said as he wished as he could knock me down."

The tears rapidly filled Sue's eyes. "Pickles," she said after a moment of thought, "'tis a wonderful, wonderful puzzlement ter me. I can't least of all break the heart of Giles. Giles wor left ter me by mother, and I promised as I'd allers tend him real faithful; but wot I 'as bin thinking is that ef yer must give me hup, and not hide me any longer, and I must be locked hup fur a time, that perhaps we might manage as Giles might still think as I wor in the country. Connie would be wery good ter him, and Mr. Harris would support him jest as well as I could have done. Giles, he's that innercent that he'd easily be made ter believe as I could not help going away. He knows nothink o' life, little Giles don't; he'd never, never guess as there were ought o' the prison 'bout me, and arter a time he'd get accustomed to doing widout me. I think, Pickles, we might manage so as not to break Giles's heart, and yet fur me to go ter prison."

"Then you really, really chooses to go ter prison, Cinderella?"

"I choose, Pickles, never to tell on Peter Harris—never, wot hever happens. I don't want ter go to prison—not one bit—but ef I can't stay hiding, why, I s'pose as I must."

"You can't stay hiding more than a day or two longer, Cinderella, and I thinks as ye're a great fool;" and Pickles walked out of the room in apparently high dudgeon.

CHAPTER XXIX

A LITTLE HEROINE

Two days afterwards it was Sunday. Pickles and his mother went to church, but Sue did not accompany them. She had hitherto, notwithstanding her disguise, been afraid to stir abroad. To-day, however, when mother and son had departed, she ran eagerly up to the tiny attic where she slept. In this attic was an old box without a lock. Sue opened it in some perturbation. There were several articles of wearing apparel in this box, all of a mothy and mouldy character. One by one Cinderella pulled them out. First there was a purple silk dress. She gazed at it with admiration. Yes; no one would ever recognize Sue in silk. It would be delightful to put it on. She did so. The skirt was much too long, but with the aid of a whole boxful of pins, she managed to bundle it up round her waist. Then came a soft, many-colored Paisley shawl. Would any one in all the world think of the little machinist if she sallied forth in purple silk and Paisley shawl? Sue did not believe it possible. She put on the shawl, and tied on her head an old-fashioned bonnet, trimmed with many-colored ribbons. There was further, in the wonderful box, an old remnant of gauze. This would act as a veil. Now, indeed, she was completely disguised. She thought herself very grand, and wondered had the Prince ever bought finer clothes for the real Cinderella. She shut the box again, tripped downstairs, and out into the street. She had not been out for a whole month now, and the fresh, frosty air, even coming to her through the musty133 gauze, was very refreshing. She walked quickly. She had an object in view. Very purposeful was her careworn little face as she stepped briskly along. She had a problem to solve. It was too weighty for her young shoulders; she must get the advice of another. She meant to consult Father Johnnot by words; no, not even with him would she dare confide her secret. But he preached now both Sunday morning and Sunday evening. She would stand with the crowd and listen to his sermon. Perhaps once again there would be a message for her in it. She had not forgotten that last sermon of his; and that last message sent to her from God by his lips had been with her all through her month of captivity.

It had been a sad and anxious month for Sue, and now its crisis had come, for the kind people who had protected her could do so no longer; she could no longer eat their bread, nor accept the shelter of their home. No; Sue quite agreed with Pickles that it would be impossible for her to stay in hiding always. Better go forth at once and meet the worst and have it over. She would be put in prison. Yes—that is, either she or Peter Harris would be put in prison. Pickles had quite brought her round to the belief that Harris was really the guilty party. He had done a very, very dreadful thing. Sue could not understand why he had acted so badly, so cruelly by her. Surely he was the right person to go to prison; she could not bear his crime for him. But then, again, it would be very like Jesus Christ if she did. It was wonderful how the thought of the Great Example was before the mind of this simple, ignorant child as she walked hastily on to meet the one who she believed would decide her fate. To-morow, most likely, Pickles would come to her and ask for her final decision. She must make up her mind to-day. She had a long way to walk, and when she reached the street where Father John held his weekly services the place was already crowded. The preacher had mounted on his chair and had commenced his discourse. Sue heard one or two people say, "Look at little Mother Hubbard." But others, again, admired her costume, and out of respect for the rich silk dress, made way for her to approach nearer to the preacher.

"Now, Lord Jesus, please do give me the right word," whispered Sue. Then through her musty veil her eyes were fixed anxiously on Atkins. Was it more than a coincidence? This was the sentence which fell upon the expectant ear:

"My dear, dear brothers and sisters, 'tis a wonderfully happy thing to be good. It gives a man rare courage. You, most of you, knew poor Bob Daily. Well, he died this morning. He was not a scrap afraid. I was with him, and he went away rejoicing. He knew he was going straight away to Jesusstraight away to the arms of Jesus. He told me a queer thing which had happened to him when he was a young man. He was falsely accused of a crime which he had not done. He was put in prison. He had to stay locked up for what he was innocent of for two years. He said he guessed who had really done the crime, but he did not like to tell on this man, who was much worse off than himself. He bore the punishment for the guilty man, and he had his reward. All the time he was in prison Jesus remained so close to him that He made his heart sing. He says that he could look back on that part of his life as the very happiest time that he had ever spent."

"I'm a bit faint-like," said Sue to her nearest neighbor. "Let me out, please." The people made way for her, and for a moment or so she leant against the nearest lamp-post. She did not hear another word of the sermon. She did not need to. When she felt better she walked back to Great Anvill Street.

That night, just before Pickles went to bed, Sue sought him.

"Pickles, I ha' made up my mindI ha' made it up quite," she said.

"Well?" asked Pickles.

"You gave me three days, Pickles, and the time 'ull be up to-morrow. Well, I'll go to prison 'stead o' Peter Harris. I ha' that in my mind which 'ull make it come uncommon light ter me. I'll go to prison 'stead o' he."

CHAPTER XXX

WHAT WAS HARRIS TO HER?

Pickles went up to the very small room where he slept, threw himself on his bed, and fell a-wondering. For the first time in his life he was completely at sea. What did Cinderella mean? For a whole month now she had been his special charge. He had rescued her; he had kept her in the safe shelter of his mother's house; he had been, he considered, very kind indeed to Cinderella. What a fate she would have had but for him! Sent to prison for a crime of which she was absolutely innocent, her whole future disgraced, blighted, ruined! All the time while he had been hunting up Harris, and bringing his ingenious little mind to bear down the full weight of his crime upon the guilty man, he had thought that no amount of gratitude on Cinderella's part nay, even a whole lifetime of devotion could scarcely repay all she owed him.

But now he kicked his legs impatiently and said to himself that it was enough to provoke the best-natured boy in the universe. After all his trouble, all his hard thoughts and anxious reflections, here was this tiresome Cinderella refusing to be set free. He had, as he expressed it, nailed his man; he had put the noose round him, and all he had to do was to tighten it, and Sue would be free and Harris sent to prison. But without Sue's aid he could not do this, and Sue most emphatically to-night had refused his aid. She would go to prison herself, but she would not betray Harris. What did the girl mean? What was this cowardly Harris to her that she should risk so much and suffer so sorely for his sake? How she had dreaded prison! How very, very grateful she had been to him for saving her! But now she was willing to go there, willing to bear the unmerited punishment, the lifelong disgrace. Why? Pickles, think hard as he would, could get no answer to solve this difficulty. True, she had said she had something in her mind which would lighten the prison fare and the prison life. What was it? Pickles could stand it no longer; he must go and consult his mother. He ran downstairs. Mrs. Price had not yet gone to bed. Pickles sat down beside her by the fire, and laid his curly red head in her lap.

"Mother," he said, "this 'ere detective's foiled at last."

"What's up now, Jamie, boy?" asked the mother.

Pickles told her. He described how he had all but brought the crime home to Harris; how he had proved to Sue that Harris was the guilty party; but that now Sue, after all his tremendous trouble, had refused to identify him. She would go to prison, she said; she would not tell on Harris. "I don't understand it one bit, mother," he said in conclusion.

"But I do, Jamie, my boy," answered Mrs. Price, tears filling her kind eyes. "I understand it very well. It means just thisthat Sue, dear child, is very noble."

Pickles opened his eyes very wide.

"Then, mother," he began, "Cinderella is" and then he stopped.

"Your Cinderella, whom you rescued, is a real little heroine, Jamie; but she must not go to prison. We must do something for her. She has been with me for a whole month now, and I never came across a more upright little soul. You surely have not been frightening her with the base idea that we would give her up, my boy?"

Pickles colored and hung his head.

"I own, mother," he said, "that I did put a little bit of the torture screw to bear on Sue. I didn't mean really as she should go to prison; but I thought as a small dose of fright might make her tell on that Harris. I do think that Peter Harris is about the meanest character I ever come across, and I'd like him to go to prison wery well indeed, mother dear."

"If he's guilty, believe me he's not a very happy man, my lad. My own feeling is that 'tis best to leave all punishment to the God against whom we sin. But about Sue? She must not sleep with the notion that she's to go to prison. I have a great mind to go to her now."

"Oh! but, mother, mayn't I tell her my own self? 'Twas I as rescued her. She's my own Cinderella, after all, mother dear; and I'd real enjoy telling her. She's asleep hours ago now, mother."

"Well, lad, see and have it out with the child before you go to work in the morning, and then I'll have a talk with her afterwards."

CHAPTER XXXI

A STERN RESOLVE

But Sue was not asleep. She had quite made up her mind now as to her line of action. There was no longer even a particle of lingering doubt in her brave little soul; she was innocent, but as the sin which was committed must be punished, she would bear the punishment; she would go to prison instead of Harris. Prison would not be so bad if she went there innocent.

Yes, Sue would certainly go to Prison. The next day she would consult Mrs. Price, and take the proper steps to deliver herself up to the police. She would go to the pawnbroker's shop and say to him, "I am the little girl in whose pocket you found that lovely diamond locket. I am very sorry I hid from you so long, but now I have come back, and you can send for the police. I will promise not to run away again when they are taking me to prison."

This was Sue's resolve, but first she intended to do something else. It was because of this something else that she lay awake now; it was because of this almost passionate longing and desire that she lay with her eyes wide open. She was going to put on her disguise once more; just once again, before she was put in prison, she would wander free and unrestrained into the streets. But she must do this very, very early in the morning, and she feared that if she closed her eyes she would sleep over the right time.

It was now March, and the days were lengthening. She rose before the dawn, put on again some portion of the remarkable costume she had worn the day before, and went out. Yes, she was going to prison. She was most likely going to prison that very day. But before she was locked up she would visit Harris's house. She would steal into his rooms to take one look—one long last look for how many weary months—at Giles. She knew the ways of this tenement house well. She had nothing to do but walk up the stairs and lift the latch of Harris's room and go in. Some of the neighbors locked their room doors at night. But Susan remembered with satisfaction that Harris never did so. It was quite dark when she set off, for she knew she had a very long walk from Great Anvill Street to Westminster.

CHAPTER XXXII

AN UNEXPECTED ACCIDENT

By dint asking her way more than once, of some of the very policemen whom she dreaded, Sue found herself at last in the old, well-remembered neighborhood. She passed the door of the house where her mother had died and where she had been so happy with Giles, and went on quickly to the other house where Connie and Harris lived. The house door stood open, as was its wont. Sue mounted the stairs; with trembling hands she lifted the latch of Harris's room. Yes, as she had trusted, it was only on the latch. She stooped down, unfastened her shoes, and took them off; then she stole into the room. There were two bedrooms, besides a sitting-room, in Harris's portion of the house. In one of the bedrooms slept Harris, in the other his daughter, and in the little sitting-room lay the lame boy. Thus Sue found herself at once in the presence of her little brother. Her heart beat high. How easily she had accomplished her purpose! How good God was to her! Stealing over on tiptoes, she knelt down by Giles. There was scarcely any light as yet; but a little streamed in from the badly curtained window. This little had sought out Giles, and lingered lovingly round his delicate face and graceful head; he looked ethereal with this first soft light kissing him. Sue bent down very close indeed. She dared not breathe on his face. She scarcely dared draw her own breath in her fear of waking him; but she took his gentle image more firmly than ever into her heart of hearts: it was to cheer her and comfort her during long, long months of prison life.

As she bent over him in an ecstasy of love and longing, Giles stirred. Instantly Sue hid herself behind a curtain: here she could see without being seen.

The lame boy stirred again and opened his eyes. He looked peaceful; perhaps he had had a happy dream.

"I think Sue 'ull soon now have found that cottage in the country," he said aloud. Then he turned over and, still smiling, went to sleep again.

Sue's eyes filled with tears. But the light was getting stronger; any moment Harris might rise. Though she would go to prison for Harris, yet she felt that she could not bring herself to meet him. Yes, she must go away with an added weight in her poor, faithful little heart. She stole downstairs, and out into the street. Yes, it was very hard to bear the sight of Giles, to hear those longing words from the lips of Giles, and yet go away to meet unjust punishment for perhaps two long years.

Still, it never entered into Sue's head to go back from her resolve, or to save herself by betraying another.

Her head was very full of Bible lore, and she compared herself now to one of those three young men who had gone into a fiery furnace for the cause of right and duty.

"Jesus Christ wor with them, jest as He'll be with me," she said to herself as she crossed Westminster Bridge. Yes, brave little girl, you were to go through a fiery furnace, but not the one you thought was being prepared for you.

Sue's trouble, swift and terrible, but in an unlooked-for form, was on her even now. Just as she had got over the bridge, and was about to cross a very wide thoroughfare, some lumbering wagons came thundering up. They turned sharp round a corner, and the poor child, weak and giddy from her morning's most unwonted exertion, suddenly found herself turning faint. She was in the middle of the crossing, the wagons were upon her, but she could not run. She had scarcely time to throw up her arms, to utter one piercing cry of terror, before she was thrown to the ground. She had a horrible sensation of her life being crushed out of her, of every bone being broken; then followed peace and unconsciousness.

One of the wagons had gone partly over her; one leg was broken. She was carried to the accident ward at St. Thomas's Hospital close by.

CHAPTER XXXIII

A POINTED QUESTION

Neither had Mrs. Price slept well. All night long she either had fitful and broken dreams, in which her small guest, Sue, constantly figured; or she lay with her eyes open, thinking of her. She was surprised at the child's resolve. She recognized an heroic soul under that plain and girlish exterior.

In the morning she got up rather earlier than usual, and instead of going directly downstairs, as was her custom, she went up to Sue's attic. She had promised her eccentric young son to allow him to tell his own tale in his own way; but she meant to comfort Sue with some specially loving and kind greeting. Having a true lady's heart, she knew how to give Sue a very cheering word, and she went upstairs with that heart full.

Of course there was no Sue in the little chamber. The bed had been lain in, but was now cold and unoccupied. Mrs. Price went downstairs, considerably puzzled and disturbed. She sent for Pickles and told him.

She was full of fear at Sue's disappearance, and told the heedless boy that she blamed him.

"You did wrong, my lady—you did very wrong," she said. "You gave the poor thing to understand that she was to be put in prison, and now doubtless she has gone to deliver herself up."

"No, mother. She only went out to have a little exercise. Cinderella 'ull be back in an hour or so," answered the boy.

But he did not speak with his usual assurance and raillery. The fact was, the calculations in his shrewd little brain were upset by Sue's disappearance. He felt disturbed, perplexed, and annoyed.

His mother being really displeased with him was a novel experience to Pickles. She blamed herself much for having allowed him his own way in this matter, and the moment breakfast was over, went out to the nearest police-station to relate Sue's story.

Pickles stayed in until noon; then he also went out. He had cheered himself until this hour with the hope that Sue had only gone out for a walk. Notwithstanding all the improbabilities of his poor, frightened Cinderella venturing to show herself in the street, he had clung firmly to this idea; but when the neighboring clock struck twelve he was obliged to abandon it. He was obliged to admit to his own little puzzled heart that it was on no ordinary walk that Sue had gone. Remorse now seized him in full measure. He could not bear the house; he must vent his feelings in exercise. For the first time in his sunny and healthy young life he walked along the streets a defeated and unhappy boy.

Suddenly, however, a thought occurred to him. He stood still when it flashed across his fertile brain. Then, with a cheerful shout, which caused the passers-by to turn their heads and smile, he set off running as fast as his feet would carry him.

Hope would never be long absent from his horizon, and once again he was following it joyfully.

He was on his way now to Harris's house. He meant to pay pretty Connie a visit, and when with her he would put to her a pointed question.

It was nearly three o'clock when he reached Westminster. A few minutes later he found himself on the landing outside Connie's rooms. Here, however, he was again a little puzzled, for he wanted to see Connie and not to see Giles. Taking a long time about it, he managed to set the closed door ajar. He looked in. Connie and Giles were both within. Connie was mending her father's socks; Giles was reading aloud to her. Neither of them had noticed the slight creaking noise he had made in opening the door. He ventured on a very slight cough.

This sound was heard; the reading ceased.

"Come in," said Connie.

This he must not do. He waited an instant, then creaked the door again.

"Dear, dear! I made certain I had shut that door," said Connie.

At this she rose unsuspiciously. "Jest wait a minute, Giles dear. I didn't catch that last bit."

She ran to the door to put it to. Pickles placed his foot in her way.

The obstacle caused her to look into the passage. There a boy, very red by nature, and with his natural color now much intensified by hard running, stood awaiting her.

He pointed to the door, put his finger to his lips, then rushed down the first flight of stairs, where he turned round, and beckoned to her to follow him.

"I'll be back in a minute, Giles," said Connie. She had ready wit enough to perceive at a glance that Pickles had something to say to her which he did not wish Giles to hear.

Closing the door behind her, she ran downstairs. Pickles could have hugged her in his gratitude.

"Ain't you a perfect duck of a darlin'?" he said, gazing hard and full into her face.

"What do you want me for, Pickles?" asked Connie.

"Fur one or two things of much private importance. First, tell me, how is the little lame chap as is fretting fur his sister wot is kept in the country?"

"He is not so well, Pickles; he is not so well as he was. Pickles, I don't believe that story about Sue being in the country."

"You don't believe me when I opens my lips to give utterance to the words of gospel truth!" replied Pickles. But his red face grew a shade redder, and his full, bold gaze was not quite so steady as usual. "Why, surely, Pickles, you ain't going to be troubled wid nerves!" he said to himself.

Connie, watching anxiously, entreated in her softest tones: "Dear Pickles, you might trust me. I should like to know, and I won't tell Giles."

"Ay, ay, that's a woman's curiosity; but the misfortune is as it can't be gratified. No, Connie. You are as rare and pretty a bit of woman as hiver I clapped heyes on. But fur hall that you ain't going to come hover this yere boy. When I tells you, Connie, that Sue is hin the country, please believe as she his in that year health-giving place. When 'tis conwenient fur me to confide in you farther, why, I'll do it. That time ain't at present. In the meantime, ef you want to real help them who ere in difficulty, you will let me know widout any more wasting o' precious time where yer father, Peter Harris, is working to-day."

"Oh Pickles! wot do you want wid him?"

"Nothink to hurt you, pretty one. Now, will you speak?

"He's at Messrs in Street," replied Connie.

"Thank yer; and now I'm off. Ef you'll listen to the words o' solemn wisdom, and be guided in that same, you'll not mention this stolen interview to little Gilesbless the little chap! You keep up his heart, Connie. As soon as hiver this yer young man can manage it, Sue shall come home. Lor', now! ain't the world strange and difficult to live in? Wot 'ull bring joy to one 'ull give pain to t'other, but the cause o' right must win the day. Well, good-bye, Connie. I'll wery like look in soon again."

CHAPTER XXXIV

PICKLES TO THE FORE AGAIN

Connie went back to Giles, and Pickles, having obtained the information which he desired, sped as fast as his feet could carry him down the street. Once more his spirits were high, and hope was before him.

"I may save you, you most obstinate and tiresome Cinderella," he said to himself. "But oh, wot a mistake gels are! Why hever those weak and misguided beings was allowed to be is a puzzlement too great fur me."

But though Pickles talked even to himself in this light and careless vein, there was (and he knew it) a pain in his hearta pain joined to an admiration for Sue, which would have made him willing to fight to the very death in her behalf.

The day, however, had been spent while he was rushing about, and by the time he reached the place where Connie had directed him to seek her father, the workmen were putting by their tools and preparing to go home.

Pickles followed Harris down the street. Harris was talking to and walking with one of his fellow-workmen, and Pickles did not care to accost him except when he was alone.

At the corner, however, of the next street the two parted; and then the boy, putting his face into grave and serious order, ran lightly after Harris. When he addressed him his very voice trembled.

"Mr. Harris, I see'd you coming out of that yer shop. I'm in much perplexity and trouble in my mind, and I thought the sight of you and a talk wid you might maybe set me up."

"You thought wrong, then," said Harris, replying in his gruffest voice, "for I'm in a mortal bit of a hurry, and I'm in no humor to listen to no chaff, so get away."

"Oh, Mr. Harris! I'll endeavor to run by yer side for a minute or two. Mr. Harris, wot does yer think? That little Sue wot I tolled yer onwhy, she has discovered who the guilty party is. She have found out who really stole the locket and put it into her pocket."

"She have!" said Harris. He was so astonished and taken by surprise that he now stood still. He stood quite still, gazing helplessly at Pickles, while his weather-beaten face grew pale.

"'Tis gospel truth as I'm telling yer," continued Pickles, fixing his own light-blue eyes full on his victim. "Sue knows hall about itthe whole thing; the great and awful meanness have been made plain to her. Yes, she knows all, Sue does; but, Mr. Harris"

"Yes; wot have I to say to this tale? I'm in a hurrytearing hurryI tell yer."

"Yes, Mr. Harris; I won't keep yer. Sue knows, but Sue, she won't betray. I know who did it," she said, "but I won't tell on him. He lent me a shilling once. He is kind to my little brother wot is lame. I know wot he did, but I won't never tell, I'll go to prison 'stead of he."

Harris's color had returned. He now walked so fast that Pickles had to run to keep up with him. Suddenly, seeing a passing omnibus, he hailed it, and in a second was on the roof. He did not glance at Pickles. In reply to his tale he had not answered by a single word.

CHAPTER XXXV

THE WINGS ARE GROWING

Connie went back to Giles, sat down by him, and he resumed his reading. He was going through the Pilgrim's Progress to her, reading short sentences at a time, for his voice was too low and weak to enable him to exert himself for long at a time.

"Connie, wot were that as I read last?"

Connie colored.

"You weren't listening," said Giles reproachfully. "It wor a most beautiful bit. But you didn't hear me, Connie."

"I wor thinking o' something else jest then," owned Connie. "I'll listen now wid hall my might, dear Giles."

"Ah! but I'm tired now," said Giles; "and besides, I want to talk 'bout something else, Connie."

"Well."

"Sue have been a whole month in the country to-dayrayther more than a month. I don't understand it at all. I never thought as she could stay so long away from me. I suppose 'tis hall right, and cottages such as we want do take a powerful long time to find. It has been a long timewery, wery longbut have I been patient 'bout Sue all this long time, Connie?"

"Yes, indeed, dear Giles."

"Oh! I'm glad, fur I've tried to be. Then, Connie, wot I'm thinking is that ef Sue don't soon come backef she don't soon find that 'ere cottagewhy, I won't want it, Connie. Sue 'ull come back and find megone."

"Gone!" echoed Connie. "Do you mean dead? Oh Giles! you're not ill enough to die."

"Yes, Connie, I think I am. I'm so real desperate weak sometimes that I don't like even to move a finger. I used to be hungry, too, but now I never cares to eat. Besides, Connie dear"

"Yes, Giles," answered Connie.

"Those wings that I told you ofwhy, I often seem to feel them flutter inside of me. I told you before, Connie, that when they was full grown, why, I'd fly away. I think they are growing wery fast. I'll want no cottage in the country now. I'm going away to a much better place, ain't I, Connie?"

"Oh! but, Giles, I don't want to think thatI don't want to," answered Connie, the tears raining down her cheeks.

"'Tis real good fur me, though, Connie. I used to pine sore fur the country; but it have come hover me lately that in winter it 'ud be dullscarcely any flowers, and no birds singing, nor nothink. Now, in heaven there's no winter. 'A land o' pure delight,' the hymn calls it, 'and never-withering flowers.' So you see, Connie, heaven must be a sight better than the country, and of course I'd rayther go there; only I'm thinking as 'tis sech a pity 'bout Sue."

"Yes, I wish as Sue was home," said Connie.

"Connie dear, couldn't we send her a message to come straight home to me now? I'm so feared as she'll fret real hard ef she comes wid news of that cottage and finds me gone."

"I'll look fur her; I will find her," said Connie with sudden energy. Then she rose and drew down the blinds.

"I'll find Sue ef I can, Giles; and now you will go to sleep."

"Will you sing to me? When you sing, and I drop off to sleep listening, I allers dream arterwards of heaven."

"What shall I sing?"

"'There is a land of pure delight.'"

CHAPTER XXXVI

A CRISIS

Connie went downstairs and stood in the doorway. She had gone through a good deal during these last adventurous weeks, and although still it seemed to those who knew her that Connie had quite the prettiest face in all the world, it was slightly haggard now for a girl of fourteen years, and a little of its soft plumpness had left it.

Connie had never looked more absolutely pathetic than she did at this moment, for her heart was full of sorrow for Giles and of anxiety with regard to Sue. She would keep her promise to the little boyshe would find Sue.

As she stood and thought, some of the roughest neighbors passed by, looked at the child, were about to speak, and then went on. She was quite in her shabby, workaday dress; there was nothing to rouse jealousy about her clothes; and the "gel" seemed in trouble. The neighbors guessed the reason. It was all little Giles. Little Giles was soon "goin' aw'y."

"It do seem crool," they said one to the other, "an' that sister o' his nowhere to be found."

Just then, who should enter the house but kind Dr. Deane. He stopped when he saw Connie.

"I am going up to Giles," he said. "How is the little chap?"

"Worsemuch worse," said Connie, the tears gathering in her eyes.

"No news of his sister, I suppose?"

"No, sirnone."

"I am sorry for thatthey were such a very attached pair. I'll run up and see the boy, and bring you word what I think about him."

The doctor was absent about a quarter of an hour. While he was away Connie never moved, but stood up leaning against the door-post, puzzling her brains to think out an almost impossible problem. When the doctor reappeared she did not even ask how Giles was. Kind Dr. Deane looked at her; his face was wonderfully grave. After a minute he said:

"I think, Connie, I'd find that little sister as quickly as I could. The boy is very, very weak. If there is one desire now in his heart, however, it is just to see Sue once more."

"I ha' give him my word," said Connie. "I'm goin' to find Sue efef I never see Giles agin."

"But you mustn't leave him for long," said the doctor. "Have you no plan in your head? You cannot find a girl who is lost as Sue is lost in this great London without some clue."

"I ain't got any clue," said Connie, "but I'll try and find Pickles."

"Whoever is Pickles?" asked the doctor.

"'E knowsI'm sartin sure," said Connie. "I'll try and find him, and then"

"Well, don't leave Giles alone. Is there a neighbor who would sit with him?"

"I won't leave him alone," said Connie.

The doctor then went away. Connie was about to return to Giles, if only for a few minutes, when, as though in answer to an unspoken prayer, the red-headed Pickles appeared in sight. His hair was on end; his face was pale; he was consumed with anxiety; in short, he did not seem to be the same gay-hearted Pickles whom Connie had last met with. When he saw Connie, however, the sight of that sweet and sad face seemed to pull him together.

"Now must I give her a blow, or must I not?" thought Pickles to himself. "It do seem 'ard. There's naught, a'most, I wouldn't do for pore Cinderella; but w'en I have to plant a dart in the breast of that 'ere most beauteous crittur, I feels as it's bitter 'ard. W'y, she 'ud make me a most captiwatin' wife some day. Now, Pickles, my boy, wot have you got in the back o' your 'ead? Is it in love you bean' you not fourteen years of age? Oh, fie, Pickles! What would yer mother s'y ef she knew?"

Pickles slapped his hand with a mighty thump against his boyish breast.

"That's the w'y to treat nonsense," he said aloud. "Be'ave o' yerself, Picklesfie for shame, Pickles! That 'ere beauteous maid is to be worshipped from afarjest like a star. I do declare I'm turnin' po-ettical!"

"Pickles!" called Connie at this moment. "Stop!"

"Pickles be 'ere," replied the youth, drawing up before Connie and making a low bow.

"Giles is worse, Pickles," said Connie, "an' wot's to be done?"

Pickles's round face grew grave.

"Is 'e wery bad?" he asked.

"So bad that he'll soon go up to God," said Connie. Her eyes filled with tears; they rolled down her cheeks.

"Bright as dimants they be," thought the boy as he watched her. "Precious tears! I could poetise 'bout them."

"Pickles," said Connie again, "I have made Giles a promise. He sha'n't die without seeing Sue. I'm sartin sure, Pickles, that you could take me to Sue nowI'm convinced 'bout itand I want you to do it."

"Why do you think that?" asked Pickles.

"'Cos I do," said Connie. "'Cos of the way you've looked and the way you've spoken. Oh, dear Pickles, take me to her now; let me bring her back to little Giles to-night!"

Once again that terribly mournful expression, so foreign to Pickles's freckled face, flitted across it.

"There!" he said, giving himself a thump. "W'en I could I wouldn't, and now w'en I would I can't. I don't know where she be. She's lostsame as you were lostw'ile back. She's disappeared, and none of us know nothink about her."

"Oh! is she really lost? How terrible that is!" said Connie.

"Yus, she's lost. P'r'aps there's one as could find her. Connie, I 'ate beyond all things on 'arth to fright yer or say an unkind thing to yer; but to me, Connie, you're a star that shines afar. Yer'll fergive the imperence of my poetry, but it's drawn from me by your beauty."

"Don't talk nonsense now, Pickles," said Connie. "Things are too serious. We must find SueI must keep my promise."

"Can you bear a bit o' pine?" said Pickles suddenly.

"Pain?" said Connie. "I've had a good deal lately. Yes, I thinkI think I can bear it."

"Mind yer," said Pickles, "it's this w'y. I know w'y Sue left yer, and I know w'y she ain't come back. It's true she 'aven't give herself hup yet, although she guv me to understand as she were 'bout to go to prison."

"To prison?" said Connie, springing forward and putting her hand on Pickles's shoulder. "Suethe most honest gel in all the worldgo to prison?"

"Oh yes," said Pickles, "yer might call her honest; but w'en she goes into a pawnshop an' comes hout agin wid a golden dimant locket a-hid in her pocket, there are people as won't agree wid yer, an' that's the solemn truth, Connie."

Connie's face was very white.

"I don't believe it," she said.

"Yer don't?" cried Pickles. "But I were there at the time. But for me she would ha' been locked up long ago. But I tuk pity on her'avin' my own suspicions. I hid her and disguised her. Wot do yer think I come 'ere for so often but jest to comfort the poor thing an' bring her news o' Giles? Then146 all of a suddn't my suspicions seemed confirmed. I guessed wot I see is workin' in your mindthat some one else done it an' putt the blame on 'er. Oh, I'm a born detective. I putt my wits in soak, an' soon I spotted the guilty party. Bless yer, Connie! ye're rightSue be honesthonest as the daynoble, toomore nobler nor most folk. Pore Sue! Pore, plain Cinderella! Oh, my word! it's beauteous inside she bean' you're beauteous outside. Outside beauty is captiwatin', but the hinner wears best."

"Go on," said Connie; "tell me wot else you 'ave in yer mind."

"It's this: yer may own up to it, an' there's no use beatin' about the bush. The guilty party wot stole the locket an' transferred it by sleight-of-'and to poor Sue is no less a person than yer own father, Connie Harris."

Connie fell back, deadly pale.

"Nono!" she said. "Nono! I am sartin sure 'tain't that way."

"Yus, but it be that wayI tell yer it be. You ax 'im yerself; there's no time for muddlin' and a-hidin' o' the truth. You ax the man hisself."

"Father!" said Connie. "Father!"

Harris, wrangling with another workman, was now seen approaching. When he perceived his daughter and Pickles, his first impulse was to dart away down a side-street; but Pickles, that most astute young detective, was too sharp for him.

"No," he said, rushing at the man and laying his hand on his shoulder. "Giles is bad, an' we can't find Sue no'ow, and yer must tell the truth."

Harris did not know why his heart thumped so heavily, and why a sort of wild terror came over him; but when Connie also joined Pickles, and raising her eyes to the rough man's face, said, "Be it true or be it lies, you are my own father and I'll niver turn agin yer," her words had a most startling effect.

Harris trembled from head to foot.

"S'y that agin, wench," he muttered.

"You're mineI'll not turn agin yer," said Connie.

"Then whywot 'ave I done to deserve a child like this? There, Pickles! you knowand you ha' told Connieit's all the truth. There come a day w'en I wanted money, an' I were met by sore temptation. I tuk the dimant locket w'en the pawnbroker 'ad 'is back turned on me; but as I were leavin' the shopSue bein' by my sideI suddenly saw him pokin' his finger into the place where it had been. I knew it were all up. I managed to slip the locket into Sue's pocket, and made off. I ha' been near mad sincenear mad since!"

"Small wonder!" said Pickles. "An' do yer know that she 'ad made up her mind to go to prison 'stead o' you?"

"You told me so," said Harris"at least you told me that she was goin' to prison instead o' the guilty party."

"Wull," said Pickles, "yer own 'eart told yer 'oo was the guilty party."

"That's true, youngster."

"Father," said Connie, "we can't find Sue anywhere, and Giles is dying, and we must get her, and you must help."

"Help?" said Harris. "Yes, I'll help. I won't leave a stone unturned. She wanted to save me, knowing the truth. Wull, I'll save and find her, knowin' the truth."

"I will come with you," said Connie. "I want to go wid yer; only wot am I to do with Giles?"

"Don't worrit 'bout him," said Pickles. "I'm 'ere to be o' sarvice to you, Miss Connieand to you, sir, now as you 'ave come ter yer right mind."

"Then I will come with you, father," said Connie. "We'll both go together and find Sue."

As Pickles was entering the house he popped his head out again.

"I forgot to mention," he said, "as hinquiries o' the most strict and dertective character 'ave been institooted by yer 'umble sarvant for poor CinderellaI mean Sue. They've led to no results. There's nothing now but one o' the hospitals."

It is very doubtful whether Pickles believed himself the clue he had unexpectedly given to Harris and Connie, but certain it is that they immediately began their investigations in those quarters. From one hospital to another they went, until at last they found Sue in bed in St. Thomas's Hospitalflushed, feverish, struggling still to hide her secret in order that when she was better she might save Peter Harris.

The poor child was rather worse than usual that evening, and the surgeon who had set her leg was slightly anxious at her feverish symptoms. He said to the nurse who was taking charge of the little girl:

"That child has a secret on her mind, and it is retarding her recovery. Do you know anything about her?"

"No, sir. It is very awkward," said the nurse, "but from the first she has refused to give her name, calling herself nothing but Cinderella."

"Well," said the doctor, "but Cinderellashe doesn't seem touched in the head?"

"Oh no," said the nurse; "it isn't that. She's the most sensible, patient child we have in the ward. But it's pitiful to see her when she thinks no one is listening. Nothing comforts her but to hear Big Ben strike. She always cheers up at that, and murmurs something below her breath which no one can catch."

"Well, nurse," said the doctor, "the very best thing would be to relieve her mind—to get her to tell you who her people are, and to confide any secret which troubles her to you."

"I will try," said the nurse.

She went upstairs after her interview with the doctor, and bending over Sue, took her hot hand and said gently:

"I wish, little Cinderella, you would tell me something about yourself."

"There's naught to tell," said Sue.

"But—you'll forgive me—I am sure there is."

"Ef you was to ask me for ever, I wouldn't tell then," said Sue.

"Ah! I guessed—there is something."

"Yes—some'ut—but I can't bear it—the Woice in the air is so beautiful."

"What voice?" asked the nurse, who feared that her little patient would suddenly become delirious.

"It's Big Ben hisself is talkin' to me and to my darling, darling little brother."

"Oh! you have a little brother, Cinderella?"

"Yus, a cripple. But don't ask me no more. The Woice gives me strength, and I won't niver, niver tell."

"What does Big Ben say? I don't understand."

"No," said Sue; "and p'r'aps ye're not wanted to understand. It's for me and for him, poor darling, that Woice is a real comfort."

The nurse left her little charge a few minutes afterwards. But before she went off duty she spoke to the night nurse, and confessed that she was anxious about the child, who ought to be recovering, and certainly would but for this great weight of trouble on her mind.

All these things, which seemed in themselves unimportant, bore directly on immediate events; for when Connie and Harris arrived at St. Thomas's Hospital and made inquiries with regard to a little, freckled girl, with an honest face and sturdy figure, the hall porter went to communicate with one of the nurses, and the nurse he communicated with turned out to be the night nurse in the very ward where Sue was lyingso suffering, so ill and sorely tried.

Now, the nurse, instead of sending word that this was not the hour for visiting patients, took the trouble to go downstairs herself and to interview Connie and her father. Connie gave a faithful description of Sue, and then the nurse admitted that there was a little girl in the hospital who was now in the children's surgical ward. She had been brought in a day or two ago, having a broken leg, owing to a street accident. She was a very patient, good child, but there was something strange about hernothing would induce her to tell her name.

"Then what do you call her?" asked Harris.

He was still full of inward tremors, for at that moment he was thinking that of all the sweet sights on earth, that sight would be little Sue's plain face.

"Have yer no name for the pore child?" he repeated.

"Yes," said the nurse. "She calls herself Cinderella."

"It's Sue! It's Sue herself father! God has led us to herand it's Sue her very own self!"

Poor Connie, who had borne up during so many adventures, who had faced the worst steadfastly and without fear, broke down utterly now. She flung herself into her father's arms and sobbed.

"Hush, wench hush!" said the rough man. "I am willin' to do hall that is necessary.Now then, nurse," he continued, "you see my gelshe's rather upset 'bout that pore Cinderella upstairs. But 'ave yer nothing else to say 'bout her?"

"She acts in a strange way," said the nurse. "The only thing that comforts her is the sound of Big Ben when he strikes the hour. And she did speak about a little cripple brother."

"Can us see her?" asked Connie just then.

"It is certainly against the rules, butwill you stay here for a few minutes and I'll speak to the ward superintendent?"

The nurse went upstairs. She soon returned.

"Sister Elizabeth has given you permission to come up and see the child for a few minutes. This, remember, is absolutely against the ordinary rules; but her case is exceptional, and if you can give her relief of mind, so much the better."

Then Connie and her father followed the nurse up the wide, clean stairs, and down the wide, spotless-looking corridors, until they softly entered a room where many children were lying, some asleep, some tossing from side to side with pain.

Sue's little bed was the fifth from the door, and Sue was lying on her back, listening intently, for Big Ben would soon proclaim the hour. She did not turn her head when the nurse and the two who were seeking her entered the ward; but by-and-by a voice, not Big Ben's, sounded on her ear, and Connie flung herself by her side and covered her hand with kisses.

"You don't think, Sue, do yer," said Connie, "that us could stop seekin' yer until we found yer?"

Sue gave a startled cry.

"ConnieConnie! Oh Connie! 'ow is Giles?"

"'E wants yer more than anything in all the world."

"Then hehe'sstill alive?"

"Yus, he's still alive; but he wants yer. He thought you was in the country, gettin' pretty rooms for you and him. But oh, Sue! he's goin' to a more beautiful country now."

Sue didn't cry. She was about to say something, when Harris bent forward.

"God in 'eaven bless yer!" he said in a husky voice. "God in 'eaven give back yer strength for that noble deed yer ha' done for me an' mine! But it's all at an end now, Susanall at an endfor I myself 'ave tuk the matter in 'and, an' hall you 'as to do is to get well as fast as ever yer can for the sake o' Giles."

"You mustn't excite her any more to-night," said the nurse then, coming forward; "seeing," she added, "that you have given the poor little thing relief. You can come again to-morrow; but now she must stay quiet."

Late as the hour was when Harris and Connie left St. Thomas's Hospital, Harris turned to Connie.

"I've some'ut to doand to-night. Shall I take yer 'ome first, or wull yer come with me?"

"Oh, I will come with you, father," said Connie.

"Wull then, come along."

They walked faralmost as far as Cheapside. Connie could not imagine why her father was taking her into a certain dingy street, and why he suddenly stopped at a door which had not yet been shut for the night.

"I thought as there were a chance of findin' him up," he said. "Come right in, gel."

Connie entered, and the next minute Harris was addressing the pawnbroker from whom he had stolen the locket.

"I 'ave a word to say with you," he remarked; and then he related the circumstances of that day, several weeks ago now.

"But we found it," said the pawnbroker, "in the pocket of the young gel."

"It was I as put it there," said Harris. "It was Ithe meanest wretch on 'arth. But I've come to my senses at last. You can lock me up ef yer like. I'll stay 'ere; I won't even leave the shop ef yer want to deliver the real thief over to justice."

The pawnbroker stared at the man; then he looked at Connie. There is no saying what he might have done; but Connie's face, with its pleading expression, was enough to disarm any one.

"The fact is," he began "this sort o' thing ought to be punished, or however could poor folks live? But it's a queer thing. When the young gel vanished, as it seemed, into the depths of the 'arth, and I 'ad got my property back, I tuk no further trouble. In course, now that you 'ave delivered yerself up, it seems a'most fair that the law should take its course."

"That's wot I think," said Harris. "Make a short job of it, man. Call in a constable; 'e can take me to Bow Street to-night."

"No 'urry, man," said the pawnbroker. "I want yer to tell me some'ut more. Is that other little party alive or dead? It seems to me as though the 'arth must 'ave swallered her up."

"I will tell you," said Connie; and she did relate Sue's storyas much as she knew of itand with such pathos that even that pawnbroker, one of the hardest of men, felt a queer softness about his heart.

"Wull," he said"wull, it's a queer world! To think o' that child plannin' things out like that! And ef she ad come to me, I might ha' believed her, too. Wull now, she be a fine little crittur. An' s'pose"he glanced at Harris"I don't prosecute you, there's no call, to my way o' thinkin'. And the fact is, I'm too busy to be long out of the shop. Don't you steal no more, neighbor. You ha' got off dirt-cheap this time, but don't you steal no more."

CHAPTER XXXVII

THE HAPPY GATHERING

There came a day in the early spring of that year when a great many pleasant things happened to the people who have been mentioned in this story.

Connie's room was very bright with flowersspring flowerswhich had been sent to her all the way from Eastborough by Mrs. Cricket. Quantities of primroses were placed in a huge bowl, and the sun came feebly in at the window and seemed to kiss and bless the flowers. There were also some early buttercups and quantities of violets.

Giles was neither better nor worse, but perhaps on this day he was a little bit on the side of better. It was so beautiful to think that Sue was coming back!

Oh, this was a wonderful day! Sue was well again; Connie was happy; Harris was never tired of doing all he could both for Connie and Giles; and other people were happy too, for Sue's return was to be marked by a sort of holidaya sort of general feast.

To this feast was invitedfirst, Mrs. Anderson; then Ronald, who happened to be staying in London and was deeply excited at the thought of seeing Connie once more; and also dear Father John, who would not have missed such an occasion for the wide world. Of course, Pickles could not be left out of such a gathering; but he could scarcely be considered a guest, for did he not belong, so to speak, to the family, and was not dear Sue, in particular, his special property?

Mrs. Anderson supplied the good things for the feast. This she insisted upon. So Connie spread quite a lordly boardcold meats not a few, some special delicacies for Giles, and a splendid frosted cake with the word "Cinderella" written in pink fairy writing across the top. This special cake had been made by Mrs. Price, and Pickles had brought it and laid it with immense pride on a dish in the centre of the table.

"Yus," said Connie, "it do look purty, don't it? Wot with good things to eat, and wot with flowers, it's quite wonderful."

When everything was arranged, Connie went into a little room to put on once again her dark-blue dress, and to unplait her thick hair and allow it to fall over her shoulders.

"It's for Ronald," she said. "Ronald wouldn't know me without my hair down."

Then, one by one, the visitors made their appearanceFather John, who sat down by Giles's side and held his hand, and by his mere presence gave the boy the greatest possible comfort; and Pickles, whose face was shining with hard rubbing and soap and water, and whose red hair stuck upright all over his head. Then Mrs. Anderson came in and sat down, and gave a gentle look first at Giles and then at Connie; and152 Connie felt that she loved her better than ever, and Giles wondered if he would meet many with faces like hers in heaven.

In short, every one had arrived at last except the little heroine. But hark! there was a sound outside as though some vehicle had stopped at the door. Giles's breath came fast. There were steps on the stairs, and two porters from the hospital carried Sue in between them.

"Oh, I can really walk," she said. "And oh, GilesGiles!Please put me down, porter; I really, really can walk."

"Jest as himpatient as ever, Cinderella!" said Pickles, who always tried, as was his custom, to be specially funny in pathetic times.

Sue glanced at him, but could not speak just then. There are moments in our lives when no words will come. She went up to Giles and hid her face on his pillow. Poor little Sue had a bitterly hard fight with herself, for that face, which belonged not to earth, unnerved her, notwithstanding the rapture of seeing it once again. But Giles himself was the first to recover composure.

"We are 'avin' such a feast!" he said. "An' it's all so beautiful! Now then, Sue I do 'ope as ye're 'ungry."

After that Ronald spoke and made the others laugh; and Sue bustled about, just as though she were at home, and Connie helped her; and very soon they all crowded round the table, except Giles, who had his dainty morsels brought to him by Sue's own hands.

Thus they ate and laughed and were merry, although perhaps the laughter was a little subdued and the merriment a trifle forced.

It was when the feast was quite over that Father John spoke a few wordsjust a very fewabout the love and goodness of God, and how He had brought His wandering sheep home again to the fold, and how He had helped Connie in dark times, and Ronald in dark times, and Sue in dark times.

"And He is helping Giles, and will be with him to the end," said the street preacher. "And now," he added, "I think Giles is very tired and would like to be all alone with Sue. Suppose, neighbors, we go into the next room."

The opening of the door of the next room was one of the surprises which had been planned by Connie and her father. As he was now earning such really excellent wages, and as he had taken the pledge and meant to keep it, he felt he was entitled to another room. It was neatly furnished. There was a fire burning in the grate, and there were white muslin curtains to the windows. Connie spoke of it with great pride as the "drawing-room," and Pickles assured her that even to set foot in that room was enough to make Connie a "lydy" on the spot.

When they were alone Sue and Giles talked softly one to the other.

"The blessed Woice," said Sue, "'ave been with me all the w'y."

"And with me," said Giles.

"You won't go jest yet, Giles," said Sue.

"Wery soonbut not quite yet," he answered.

Sue smiled and kissed his hand, and they talked as those who have been long parted, and know they must be parted soon again, will talk, when heart meets heart.

In the other room people were not more cheerful, but at least more glad.

"There is nothing left to wish for," said Pickles. "It's just the best thing in all the world for little Giles to get quite well up in heaven. Ain't it now?" he added, looking at Father John.

"Yes," said Father John very briefly. Then he turned to Connie.

"You must never forget all that you have lived through, Connie," he said. "You'll be a better and a braver girl just because of these dark days."

"She's the best wench on 'arth," said Harris.

Suddenly Ronald sprang forward and spoke.

"Uncle Stephen said I was to tell you he has bought the cottage in the country where Mrs. Cricket lives and he's adding to it and making it most beautiful, and dear Mrs. Cricket is to be housekeeper, and you're all to come down in the summerall of youeven Giles; and Giles is to stay there as long as he lives. Uncle Stephen is a splendid man," continued Ronald. "It was after him my darling V. C. father took when he became so great and brave and manly, and I love Uncle Stephen better than any one except father. Father hasn't come home yet, and perhaps I won't see him until Giles sees his father. But I'm a very, very happy boy, and it's all because of Uncle Stephen. Now, the rest of you can be happy too in my cottageUncle Stephen says it is my cottagein the beautiful country."

These things came to pass, and even Giles went for a short time to the beautiful country, where the flowers grew in such abundance, and where the birds sang all day long.

"Now you can guess," he said to Sue after they had been there a fortnight or more, "some little bit about the joys of the Land of Pure Delight."

THE END